The
Helpline

The Helpline

- a novel -

Katherine Collette

ATRIA BOOKS

New York   London   Toronto   Sydney   New Delhi

An Imprint of Simon & Schuster, Inc.
1230 Avenue of the Americas
New York, NY 10020

Copyright © 2018 by Katherine Collette
Originally published in Australia in 2018 by The Text Publishing Company

First Atria Books hardcover edition July 2019

ATRIA BOOKS and colophon are trademarks of Simon & Schuster, Inc.

For information about special discounts for bulk purchases, please contact Simon & Schuster Special Sales at 1-866-506-1949 or business@simonandschuster.com.

The Simon & Schuster Speakers Bureau can bring authors to your live event. For more information or to book an event, contact the Simon & Schuster Speakers Bureau at 1-866-248-3049 or visit our website at www.simonspeakers.com.

Interior design by Jill Putorti

Manufactured in the United States of America

1 3 5 7 9 10 8 6 4 2

Library of Congress Cataloging-in-Publication Data

Names: Collette, Katherine, 1981– author.
Title: The helpline : a novel / Katherine Collette.
Description: New York : Atria Books, 2019.
Identifiers: LCCN 2018058750 (print) | LCCN 2018061499 (ebook) | ISBN 9781982111359 (eBook) | ISBN 9781982111335 (hardback) | ISBN 9781982111342 (paperback)
Subjects: | BISAC: FICTION / Contemporary Women. | FICTION / Humorous.
Classification: LCC PR9619.4.C644 (ebook) | LCC PR9619.4.C644 H45 2019 (print) | DDC 823/.92—dc23
LC record available at https://lccn.loc.gov/2018058750

ISBN 978-1-9821-1133-5
ISBN 978-1-9821-1135-9 (ebook)

For my parents,
Julie and Greg Collette

- 1 -

The night before I started work, Sharon called. She was as encouraging as always.

"You're still planning on going? It's not too late to change your mind."

"Of course I'm going. I can't wait, I'm so excited." This was an overstatement, but contradicting Sharon is a kind of compulsion. Like a form of Tourette's.

She sighed. "You know, when that insurance place gave you the flick, I hoped you'd see the light. Take some time out and think about what you really want to do."

"They didn't give me the flick," I said. "I tendered my resignation, and they were quite upset about it."

"I mean, you're not stupid. You're not great with people, obviously. And you're a bit of a self-promoter. But that's the Douglas in you." She says it casually, like the Douglas family has been a feature of my existence, but that's not the case. I've never met my father—he left before I was born. I try not to take it personally; it was her he was getting away from.

I checked the clock. "I better go. I have to . . . get to bed."

"Now? It's seven-thirty."

"The early bird gets the worm, Sharon."

"Oh, please, not the early bird again. The one I feel sorry for's the poor bloody worm. That worm got out of bed early, too, for all the good it did . . ."

I didn't hang up the phone, not officially. I put it facedown on the table and left the room. Sharon could be very sympathetic to things like hypothetical worms. Not so much daughters.

It was raining in the morning, which I anticipated. I brought with me an umbrella that was very large, and very waterproof. When I got out of the car and walked towards the front doors of the town hall, it covered me, my disposable hooded poncho, the matching pants, *and* my wheeling briefcase.

Unfortunately, my timely arrival had not taken into account the opening hours of reception and, as it was 8:57 a.m., the sliding glass doors remained stubbornly inert.

Lucky I had a sudoku in the inner pocket of my jacket. I wiggled one arm from the sleeve of the poncho and maneuvered inside the plastic sheath to get it out. Then I stood and filled it in.

This was called Making the Best of Things. I'd become a seasoned veteran of Making the Best of Things these last few months. Specifically, since the day I left Wallace Insurance.

About a year ago, just after Easter, Peter called me into his office. He and I used to meet there on Friday nights after everyone else went home. I'd stay back filing difficult claims and drafting advisory notes for my inferiors, while they laughed and joked over after work drinks in the kitchenette downstairs.

During the week Peter could be gruff. He was under a great deal of stress—as manager, he had a lot on his plate. But on Friday nights, between 7:32 p.m. and 8:17 p.m. (approximately), he was a different person. I'd sit in his chair and he'd massage my shoulders. He was a lazy masseur—maybe he'd lost some of the strength he once had in his hands—but it was nice to be touched. I'd feel my back soften, the knots unraveling, and then he'd say how much he liked me and how smart I was. "Germaine," he'd say, "you're the only one with any intelligence around here." He told me that *several* times.

But the last time I saw Peter was not on a Friday night; it was a Wednesday afternoon. And it was not only him in the office; Helen from the HR department was also present.

I wasn't worried. There'd been a recruitment process; I was pretty sure they were going to tell me . . . I thought it was good news, as shown in Figure 1:

1. Career Trajectory (Anticipated)

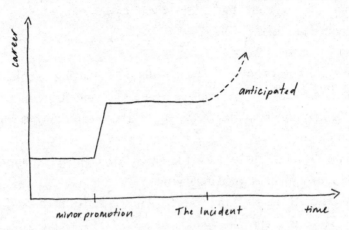

But when I entered the room, it had an air of formality that made my skin prickle.

"Germaine," said Peter. His voice was stiff. "This has been a very difficult decision. We had lots of high-quality applicants, and some of them had been team leaders before." His eyes wandered to Helen from the HR department, who gave an encouraging nod. "And I know you've been here before, too, Germaine. I know you've been down to the last few candidates more than once."

Four times, in fact, in the seventeen years I'd been at Wallace Insurance (five as senior mathematician). Once upon a time there were *six* mathematicians, one whole department, but the others had moved on and their replacements were statisticians and computer programmers. I was the last of the old guard, and it was my time, my turn.

And Peter knew that. We'd talked about it, on a Friday. He'd *intimated* things were about to change.

But now look at him. He was perspiring. Little beads of sweat had appeared on his brow, highlighting the silver regrowth at the hairline. "Did I say it was a difficult decision? It was a very difficult decision, but *unfortunately*—"

I don't know what he said after that because I stopped listening, but I got the gist of it, and the gist was they were promoting Susan Reynolds from the Customer Service team.

"But I'm older," I said, "and I've been here longer. I have seniority."

"Actually, no," said Helen. "Susan will have seniority."

I looked at Peter.

Peter looked away.

"We don't want to waste your skills on managing people, Germaine," said Helen. "We want someone like you sitting in a room crunching numbers all day long. Not everyone can do what you do, you know."

I said, "But . . . Susan doesn't know basic calculus. Her appreciation of polynomials is worryingly limited."

Helen used the soothing voice. "I know . . . It's hard. And Germaine, you are a very valued employee."

I said if I was so valued, maybe they'd like to give me a pay rise? Helen said they weren't in a position to increase my wages, but perhaps she could see about some movie tickets. To acknowledge all my hard work.

There was some conjecture about what happened next. As I recall, I expressed a degree of disappointment and asked them to reconsider.

Helen and Peter alleged I kicked the table over. They claimed I called Peter an expletive—a word I would never use—and exited the room in such a manner that the door required attention from the Maintenance department. That is not my recollection. For clarity, in Figure 2, I have accurately apportioned blame.

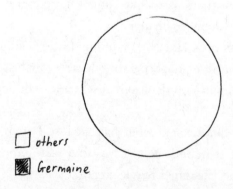

2. Persons at Fault for The Incident

☐ others

▨ Germaine

In any case, the next morning my security pass didn't work. Helen informed me through the intercom that they'd accepted my resignation and requested that I not contact Peter.

In the search for another job I approached every insurance company in Melbourne, Sydney, and Adelaide, outlining my capabilities. I explained that given a few simple data points I could estimate the probability—using a calculator and pencil, no less—of any conceivable scenario. I could say with ninety-three percent accuracy that a sixty-eight-year-old smoker (male) on holiday in Thailand would lose his wallet within a week of arrival. I could tell them a family of four from Melbourne en route to the Gold Coast was unlikely to miss a flight but highly likely to require medical assistance at some point. Age, place of residence, claims history—whatever the variable, I could make the numbers not only sing, but extemporize in four-part harmony. I could devise algorithms that estimated the likelihood of an event occurring and cross-reference this against the cost of that occurrence. I could identify the sweet spot, the point at which we were insuring people for things that wouldn't happen and not covering them for things that would. "I can save you millions," I assured them—correctly.

They were, to a person, unconvinced. It seems people no longer understand what mathematics is and uniformly fail to see the possibilities it presents. "We've got computers for all that," they said. And: "Can you do Twitter?"

I had to broaden the search, sending letters for positions in finance, bookkeeping, payroll, and real estate, but it was all for nothing. Not one phone call; not one interview.

I went for a job in the café down the road.

"Why should we hire you, Germaine?" said the manager, whom I'd hitherto avoided because his lattes were always lukewarm.

"Well, Graham," I said with as much enthusiasm as I could muster, "I think you know what a people person I am."

The arsehole hired some other people person.

As each month passed, life seemed to get bleaker. It wasn't just that no job meant no money, and not going anywhere and not speaking to anyone. It meant . . . no Peter.

I sat on the couch watching old sudoku competitions on YouTube and eating beans out of the can.

Enter Cousin Kimberly.

"Auntie Sharon says you're having a breakdown," she said through the receiver.

"I can't hear you, Kimberly. It's a terrible line."

"Might be able to get you a job at the council. I know the mayor. Verity and I go way back."

This gave me pause. Maybe Cousin Kimberly wasn't entirely useless.

"Something in management? I'd like to be a team leader."

"You'd have to promise not to fuck it up, Germaine. Promise you won't be weird. No asking questions and no arguing. You just shut up and do whatever it is they tell you to do. I'll let you know what she says." She hung up quickly.

At eight minutes past nine, the disposable poncho and pants had been removed, folded, slipped into a ziplock bag, and secured in my briefcase. *Then*, the doors to reception finally slid open. Two women had appeared and were sitting at the desk. Neither looked the slightest bit sheepish. "Hello," called one. She smiled brazenly. "You're early," said the other, without a hint of irony.

I gave a chastising smile, which, in hindsight, was probably too subtle. The women were oblivious.

"I'm Germaine Johnson," I said. I expected they would have heard of me, being the cousin of the mayor's oldest friend, but their faces remained blank. Perhaps this was their default position; it was difficult to say.

"Here for Francine Radcliff," I added. Francine was my new manager. She was in her fifties and had frizzy hair and big teeth. In my interview she'd worn a brown dress and the kind of ergonomic shoes you get at the chemist, the ones with the built-in orthotics.

With what appeared to be considerable effort, the one holding the phone receiver placed a call, and Francine appeared a few minutes later, sticking her head through the security doors like a turtle peering out of its shell.

"You're here," she said.

"I've been here for ages. Since at least a quarter to." We went inside.

I'd been in the staff area for the interview, but this time it seemed smaller and sadder. Low partitions formed a corridor, and on either side were cubicles. Neat little boxes, one after the other.

"We're a bit short on space at the moment," said Francine. "We used to be down the other end, but last week they decided to move us. The team's still adjusting to the new layout."

We turned a corner and wound our way through the partitioned maze. I kept waiting for Francine to stop and point out my seat. I was prepared to appear enthusiastic or, at the very least, not horrified when this occurred, but she didn't stop. She didn't slow down, and it struck me that perhaps the mayor had moved the team, anticipating my arrival? Perhaps she felt I ought to sit somewhere a little more salubrious? It wouldn't be the first time I'd had an upgrade.

At Wallace I'd had my own office—I wasn't really senior enough, but Peter said it was better that way—and I loved it. Often I went in early just to soak it up. I'd sit in silence and imagine the future, spending time perfecting each part of the fantasy, restarting when I came up with additional good bits that needed to be slotted in. One day, I'd have a whole team that reported to me. One day, the people upstairs would say things like, *Don't know what we did before you, Germaine* or *What a great idea, Germaine.* I'd have special open-door times when people could come and ask me questions or get my opinion on things. I'd be the one with the answers if there was a problem. *Germaine will know,* they'd say. *Germaine should be able to answer that.*

As it was, no one much did come to visit. I kept the door open permanently so I could participate in conversations, but the people around me seemed to talk in whispers. I had to come out and tinkle a bell if I wanted to make an announcement or tell a funny story.

Francine and I kept walking. "How's the mayor today?" I said. I thought Francine might have a special message for me, but she didn't seem to.

"The mayor? Fine, I guess."

Our feet padded softly against the carpet.

"You know," said Francine, "you won't even notice the space after a while, Germaine. You'll be too busy answering the phone. Some days I think every senior citizen in the country is trying to get through."

When Francine had called and said they had an opening for some-one interested in working with old people, I thought it was a joke, some elaborate Gotcha. "Very funny, Kimberly," I said, and went to the mirror to fluff out my hair. I didn't want a flat bob if cameras appeared and started to film my reaction.

But it was not a joke.

At the interview, Francine explained the position was on the Senior Citizens Helpline, which was a number old people could call if they needed help showering or cooking or whatever it was they couldn't do for themselves. This initial description made me shudder. I didn't want to clean toilets or towel anyone's crevices dry.

But Francine said that wasn't how it worked. I wouldn't have to *do* the things that needed doing, I just had to organize for them to be done.

"And a lot of people don't even need anything," said Francine. "They're lonely and they just want someone to talk to. In fact, that's probably the most important skill you can have in a position like this: the ability to listen. And empathy. People really open up over the phone; they'll tell you all sorts of things. You get someone's whole life story some days."

"And what would my key performance indicators be?" I said. "Do you operate on a bonus system? I'm very motivated by incentives."

I heard Francine swallow. "The pay is twenty-five dollars and twenty-seven cents an hour," she said.

I accepted the position.

– 2 –

We reached the last of the cubicles and followed the passage around in a tight U. "Here we are," said Francine. Her voice was upbeat, as though if she appeared cheerful, I mightn't notice how depressing it was. Less a room and more a widening of the corridor, it was so compact there were only two desks. They were wedged in, side by side, no partition in between.

One desk—"Yours," said Francine brightly—was empty. The other was covered in notebooks and takeaway menus, tissues scrunched in balls and crumbs of indeterminate origin. Sitting in front was a large woman in a brown T-shirt. She was holding an enormous Slurpee.

"This is Eva. She's the other half of the Senior Citizens Helpline."

"The other *half*?" I said.

"Yes, it's just you two. You're the dynamic duo, eh, Eva?"

In the ensuing silence, Eva used her straw to funnel Slurpee into her mouth. Some of the liquid spilled on the desk, and she rubbed at it with her forearm.

Francine examined her watch. She had to go to a meeting. "I had hoped I'd be around to help you settle in, but things are so busy right now. Just wait, you'll see. In the meantime, Eva's going to show you the ropes. She'll give you the tour and tell you what to do, won't you, Eva?" Eva did not respond. "Or you can look at the handbook in your desk drawer," said Francine as she started to move away. "It'll tell you everything you need to know."

When Francine was gone, Eva put down her Slurpee. "Nice shirt," she said.

"Thanks." It was my best one: white with tiny black numbers all over. People always commented on it. Once, I wore it to a sudoku convention and met the national champion, Alan Cosgrove. I had to line up for three hours to get his autograph. First thing he said when he saw me was "That's an impressive shirt." He didn't have to say that. But that was the standard of the shirt it was.

"I might go to lunch soon," said Eva. "Been up since four a.m."

"Four a.m.? Why?"

She shrugged. "I get up early. Don't need much sleep. I'm like Napoleon."

"Who's Napoleon?"

"*Napoleon*. The French guy? The little one that fought the battles?"

"Napoleon Bonaparte?"

"Whatever his name is, I don't know. He only slept four hours a night. I sleep five." She waited.

"Eight and half," I said. "Most nights."

"Mind you"—she waved the Slurpee about—"I drink three of these a day."

"They say the minimum you should get is eight hours."

"Yep, three hundred and sixty-five days a year, three hundred and sixty-six in leap years. It's all I drink, Coke-flavored Slurpees and iced tea. Don't do hot drinks, don't see the point of them."

"What about water?"

"Don't do water. Don't like the taste of it. I haven't had water in probably thirty years."

At that moment, the phone rang. "Suppose I should show you what to do," Eva said, picking up and barking "Senior Citizens Helpline" into the receiver.

But it was not whom or what she expected, that much I could ascertain. "Oh," she said, three times, each with a greater upward inflection, each suggesting something more curious was unfolding at the other end.

"What did you do?" she said when she hung up.

"Nothing. Why?"

"That was Stacey. The mayor's assistant?" Eva raised her eyebrows and leaned back like she had such enormous news she had to physically give it more space. "The mayor wants to see you."

"How come?" I was careful to appear as surprised as Eva was. No point inflaming things with the suggestion it was inevitable. I've borne the brunt of jealous colleagues before, and it's never pretty. People start to pick fights in meetings or say things like, *Here we go again, Germaine*, and, *We didn't actually ask for your input*, when all you're doing is trying to help them out.

Eva shook her head. "Stacey didn't say. It's weird. Why would the mayor want to see you? You only just started. I've been here twelve years, and the mayor's never wanted to see me."

I shrugged and hung my bag on the chair. When I sat down, it was casually, like it wasn't *that* interesting. "What's she like?" I said. "The mayor, I mean."

I'd looked her up online, but that didn't tell me anything. Everyone looks good online, unless they look like a serial killer. Even I had a sizable Internet presence, with a devoted following: On World Puzzle Forum's sudoku website I called myself Mathgirl and had 1,300 friends.

When you googled Mayor Verity Bainbridge, City of Deepdene, a woman in her fifties came up. She had long brown hair, tanned skin, and teeth so shiny and white she might have modeled toothpaste. In every photo, and there were a lot of photos, she was smiling and looking at the camera. There was not one picture in which she was sneezing or slouching or taking an inopportune bite of a sandwich. She was smart, too. She had her MBA, and before she was mayor she was a partner in a large multinational that had an acronym instead of a name. On paper at least she seemed like a kindred spirit.

Eva scrunched her nose up as if something smelled bad. "They're all the same. Good at schmoozing; better at getting her face in the paper. She picks Employee of the Year. Those bitches on Customer Service have got it the past two years running; the whole thing's rigged. Still, most people love her."

Eva, I gathered, was not "most people." This might have been a commendation—or not. I would have to find out.

"When does she want to see me?" I asked.

"Like, ten minutes ago."

There were multiple surprises in the mayor's office. In order to provide the most accurate account of what transpired, I will list them in the order in which they appeared.

Surprise 1: The mayor's office was huge. It was bigger than any of the offices at Wallace Insurance, even the CEO's. It could have fitted a swimming pool or, at the very least, a decent-sized spa. There was a beautiful oak desk, a silver computer, and *windows*. Sunlight streamed in, bathing the mayor, myself, and the Other Party in warm, golden light.

Surprise 2: The mayor was *not* wearing the signature twinset that was featured in all her Google images. She wasn't even in business attire. She had on a pink jumper with the council logo on the breast, tan pants, and crisp white runners.

Surprise 3: The mayor was not alone. There was a man with her (the Other Party).

Surprise 4: This was the biggest surprise of all—I knew the Other Party. He and I had met before, though it was unlikely, given the previous circumstances of our meeting, that he would remember.

The mayor's assistant announced me. "Germaine's here."

The mayor said, "Hi, Germaine."

I didn't say anything. I was too busy *not* looking at the man, which was as much effort as not staring at the sun or the moon when an eclipse is occurring.

"It's good to finally meet you," said the mayor.

And I said, "Yes."

She held her hand out and we shook. Think of the differential between Eva and me and multiply it by ten. The mayor's self was cool and calm, and *my*self, which a moment ago had seemed capable, up to whatever task it might be set, suddenly inadequate.

She gestured at Him. "Germaine, do you know Don Thomas?"

Don Thomas? It must have been some kind of alias. I guess it got difficult being accosted by fans all the time. I smoothed my shirt down at the front.

"Don," I said. "It's a pleasure to meet you."

I didn't say we'd met before. Even though a localized fog had descended on my person, I had the wherewithal to realize his *not* remembering the first time we'd met was a gift. I had a chance to make a *second* first impression. A chance I was squandering, right now.

The mayor said, "I know what you're thinking."

She didn't, because I wasn't thinking. It was too hard with Him standing there.

Luckily, I had The List, folded in my notebook: a series of dot points comprising potential conversation topics and my current thinking on each one. If you want to be insightful, you need to pre-prepare. I needed only to open the notebook and unfold the paper, and I'd have access to a number of interesting remarks. That was all I had to do.

But I was having trouble moving. I could only stand there, still, like a very lifelike statue.

The mayor said, "You're thinking . . . Why are they wearing golf clothes?"

No, but a fair guess on her part. The pants, the sneakers, it *was* unusual.

"There's a tournament at the club this afternoon—Don's club. Fund-raiser for Alzheimer's. Speaking of which . . . Don, do you have to get back? I can deal with this."

He cast an apologetic look at her, at me. "I ought to. See you this afternoon, Verity . . . And Germaine." A nod. "I'm sure we'll meet again."

And just like that he was gone. Disappeared, leaving me feeling like the remainder in a long-division equation. I didn't show it. If there's one thing I'm good at, it's hiding feelings. Most people don't know I have them.

In addition to the desk, the acreage of carpet held a table with four chairs. The mayor gestured that we sit down, and poured me a glass of water. "Your cousin's told me a lot about you, Germaine."

"Don't believe everything she says," I said. "Kimberly's not very astute."

She laughed—I don't know why. Kimberly was not very astute. Sometimes I wasn't even sure we were related.

I took a sip of water. "Thank you for getting me the job," I said.

The mayor flapped her hand. "I didn't get you the job. I don't do any of the hiring and firing around here, Germaine. Well, perhaps a little firing—ha. That's a joke; I'm joking. Did Kimberly tell you I have a wicked sense of humor? You'll have to watch out. No, I just passed your résumé on. I thought it was very impressive. You don't meet many mathematicians these days."

"Or *senior* mathematicians."

"Or senior mathematicians."

"I guess it's in my blood." Not the blood I inherited from Sharon, which was pretty ordinary, to be honest; the blood that came from Professor Douglas.

"You must be good with numbers."

"It's not just numbers," I said. This was a common misconception.

"Of course not, no. That's oversimplifying, isn't it? I suppose I mean to say you're logical."

"And I have a good work ethic. I can write a thousand words in two hours."

"Indeed."

It was in my résumé, all of this. I wasn't telling her anything new.

"Are you excited about working on the helpline, Germaine?"

I shrugged. "I don't want to answer the phones for too long. I'm hoping we can automate it. I want to be a team leader—that's my ultimate goal."

Another inexplicable laugh. "You're a breath of fresh air, Germaine."

I wished I had my phone so I could record the conversation. I'd have sent the audio to Peter. Not just Peter, the whole of Wallace Insurance.

"What's your position on internal promotions?" I asked. The more we talked the more relaxed I felt.

"I'm all for them." She pointed at the door. "You know Stacey, my EA? She started off in Customer Service. Someone does well and it gets recognized around here. At least, I hope so."

I smiled into the glass of water. I was about to open my notebook and extract The List when the mayor got up and went to a filing cabinet set against the wall. She opened the drawer, pulled out three manila folders, and brought them back.

"I need your help with something," she said. "If you're interested."

I didn't have to know what it was to know I was interested. But when she said it had to do with Don, my interest doubled.

"Poor old Don. He's been having issues with a few people. You'll never guess who."

Oh, a guessing game. My first guess was sudoku enthusiasts—you'd be surprised how crazy they are. My second guess was troubled youth. For my third guess I was going to ask if drugs were involved, but the mayor interrupted.

It was nothing like that, she said. It was the *old people*, the senior citizens. Not all of them but a specific subset:

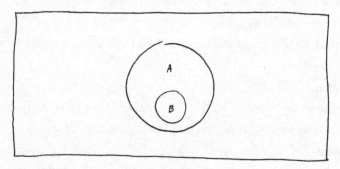

A = old people
B = members of senior citizens club

The issue, said the mayor, was car parking. *"Technically*, the golf club should have put in more parking a few years ago, when they expanded. But you know how it is, Germaine. You have to be a little flexible about these things. You're better off having a golf club with all the bells and whistles and a little parking problem than no golf club, no bells or whistles, and no one parking anywhere," she said.

I said I agreed.

Not everyone did, she told me. From time to time—like today, in fact—the golf club would host a big event, a charity dinner or some sort of fund-raiser. "Don's a real philanthropist. Not many people know that, but he is. Honestly, the amount of good work he does behind the scenes, people don't talk about that, do they?"

How sad, I thought, always to be underestimated and thought the worst of.

The mayor explained that when these philanthropic and other events were on, people would park their cars at the golf club and, when it was full, they'd spill into the parking lot at the senior citizens center next door. It should have been fine. The senior citizens center and the car park attached to it were both owned by the council, and anyone could park there. But the old people had started getting upset about it.

"Don't tell me . . . Old people are the worst in insurance."

"I understand where they're coming from," said the mayor with a patience and a sympathy I could never pretend to feel. "But it's getting worse. Don came by to talk about it."

There'd been an incident over the weekend. The "usual" story: too many cars, not enough space, people having to park next door. The only difference was, when people came back to their vehicles at the end of the evening, there were chains on their wheels.

"What, metal chains?" I said.

She fluttered her eyelids to show how crazy it was. "They had to catch taxis home. And when they came back in the morning? The chains were gone. Someone's idea of a joke, you might say, and if this was an isolated incident, I'd agree. But it's not an isolated incident." She gestured at the files on the table.

This was where I came in. I'd been employed to work on the helpline, but the mayor had something for me to do in the downtime, between calls. The next time the phones were quiet she wanted me to go and have a "discussion" with the senior citizens. Let them know chaining up cars was not the sort of thing the council condoned.

It was an okay project, I supposed. I'd hoped for something more substantial, but on any test you start with the simplest questions.

The mayor looked at her watch. "Is that the time? I have to get through a mountain of work before this tournament. Shall we . . . reconvene at a later date? Oh, and Germaine?" She waved her hand over the folders like she was a magician casting a spell to make them vanish. "Keep this to yourself for now. You know how people are."

– 4 –

Eva wasn't there when I got back to my desk. I transferred the files to my briefcase to take home and read later and then sat for a moment, thinking. I wanted to understand how I felt about what had just happened, and the first step was to identify my feelings.

I was *pleased* to have met the mayor. I was even more *pleased* she'd given me my own special project. While the project itself was rudimentary to the point of anticlimax, it was exciting to be singled out. And so early in my tenure. The complexity of tasks would inevitably increase over time, as she got to know me and my skill set, and maybe, possibly, she'd pass this information on to Don Thomas.

Don Thomas. I turned the name over in my head. It was strange calling him that, even if only silently. Mainly because it wasn't his name. His name was Alan Cosgrove. He was the national sudoku champion in 2006 and should have been again in 2007, only . . . a thing happened. Alan Cosgrove had been unfairly dealt with, a mode of treatment I had some experience of.

I wished I'd said something. Other than it being a pleasure to meet him, which it was. But I could have said, *You're not alone, Alan Cosgrove. I'm here.* I wanted to help him; he'd been a very positive influence in my life at one point in time. Sort of like the father I never had. And quite unlike Sharon, the mother I did have.

After what happened at Wallace she'd taken to calling me every day, wanting to "talk." It was like being stalked by a telemarketer.

"What'd you do this morning?" she'd say.

"Different things. This and that."

"What exactly?"

"Can't remember."

"Germaine." She'd sigh and threaten to come over.

"Don't come now," I'd say. "I'm about to go for a walk with the girl from next door." This was a lie, but one I'd cultivated over a long enough period of time to make it seem plausible.

"So long as you're not wallowing in self-pity," Sharon said.

I wasn't wallowing in self-pity. I'd discovered old YouTube clips of Alan Cosgrove, competing in his heyday. He was a shining light in an otherwise dark room. My financial situation meant I'd been restricting electricity use.

At my new desk, at the town hall, I stared at the computer screen the same way I'd stared at the television.

Don Thomas, Alan Cosgrove. What was he doing right now, in this very moment? Was he thinking about me, just as I was thinking about him?

I remembered I was meant to be categorizing feelings. I could never remember all the feelings that existed. Perhaps I should write them down?

Optimistic was a feeling.

Enthusiastic was a feeling.

Was *wishful* a feeling? I looked it up. It was not a feeling but a way of thinking:

The formation of beliefs based on what might be pleasing to imagine instead of what was supported by evidence, rationality, or reality.

No, I wasn't feeling that.

Eva didn't come back for some time. I was forced to consult the handbook in my drawer in order to work out what my official duties were.

The Senior Citizens Helpline Handbook was eighty-nine pages long and appeared to be very comprehensive, far too comprehensive to read in full. The first section was on ergonomics and how to set up my desk. The next was phone etiquette, instructions on how to use the phone, what to say when picking up, presenting a professional image, and appropriate responses to complaints . . . I skimmed this. There was a lot to get through. The last section was an alphabetized list of common requests. Theoretically, this was a good idea, but I could tell immediately it was inadequately cross-referenced.

I flicked through a couple of pages, and then the phone rang. I put on my headset and pressed the button to pick up. "Senior Citizens Helpline."

There was a woman at the other end. She asked to speak to Eva. When I advised that Eva was currently unavailable, the woman said, "When's she back?"

"I cannot give out that information. It's classified."

"Who are you?" she said.

"Who are *you*?"

"I'd rather not say."

"I, too, would prefer to remain anonymous."

A pause. The woman sighed. "Look, I'm calling about taking food home from restaurants. That's all I want to know about."

I picked up the handbook again. Nothing under R for Restaurants or T for Takeaway. Under D for Dining there was this:

"Many local restaurants and cafés in the City of Deepdene provide takeaway foods," I read aloud. "Refer to the online business directory on our website for a listing of those that offer a seniors discount. Do you want me to look it up?"

"Not takeaway, you idiot. *Leftovers*. Last week I ordered two dishes at the Red Emperor. I got beef in black bean and fried rice. I couldn't eat it all, but when I asked them to put it in a container to take home, they said they weren't allowed. They said the council had changed the rules. *Have* you changed the rules? If so, who made that decision and how do I lodge a complaint?"

Predictably, there was nothing in the index for History of Take-away or Food Hygiene Practices. Why did she have to order two meals, though? It wasn't surprising she couldn't finish it; the Red Emperor's serves were huge.

When I asked, she said, "It was our wedding anniversary. Mine and my husband's. We used to eat the beef in black bean and fried rice at the Red Emperor every Thursday."

"That's nice. Why didn't he finish the food? Late lunch?"

"Because—"

"They haven't changed the recipe, have they?"

"No, because he's dead."

If he was dead, why on earth did she order for him? I looked in the handbook for Inexplicable Behavior with a quick detour through Dementia—maybe I was obliged to report it—and while turning through pages, I came to F for Food. That might be useful. A quick scan revealed that most of the information pertained to Meals on Wheels. "Have you thought about a delivery service?" I said.

But she was still going on about her husband. "I just wanted to remember how it used to be," she said.

I told her she could have meals delivered for $16.50 per day, $17.50 if she was diabetic. That was for three courses, which seemed reasonable.

"I thought for a few minutes I could just sit there. Pretend he was in the toilet and might come out any minute. I should have known not to bother."

"Sorry, diabetic is the same price; it's gluten-free that's extra. Meals can be delivered on Wednesdays and Fridays. No, wait. Depends which neighborhood you live in."

"My husband was diabetic."

I was confused. "Isn't your husband dead?"

Her voice went soft. "Three years last Tuesday."

I turned the volume on the phone up. "I'd say just get the normal meal. Diabetic, gluten-free, they never have the same flavor. Or you could try the Golden Duck on Cotham Road. They're quite good."

"But—"

"Enjoy the rest of your day." I hung up. The line went silent and then a very cool thing happened. The computer, which had been humming away in the background, flashed the following on screen:

—LINE 1—
Call duration: 3 minutes 07 seconds.
Total calls today: 1
Total calls this month: 1

—HELPLINE—
Total calls today: 3
Total calls this month: 47
Average call duration: 19 minutes

They were collecting statistics. The computer was recording quantitative data on each phone call, both cumulative and individual. This was exciting in itself but doubly so given my call time was already well under the average. I had taken three minutes to get rid of my first caller, and Eva, who had answered calls in the previous month, was taking nearly twenty to achieve the same thing. How long had Eva been working on the helpline? I'd been there one day and already I was the best. I sat up taller and swished my chair from side to side. But before I could really soak up the moment, before I could fully revel in its glory, the phone rang once more. I pushed the pick-up button, and a box flashed up on the computer screen.

It had a black background with red numbers. It was a timer, ticking off the seconds as they passed. Wow. Not only were they collecting cumulative statistics, but I could see how I was faring in real time. This was immediate feedback on performance and

It

Was

Wonderful.

If they'd had this at Wallace, they'd never have got rid of me. It was hard data, objective proof, that I was not just good *enough* but *very* good. I felt a rush of elation. "Senior Citizens Helpline," I said.

Nancy was on the other end. "I broke my hip in January," she said, and embarked on a long-winded tale of woe. I tuned out, reduced the size of the on-screen timer, and opened a spreadsheet. I plugged in the average call time and the number of calls waiting and tried to establish how many calls I would have to answer and how quick they'd have to be if I wanted to get the average down under fifteen minutes.

"—and I think someone needs to come out and clean my gutters. It hardly even rained on Sunday, and they started overflowing."

According to my calculations the next twenty-seven calls needed to be under nine minutes. The counter was at 6:19. "Clean the gutters?" I said. "Sounds expensive. Listen, Nancy, is it? Nancy, if I were you, I'd save myself a good bit of money by doing it myself."

"I called last week, and the woman said it was a free service."

"Do you have a ladder? Get a ladder and a broom. Lean the ladder against the wall and angle the broom into the gutter. If you get the angle right, you should be able to dig the leaves out. Just jiggle a little and they'll come off the side. You could have the whole lot done in less than an hour."

"It's just my hip is—"

"Up to you, Nance. If you want to spend a couple of hundred dollars on gutters, that's fine, but it if was my money—" I suppose I could have checked the handbook to see if there was anything in her claim for a free service, but this seemed unnecessarily bureaucratic. No matter how you looked at it, it was more cost-effective to encourage people to do things themselves. It was empowering, too. Nancy, though she was difficult to convince (8 minutes, 42 seconds), in the end agreed.

By the time I hung up, I felt more like my old self than I had in months. This might be my Waterloo. Of all the places and all the jobs. By the time Eva got back our average call time was 17:57 and the queue was empty.

"Seventeen minutes," I said, pointing. "Call time's down to seventeen minutes."

"Not for long," she said, and eased herself down.

The phones rang through lunch and into the afternoon. I was pleased for both statistical and avoidance reasons, but of course there was a lull eventually. First thing Eva said was, "What did the mayor want?"

"Nothing. She just introduced herself. I guess she does that with all the new people."

"No." Eva was very firm. "She doesn't."

"Doesn't she?"

Eva took a long, slow sip of Slurpee. She seemed to be scanning my face, sensing deception. I maintained a fixed expression.

"Where did you work before here?" Her tone was more interrogatory than conversational.

"Wallace Insurance."

"Doing?"

"Data analysis."

"Data analysis? Why you working here?"

I shrugged. She put the Slurpee down, setting it between us like a recording device.

"How'd you get the job?"

"I applied."

"Did you know someone?"

"Like who?"

The phones were quiet, but I put my headset on anyway. Then when her lips moved, I mouthed, "I can't hear you." She persisted for a while but eventually capitulated and picked up the Slurpee again. Then she sat there for ages, staring at her screen and chewing on the straw.

- 5 -

On the way home I stopped at the food court near the cinema. The Indian place was selling containers of leftover rogan josh for $4 each, and I bought three: one for dinner tonight, one for dinner tomorrow, one for dinner on Wednesday.

In the elevator up to my apartment I ran into Jin-Jin from number 22. She's in her twenties but dresses like a four-year-old. Tonight she had on tight pink pants, a pastel blue jumper, and a Hello Kitty backpack. It took forever to get to level four. The smell of spices and lamb permeated the small, rectangular space.

"Takeaway?" she said.

I was not responsive. The less you said to Jin-Jin, the better.

She pointed at the bag. "Lots of food for one lady, ha."

Once Jin-Jin and I ran into each other in the car park downstairs and she saw me throw some rubbish into number 21's bin. There was space in mine, but the bags were full of fish bones and I didn't want to stink it out. I said, "They gave me permission," and she giggled.

It was a skeptical giggle, a giggle that said, *I got you now, lady from number 23.* Ever since, she'd tried to strike up a conversation every time I ran into her. It was like being held hostage. We'd see each other in the corridor and it was, *How was your day, Germaine?* Or, *Isn't the weather nice?* I lived in fear she'd knock on the door and I'd have to put aside my sudoku and make her a cup of tea. We might spend a whole hour, sitting there, talking and wasting time. It was not going to be a profitable enterprise: Jin-Jin was a student at the university, and she wouldn't have known anything I hadn't already read about.

"It's for a friend and me, actually," I said as the lift doors opened and Jin-Jin followed me into the hall.

"You have a friend?" She grinned and squeezed my arm. "That makes me very happy."

I wheeled my briefcase down the hall. Inside, I put one serving of curry in the microwave and the others in the fridge. I hung up my work clothes, put on a pair of tracksuit pants, and sat on the couch to eat and read the mayor's files.

They were very comprehensive, a complete history of everything that had ever happened in relation to the Deepdene Senior Citizens Center and associated car park. There were plans for the original building, including estimates of construction costs, council audits, documents detailing electricity usage and the cost of cleaning contracts, and information pertaining to current booking fees. There was even a recent land valuation.

While it was a council building, there was a committee that oversaw its day-to-day operations. They were the ones who organized the knitting group and the book club, the buses for group outings, and the community lunch on Sundays.

The name *Celia Brown* appeared multiple times. She was the long-serving president of the committee (fifteen years) and, in recent times, a prolific correspondent.

She'd sent letters complaining about everything: the golf club, the council, the building. There were highly detailed lists of things that needed fixing—*the walls are falling down* and *the roof is leaking*—and requests for more money and more space. I had a good image of her in my head: Actually it was more or less a picture of Sharon. The words *serial pest* came to mind.

I finished eating, put the empty container on the coffee table, and opened the last file. Inside was a black-and-white photograph. Three older women standing side by side. The wind was blowing and they were laughing, their eyes squinted and their hair arced in strange shapes around their heads. They looked wild and crazy and unpredictable.

I lay back on the couch. Some people have no respect for rules and no sense of order. It was lucky for the mayor, for the council, for my career in general, that I had both these things in excess. I was just the one to put things right.

When I got to work, Eva was unexpectedly chipper. "Good morning," she sang out. "Guess what day it is?"

I gave her a wry glance. "Tuesday?" It sounded like a trick question.

"It's not Tuesday," she said. "It's *Biscuit* Tuesday."

I didn't ask. If she wanted to tell me, fine. If not, fine. I had things to do. I turned the computer on.

Meanwhile, Eva rolled back in her chair and bent down to reach under her desk. When she reappeared she was holding three tall glass jars.

"On Tuesdays and Thursdays they put biscuits out in the tearoom upstairs. They're complimentary—free, I mean. They're not going to give you a standing ovation or anything." She waggled a jar at me. "We take turns to fill these with biscuits and guess what? It's your turn. I did it last time."

I could have said I wasn't here last time. I could have said I didn't know where the tearoom was. I could have said a million things, but none of them occurred to me. All I was thinking was, *Free biscuits. Francine didn't mention* that *in the interview.*

"Kitchen's upstairs," said Eva. "You'll find it."

The tearoom had rows of plastic tables with plastic chairs and vending machines with fake wooden panels around the glass. There was a kitchenette in the corner and on the bench an urn and three big barrels, all in a row. They were labeled:

CREAM-FILLED
RICE CRACKERS
SWEET

I pulled the lid off one and began to fill the jars, placing the biscuits on their side to maximize capacity. I finished the first one and the second and was partway through the third when a portly man in fluorescent safety vest appeared. He had short black hair and was holding a clipboard under one arm.

"Hi." He clicked his heels together. "I'm Ralph, Ralph Garner. Risk management and health and safety coordinator."

"Germaine Johnson. Just started, Senior Citizens Helpline."

He nodded, and I picked up the lid for the jar. "Well, Germaine," said Ralph. "You being new and all you probably don't know about the biscuits."

"Oh no, Eva filled me in. Complimentary biscuits. Free, that is— no standing ovations. Ha-ha."

"Yes." There was a long pause. Ralph looked at the jars, lined up in a row. "Just so you know, we budget two biscuits per person per day."

At this point, I began to blush.

"Unless you have the rice crackers," he continued. "Then you can have eight."

Another guy and a lady came in to make tea and coffee. They seemed to be moving very slowly: More pricked ears than parched mouths, you might say.

"It's so there's enough for everybody; otherwise, people miss out."

More people came in. Another man with a mug, a bearded man, a thin woman who didn't look like she could possibly even eat biscuits. All of them, eavesdropping and passing silent judgment.

I was still blushing. My hands got sweaty, and slippery clouds started to appear on the glass of the jar.

This was not how I'd intended to meet my colleagues. I'd envisaged a get-to-know-you morning tea in which I told them interesting stories about data analysis and the insurance industry and they listened and asked questions at the end. It was misrepresentative to have them see me this way, because if anyone's a stickler for the rules, it's me. I return library books on time. I stop at give-way signs even when it's obvious no one else is coming.

The smell of biscuits was sickly and overwhelming.

"I didn't know," I said. "I'm new. These are Eva's jars." I was projecting my voice, for the people in the back.

"It's an easy mistake to make." Ralph looked skeptical about the ease of the mistake. I'd have been skeptical, too, if it had been someone else standing there instead of me.

"If you wouldn't mind?" He tilted his head from the jar to the barrels. He wanted me to put the biscuits back. The assembled throngs didn't formally divulge their opinions, but they seemed to agree.

I wrenched the lid off the jar and shoveled them back into the barrel with both hands.

"*Stop*," said Ralph, but I didn't listen. I kept on shoveling. The crumbs that didn't stick to my palms sprayed onto the bench. It would have been quicker to tip the jar upside down, but I'd packed them in so efficiently they were stuck together.

"*Stop*," said Ralph. "*Use the tongs.*"

Tongs? I stopped shoveling. As I looked across to the barrels, I noticed something I hadn't seen before. There were three pairs of tongs, one attached with string to each barrel. The room went quiet.

Ralph asked if I'd used the tongs to get the biscuits out.

I did not answer this question.

"Probably best you hang on to them," he said, and the bearded man tittered audibly into his mug. "We don't want a bacterial outbreak."

I avoided eye contact, hugged the jars to my chest, and backed out of the room. When I was halfway down the corridor, Ralph yelled, "You should be using a trolley. *It's bad for your back.*"

Eva took no responsibility when I told her. "Can't spell everything out," she said. "Anyway, you did good. Often the cream-filled run out by the afternoon."

– 6 –

The phones didn't stop for the rest of the day, and it wasn't until the following afternoon that I was able to make any progress on my special project. I waited until Eva went to the bathroom and then slipped away.

Driving down High Street past the Fitzsimmons Golf Club and into the long drive that led to the senior citizens center, the contrast was stark. On one side of a tall cyclone-wire fence were rolling green hills and crisp sand bars and on the other was a square of patchy asphalt, a picnic table with no chairs, and a weatherboard building with a slumped roof.

Inside was just as bad. In the foyer were two armchairs with stuffing bursting through the fabric, a bookcase filled with books (nothing contemporary), and on the far wall, a photo of the queen looking, frankly, disappointed. It reminded me of the co-op Sharon and I used to get our food at. Smelled the same, too, like old eggs overlaid with lentils and dust.

There was a door marked Office and on the bench beside it, a bell. I dinged it.

Ding.

No response.

Ding.

Ding! Ding! Ding!

The door opened halfway and two stern bespectacled eyes peered out. They were attached to a woman in a green T-shirt and a pair of elasticized black pants.

"What," she said. It wasn't a question.

I flashed my ID and said I was from the council.

"Are you here to fix the roof? It's about time someone came out about that roof."

I said I was there to see Celia Brown.

She didn't exactly open the door; it was more like she let it go and it didn't swing itself shut.

Inside, four chairs were arranged around a coffee table. She shifted some junk off one and dumped it on the desk behind. Then she sat down; I sat opposite. She didn't say anything.

"So that's you, is it?" I said.

"That's who?"

"You're Celia Brown." It was a lot of effort, trying to maintain my professional demeanor.

"If you say so."

I'd allocated eight minutes for small talk but elected not to utilize all of them. Instead, I got my notebook out.

"I'm doing an investigation for Mayor Verity Bainbridge. Not sure if you're aware but there was an incident with some parked cars recently. We had a complaint from the golf club next door."

It was strange, but at this her face seemed to brighten. Her eyes softened and the beginning of a dimple appeared in one cheek. "An incident?" she said. "Fascinating. What happened?"

"You haven't heard? About the chains?"

"Chains?" she said, and the dimple got bigger.

I gave a succinct explanation: The golf club had an event, their car park got full, and attendees had to park "elsewhere."

She pounced on that word *elsewhere*, like a cat toying with a ball of wool. "Elsewhere?"

"Here, specifically. And when people came back to get their cars at the end of the evening, there were chains on their wheels. Big chains . . . metal ones. They couldn't get them off. They had to catch taxis home, some at considerable expense."

"They had to catch taxis? Horrifying. And Don—Don Thomas,

was it?—he called the council, did he? I expect you're all on red alert. Working in shifts, are you?"

It felt like a fly was buzzing around, annoying me. Celia didn't seem to comprehend the gravity of the situation. "The mayor is very upset."

"Oh, she is, is she? Oh, dear. Was she upset that people from the golf club were parking their cars here? Because the car park is part of the senior citizens center? Was that what upset her?"

I could feel red blotches start to appear on my chest and neck. I did what Dr. Smithfield had told me to do: *Breathe in—two-three-four-five-six, out—two-three-four-five-six.* "No. She was upset about the chains."

"Oh, the *chains*."

"Also: It's the *council's* car park. It doesn't belong to the senior citizens center. Anyone can park there."

"Is that so?" She folded her arms across her chest.

"That is so." I folded mine, too.

In the ensuing silence we heard the front door open. Hurried footsteps came down the hall, and then a woman in a yellow cardigan appeared. She had short gray hair and was in a state of excited agitation.

"Celia," she said—rudely, because she was interrupting an important meeting-cum-investigation. "She *won*. Betsy won."

At this, Celia seemed to turn into a different person. One who was almost pleasant. "She did? All five categories?"

"Four, the fifth is still going. They'll announce later today."

"Who won?" I said. "What did they win?" I didn't càre what it was they were talking about, I asked only to make them aware that I had not suddenly become invisible.

Celia's quasi-cordial aspect vanished. *"No one won anything."* Her voice was very cold, like icicles were hanging from it. Then, to stop the interrupter from explaining, she gestured at me. "Gladys," she said, "this woman is from the council."

Gladys took a step in a backwards direction. She claimed it was nice to meet me but did not sound convincing.

Celia's normal obnoxious self had reasserted itself. "Gladys is the club's vice president," she said. "Her main area of responsibility is— or rather, is *supposed* to be—communicating with the subcommittees. Isn't that right, Gladys?" This had the feel of a leading question. Leading questions are ones that have known answers but take you to an unexpected destination. The sort of question *I* should have been asking all this time.

In any case, Gladys was not excited anymore. "Yes," she said, slowly.

"Yes," repeated Celia, at a similar pace. "Which means *you* should have been the one to *communicate* with the Christian choir that they cannot eat biscuits in the John Stanley Room. Gladys, there were crumbs again. *Crumbs.*"

"They are allowed to—"

"Call them and tell them that they're not to eat biscuits for supper if they can't clean up after themselves. I mean it. If they do it again, I'm going to kick them out. *And then I'll burn their hymnbooks.*"

"Celia," said Gladys. She gave me an apologetic look.

"And some idiot's taken all the chairs from the bingo room. They better not be using them for mahjong. Bingo's tomorrow and no one's going to be able to sit anywhere. I want them back in there by three o'clock this afternoon. On the dot, Gladys. Three o'clock."

Gladys shook her head at Celia and turned to me. She asked (nervously?) if I was there for something in particular.

I most certainly was, I told her, and was quite prepared to commence a cross-examination when Celia interrupted once more. "No," she announced. "We're done. You and I are finished here."

Finished? We hadn't discussed anything. I said, "There was an incident, and we need to determine its root cause." But Celia would not have it.

"What's there to discuss? I don't know anything. And neither does Gladys."

"But Gladys doesn't know what we're talking about."

"Nothing. She knows nothing. Do you, Gladys?"

Gladys said no, but this was not credible. One cannot be sure they know nothing when the subject matter has not been disclosed.

Celia got out of her chair and went and stood beside Gladys at the door. They were like two guards, one head guard and one of lesser ranking, escorting me from the building. If it wasn't a new job, if I hadn't been on probation, I would have stayed until they confessed.

Celia smiled as I squeezed past. "Thanks for coming," she said. "Send our love to Mayor Bainbridge."

– 7 –

I went to the office early in the morning to type the notes from my meeting with Celia Brown. I included a comprehensive overview of the salient events, plus a number of additional insights. Like how I could tell (even without a polygraph) that Celia was lying and how she didn't seem to understand the hierarchy that was operating in the situation. Perhaps in future I should take a printout of the council's management structure, something to show my official status?

I was convinced Celia had coordinated the chaining-up of cars but couldn't conceive how it had been achieved. Chains were very heavy. Either the old people were more agile than they appeared or they'd had help.

I printed the notes and put them in my briefcase. I wasn't sure how to get them to the mayor. Maybe I should put them in the internal mail; there was a tray by Eva's desk that said "Outgoing."

Before I could decide, the phone rang.

The helpline didn't open until nine, so I was not required to pick up, but I did and it was lucky, because it wasn't an old person or Eva or even Stacey, the mayor's assistant. It was the mayor herself.

"I was hoping you'd be in," she said.

"Were you?"

"Yes. I was wondering if you had something to tell me." She was talking in code, not saying what it was exactly but knowing that I'd know.

"I have completed the task," I said.

"Excellent. Why don't you and I go get a coffee?" More code. *Let us discuss the matter elsewhere, away from prying eyes and ears.* It really was a special project.

The mayor was wearing a black pantsuit that tapered in at the ankles. It made her look like a Power Ranger but in a really good way. She had her handbag in one hand and car keys in the other. She waved the keys at me.

"I'll drive," she said.

We had no trouble making conversation in the car. We were like old friends—I imagined this was what having old friends was like.

"Your car's nice," I said. It was a BMW, black, like her outfit and her handbag.

"Thanks."

"Is black your favorite color?"

"Is black a color?" she said, and we laughed at my stupidity—black, a color!

We pulled out of the car park onto the main road. The mayor didn't say where we were going but seemed to have somewhere in mind, as she cut through backstreets and zipped around corners.

At a strip of shops, she parked outside a sleek-looking café where, it turned out, the barista knew her. "The usual, Verity?" he said. "Skinny cappuccino?"

When he asked what I wanted I said, "The same." I'd never had a skinny cappuccino before, but the way the words rolled off the tongue was so satisfying I thought it might become my regular order.

We sat at a booth along the wall, her looking out, me looking at her. I watched her get a compact mirror and lipstick out of her bag and start putting the lipstick on.

"I come here a bit," she said. "Christos and I—Christos is my husband—live just around the corner."

Would it have been odd to ask where exactly?

"What does Christos do?" I asked instead.

"He's on boards."

"I was on a board once." Sort of. Sharon asked me to take the minutes at a Friends of the Animals meeting. It was very tedious and I left halfway through. "It was to help endangered species."

"That's very altruistic of you."

I hope I didn't blush. I tried not to.

Our coffees arrived. The mayor snapped the compact shut and put it away. She waited until the barista was back by the coffee machine and then lowered her voice and said, "Tell me everything."

I provided a thorough overview: "Call volumes this week have been quite erratic. Monday and Tuesday we received twenty-five phone calls before lunch, but yesterday we received four in the same time period. One possible use of the unexpected free time was to continue the statistical analysis I had commenced previously but given you'd asked for my assistance on a special project . . ."

I had her full attention. It was glorious, to be so seen. And by her. She was the mayor of a whole municipality, in charge of *everything*.

"I decided to visit the senior citizens center. I didn't tell them I was coming—I wanted to see what it was like, how it operated, what the people were like, on a normal day."

"And?"

"Underwhelming. Quite old and uninviting . . . and so is the building."

"That lot aren't even the worst," said the mayor. "You should meet the miniature train society. Did you see Celia?"

"Yes. She was *interesting*." Interesting was a euphemism—the mayor got it straight away.

"She's very *interesting*, isn't she?"

I adopted a tone of forced diplomacy. Just enough so she'd know that was what I was doing. I said how "refreshing" it was to meet someone so "direct" and "matter of fact."

The mayor was amused, internally. "Celia used to be fairly normal, you know. I don't know what happened. What did she say about the car parking?"

"She claimed to have no knowledge of the incident in question," I said. "She told me she knew nothing about anything. On the night it happened she was home by five and in bed by six."

The mayor rolled her eyes.

"I don't believe her," I said.

"No, I wouldn't have thought so."

The barista did something with the sound system, and the music changed. It had been light and upbeat, but now it got darker and moodier. The mayor rubbed her temples. "Drives me crazy," she said, half under her breath. "This is not what you get into politics for, Germaine . . . Do you have any idea how many people there are in Deepdene?"

I said no but I could probably estimate.

"Let's just say Celia Brown isn't the only one. But everyone thinks them and their backyard are all that's important."

I maintained a fixed expression. I was waiting for her to tell me what to do next, but she was talking about how idealistic she used to be, how you can't be everything to everyone, and how no one wants to pay taxes but everyone wants unlimited curbside collections.

I suppose she saw me glance at the clock. "Sorry." She grimaced. "It gets wearing, that's all. Closer you to get to the 'community,' the further away you wish you were."

I understood that.

The mayor sighed. "Write them a letter. Tell them it's not their car park, they don't have exclusive use of it, and if they don't want to share, we'll make them. If they're not careful, it won't be the *senior* citizens center, it'll be the *every* citizens center. Or the *no* citizens center—" All at once she stopped and looked behind me. "Don?"

I started to turn around, but he was in motion, a moving pink polo shirt. He stopped in the gap between our table and the next. The mayor got up and the two of them kissed the air beside each other's cheeks.

"How are you?" he whispered, holding her arm under the elbow.

"Good. How are *you*?"

"Good, good."

I got up, too, so we were all standing, and quite close.

"Don, you remember Germaine?"

"I do. Hello, Germaine."

FACT: He remembered me—this time.

FACT: People only remembered people they felt were important *to* remember.

FACT: I had reached this level of importance.

The mayor said, "Germaine met Celia yesterday."

Don winced. A sympathy wince—for me. "Sorry," he said.

I told him it was fine, no problem, anytime, whenever.

Meanwhile, the mayor bent down and picked up her handbag. I had a sinking feeling in my stomach, thinking we must be leaving. But, no. The mayor only needed to use the bathroom. If there was ever a more timely toilet interruption, I hadn't experienced it. And it got better: "Don, can you hang around?" she said.

He sat in the seat the mayor had vacated, opposite me. He and I were at the same table. The only other time we'd been so close was at Sudo-Con 2006. I was glad he'd forgotten. After he'd said what an impressive shirt I was wearing, he said, "Name?" and I said, "Alan Cosgrove." He'd laughed. Not unkindly, but not amused either. What kind of person couldn't remember their own name? I got a cold sweat from remembering.

Don said, "I hope Celia wasn't too hard on you."

"She was fine." I didn't want to talk about Celia. "You remind me of someone," I said.

Don averted his eyes. "Do I?"

"Yes." I was watching him carefully, but he wouldn't look at me. "Do you know Alan Cosgrove?"

"Alan who?"

"Cosgrove. He plays sudoku."

"What's sudoku?" Don's face was a picture of innocence. Did I have it wrong? Did they look the same, or only similar? Maybe I should get my eyes tested.

The mayor returned, smelling of peach perfume. "Don," she said. "We have to talk."

Don was happy to talk. I was also happy to talk—or do anything that would keep me there.

Only:

"Do you mind, Germaine?" said the mayor.

"Not at all," I told her. The three of us could sit and talk and get to know or possibly just watch each other. We could forget the last few minutes had ever happened. Alan who?

The mayor nodded and smiled. Don nodded and smiled, and so did I. Should we get another chair? I wondered. A long moment passed in deliberation.

And then the mayor coughed. Perhaps she wanted *me* to get the chair.

"Do you need a Cabcharge?" she said, and I realized my mistake.

I got up. "No, I can walk."

How far was it? It must have been three kilometers.*

"Are you sure?"

I was quite sure, I said, and hitched my handbag on my shoulder. The bell above the door signaled my departure, but when I waved from the footpath, even though I was at the window right in front of them, they didn't notice.

"What time d'you call this?" said Eva when I got back.

I didn't tell her I'd been in already. Coffee with the mayor, meeting Don—how much of it was secret? I wasn't sure. And I didn't want to talk about it, not right now. Had I ruined it with Don? I crossed my arms and hugged myself.

"Phone's been ringing off the hook." Eva's tone was accusing, as if this were my fault.

"Has it?"

"It has."

Oh, well. Call stats were important, but they weren't the only measure of performance. I had other tasks with other indicators.

---

*It was 4.65 kilometers, thirty-two percent of it uphill.

"Isn't that why they employed you?" she probed. "To answer it?"

"It's part of my role, yes." An increasingly small part, I hoped.

The biscuit jars were on Eva's desk. There were not many left. She extracted a handful of rice-cracker shards, her face thoughtful, reproachful. Then all at once her expression changed completely. She started laughing.

"I'm joking," she said, between breaths—she was struggling to breathe. *"Isn't that why they employed you?* That was a joke. And you believed me."

I didn't understand. What was funny about aspiring to improve our collective performance? For a moment I'd almost liked her.

Eva dabbed her eyes with her sleeve. She picked up a biscuit jar and offered me the crumbly contents. I declined.

"A few of us are going to lunch today," she said. "You want to come?"

It was a kind offer but deeply unappealing. It was hard enough sitting next to her. "I brought lunch from home," I said.

"So eat before you come."

"What about the phones?"

"You know what? No one cares if we don't answer them. Nothing happens."

"Maybe next time," I said.

"Who knows if I'll invite you next time?" She cackled like a hen.

Before I put my headset on, I checked the current stats. They were worse than I thought they'd be. Total call time had increased significantly since yesterday morning, with almost no corresponding increase in total number. It was as if Eva answered the phone once and never hung up. That was the only way of accounting for what the average was.

When I was ready to take my first call I switched the phone to *online*. It rang immediately. "James" was on the line. He sounded distressed; his voice had a desperate pleading edge to it. "Can you help me?" he said.

"Maybe. Not sure yet, need more information." I wasn't promising anything. People usually held you to it if you did.

"It's about the pension," said James.

As soon as he said "pension," I groaned. Pensions had nothing to do with council. They were up to the Department of Social Services, a federal body. But even with my limited experience, I knew how people got when you told them that. They just wanted someone to complain to, and call times at Social Services were even worse than ours. Which was an achievement in itself.

I did wonder if the number of complaining calls we got had anything to do with Eva's making the problem worse by sympathizing with people. She didn't do anything to assist them, but I often heard her say, "That's terrible" or "Those guys are such arseholes." This, I surmised, had the effect of making people feel they could call back.

I, on the other hand, was putting my efforts into education. "What do you know about the tiers of government, James?"

"They said I had to fill out a form. I filled out the form and sent it to them, but then they said it wasn't the right form. But they were the ones that sent *me* the form in the first place."

I told James I could be of assistance on this occasion. I got his full name and address and told him to keep an eye on his letter box.

"Thank you," he said. "Thank you *so* much. *Thank you.*" The change in his demeanor was marked. And it was hardly any effort, clicking on the How Government Works website and finding him a suitable factsheet.

After that there were four more calls in quick succession, and two of them were pension-related. It was at this point that I had my great idea.

I'd been thinking about all the data the council was collecting. It was great to have this information but, as Professor John Douglas always said, "Data is meaningless if you don't understand how to use it."*

The current information was limited to volume, average call

---

*He may not always have said this, technically, but he did say it in a newspaper article circa 1988.

length, and total call times. But there was only so much you could do with that. We could do a lot more if I started to *classify* the calls. I could create categories and at the conclusion of each call decide which category the call was in. This would facilitate trend analysis. I'd be able to demonstrate, for example, *with evidence*, that half the calls were unrelated to our sphere of influence, or that there was a twenty-five percent increase in requests for domestic assistance.

The possibilities. It was—and I would say this regardless of *whose* idea it was—brilliant. I could already see what a big impact it could have on this place.

Categories just started coming to me; I hardly had to think, all I had to do was write them down. And it was not only categories that came to me, I could see the spreadsheet itself: what things would go in columns, what would go in rows, what formulas I'd need.

I was writing it all down in my notebook, having the best time I'd had at council, notwithstanding meeting with the mayor, but then I was rudely interrupted—the phone again.

Not only that, it was my anonymous friend, the woman with the previous inquiry relating to takeaway foods. Apparently she was as underwhelmed by my answering as I was by her calling, because the first thing she said, the same as last time, was: "Is Eva there?"

"No."

"Where is she?"

"On her lunch break."

"At eleven o'clock in the morning? Council workers. Wish I could sit around and eat lunch all day." Her voice reminded me of someone when she said this. Maybe Kimberly? She was a big luncher.

"Can *I* help you?" I said.

"Probably not. It's . . . personal."

"You mean some form of domestic assistance? Home nursing?" I was testing out the categories. But it was a new one.

"My house is too quiet."

No relevant categories in the spreadsheet; nothing under Noise Guidelines in the handbook. I was baffled.

"There's no one in it," she went on.

"What about you?" Where was she living?

"No one *except* me. I'm the only one."

"You live alone," I clarified.

"I do now." Her voice softened. "It's the anniversary next week. Three years since he passed." The husband again. "It's just me now."

"I've always lived alone," I said, "except for when I was living with my mother." Why was I giving personal information? What if this person was a serial killer, and this was an elaborate plot to target me?

"Do you like it? Living alone?" she said.

"Most of the time. But I've had a while to practice." Thirty-seven years. I'd practiced being on my own all my life, regardless of the environment in which I lay my head. "You have to keep busy," I said, "doing things. Doesn't matter what they are—you just keep the day filled up." I would have suggested she focus on her career, but she was too old for that.

"I *do* keep busy, in the day. It's late at night that's the problem."

Nights could be hard, of course. That was the time for a level-five sudoku. Somehow the empty squares on the page made the empty spaces in the house less obvious.

"Cancer's cruel," she said. "I knew he was going, but . . ." Her voice trailed into the ether. Much like her husband had. "Do you believe in life after death?"

Sharon would be better—not more accurate, but certainly more voluble—with this sort of question. She had a lot of theories. Reincarnation, past lives, spiritualism. Nothing subject to peer review.

"No," I said.

"Me neither. When you're gone, you're gone."

"But you're not gone yet," I pointed out.

"No," she said. "I'm not gone yet."

- 8 -

When Eva went to lunch, I turned the phones off. I checked that no one else was around and typed: *Alan Cosgrove* and *Don Thomas* into the Internet search bar. When their photos came up, I downloaded one of each and put them side by side. Looking at them this way, I was sure they were the same person, even if their Wikipedia entries were different. I even did two eye tests: I had 20/20 vision.

I couldn't understand why Don would lie. What was the point of denying your greatest achievements? If it were me, I would have told everyone. It would have been the first thing I said when introduced to someone new. *Have you ever met a world champion? Trick question! You're meeting one right now.*

I used to love Alan. As a teenager, I went to every major sudoku event there was in the hope of seeing him. This was when public transport was even more inefficient than it is now and it took two hours to get into the city. Sharon would tease me and call me his "number one fan," sometimes upgrading this to "number one super-fan" in typical Sharonic disregard of the implied tautology.

He was hardly ever there, and we spoke only one time, but we had an unspoken connection: It didn't require acknowledgment on his behalf. Although, that said, it would have been better if he *had* acknowledged it.

I thought a lot about how life would be different if Alan was in it. Monday through Thursday I'd have homework, but on Friday nights we'd go to the Knox Mall and attend a movie. I'd say, "I'll make popcorn for us and bring it along," and he'd say, "Don't worry about it," and buy an extra-large one *each*, so we didn't have to share. People from school would see us and wonder who he was, this handsome, rich man I was standing with. Maybe they'd rethink their behavior towards me, without teachers having to get involved.

On Saturdays Alan and I would go to a sudoku competition if one was on or, if it wasn't, we'd sit around and do sudokus together. We'd do the same sudoku at the same time and keep a tally in a book of who was quicker, which, to start off with, would be him; over time, with a bit of encouragement, I'd get better. Alan would say, "Well done" or "That was quick." Rather than, for example: "Are you finished yet?" or "Germaine, I'm worried about you."

In time, we might go on holidays together, and not only in winter when everything was on special, but all the time, whenever we wanted. Of course, Sharon would have to come, too, and I'd sleep with her in the big bed and Alan would be on the fold-out couch. The three of us would share a single mini-soap to wash our hands or in the shower, and when the holiday was over Alan would let Sharon and me take the unopened ones home.

I didn't think having Alan in my life would change me, but I did think it would improve the experience of being me. My glass would be fuller, or at least it would *feel* fuller, instead of feeling like everyone else had got together and agreed on a specific size of glass and volume of liquid and I was wandering around holding a giant mug with a tiny splash of water in it.

The problem was that everyone wanted Alan. When Sharon said I was the number one fan, this implied there were other, lesser fans. She called them "groupies." I was not a groupie. I didn't have a group.

Groupies were older, anyway. Most of the sudoku fraternity were in their twenties or thirties. I'd tried meeting people my own age with similar interests, but my success rate was low. It peaked in 1997, when the Internet first started. I used to log on to World Puzzle fan page after school and chat. [Sharon at the door: *Germaine, is everything okay in there?*]

I had my first relationship with someone I met on Alan's website—we were Mathgirl and Blackadder—but the mistake we made was meeting up IRL. The idea of a guy my own age who liked the same things as me turned out to be much better than the reality. Sometimes the less you know the better, sometimes you *have* to delude yourself and pretend to believe in things that aren't real. Like imaginary numbers:

$$i^2 = 1$$

"*i*" is a concept, it doesn't exist. You can't multiply the same two numbers and get a negative, but we pretend it *does* exist. We pretend other things exist, too: Santa Claus, the tooth fairy, cryptocurrencies.

They're not lies, exactly. Like how a secret isn't exactly a lie.

Peter said, "Let's not tell anyone, Germaine. Let's keep this to ourselves."

I don't know why I said, "What *is* 'this'?" I knew Peter didn't like definitions. I'd put extensive glossaries in my reports and he always got rid of them.

It was only a question, but he refused to answer.

I should have said to Don: "Alan Cosgrove was a great man, a man I have always admired," and *then* asked if he was him.

I made the photos bigger on the screen, zooming in on both Alan's and Don's faces.

Poor Don. Where Alan's face was young—younger, anyway—and full of optimism, Don's was sadder, more resigned. It seemed to brim with disappointment.

I could see how lonely he was. I felt the way Sharon feels around cats or Eva around sandwiches—I wanted to hold him, hug him to my chest, and whisper compliments in his ear. *You're great, Alan. Everybody loves you.*

– 9 –

The following week, on Biscuit Tuesday, Eva tried to fob the jars off on me again, but I was wise to her. Not only was it (a) her turn but (b) I knew better.

"No, thank you," I said. But I did go upstairs to collect my personal allocation, as was in keeping with the official policy.

The tearoom was empty, except for a man in shorts and hiking boots standing near the sink. He was in his early forties and not unattractive (maybe a 6.3?) but sloppy-looking and too laid-back for my liking. His shirt wasn't ironed and the collar had crumpled, folding down around his neck and curling upwards at the ends.

I observed the man remove the lid from the cream-filled barrel. He put his bare hand inside and fished about for a biscuit, paying no heed to the newly erected signage fixed to the wall behind him:

TONGS MUST BE USED FOR BISCUITS.
IT IS FOR HYGIENE REASONS.
MAXIMUM BISCUIT ALLOWANCE:
2 BISCUITS PER PERSON PER DAY
(8 IF RICE CRACKERS)

I frowned and made a low tsking sound, and when this failed to garner his attention, said, "No tongs?"

When he looked up, his face was not embarrassed or apologetic.

There was a gap between his front teeth some people might have found endearing.

I pointed at the sign, which he did not look at.

"I won't tell if you don't," he said.

That was the difference between us. Mine was an innocent mistake whereas his was a transgression in full knowledge. *And* he wanted me to be an accomplice.

I increased the severity of my expression, but he was oblivious. He pulled out four (4) Monte Carlos and a cream-filled yo-yo. He offered me the yo-yo, then, when I declined, tossed it back in.

By now I had decided he was a 6, maybe even a 5.9. The gap between his teeth was not appealing enough to override certain other personality traits.

Having selected his biscuits, he moved to one side so I could access the barrels. He watched as I used the tongs to extract rice crackers and began to count out aloud as I set them on the bench.

This "assistance" was doing nothing to improve the experience of our interaction. I cut him off at six. "Aren't you cold?" I said.

He looked down at his legs, as though he hadn't realized he had shorts on. Then he said, "Actually, no . . . Did you know you only lose ten percent of your body heat through your legs? Most of it comes out through your head and your feet. You're better off wearing a beanie and a pair of socks than pants."

"I know," I said. "I've known that for ages."

"Really? I thought I just made it up."

"No, I've read it before. Quite a few times."

"Huh . . . Where?"

He was a 3.7 now and plummeting rapidly. "In different articles . . . Can't remember which ones."

"Well, if you do remember, can you let me know?" He held out his hand, an infuriating gesture. "I'm Jack. I'm in IT."

I didn't shake. I pretended it was too difficult, on account of holding four rice crackers in each of my hands. But I gave him my name. "Germaine Johnson, Senior Citizens Helpline." It would have been good if I could have said, "Germaine Johnson, Senior Citizens Helpline *and* Special Projects," but it wasn't official yet. Or not public knowledge anyway.

"Well, Germaine," said Jack. "Enjoy those eight rice crackers. And if you do happen upon any reading you think might be of interest, let me know."

Twenty-two hours later, eleven of which were spent perusing online databases and scientific journals:

To: Jack Bowe, IT

From: Germaine Johnson, Senior Citizens Helpline

Please find attached article from *Journal for Scientific Medical Studies of Australian Sciences* (v. 3, 2013) regarding body heat loss via head and other limbs.

To: Germaine Johnson, Senior Citizens Helpline

From: Jack Bowe, IT

Thank you for the article.

One question: You write, "heat loss via head and other limbs." Is the head a "limb"?

To: Jack Bowe, IT

From: Germaine Johnson, Senior Citizens Helpline

Please find attached an article from the *Journal for Scientific Medical Studies of Australian Sciences* (v. 3, 2013) regarding body heat loss via *head and limbs*.

To: Germaine Johnson, Senior Citizens Helpline

From: Jack Bowe, IT

Thanks, Germaine.

Maybe we can talk through the contents over lunch?

Lunch?

I pushed the chair back from the desk and looked to see who was watching. First Eva and now Jack. Two invitations for lunch in less than one week. It must be some sort of joke. Maybe they were evangelists, recruiting for some religion? Neither of them seemed the type, but maybe that was their strategy. Send in the most unlikely candidate, make the target comfortable, and then when their defenses are down and they are at their most vulnerable, ask, *Do you believe in God?*

I glanced at Eva, who was on the phone.

"I *suppose* I could organize a cleaner. Yes, yes, you qualify. Look, I'll have to ring around. I'm not promising anything."

There was no evidence to suggest religious fervor. Quite the opposite. Pinned above her desk was a sticker that said, IN CASE OF ZOMBIE APOCALYPSE, FOLLOW ME.

What a strange thing for Jack to do. It was not as though our interaction in the kitchen had been so satisfying as to warrant further contact. In fact, it had been entirely *un*satisfying, so far as I was concerned. It was reminiscent of—

Oh. Oh no.

Last time I agreed to go to lunch with co-workers. Susan, David, Wayne. *Come, Germaine*, they said. *We'll meet you there.* Then: an empty table in the tearoom, smirking faces in the hall, whispers in the meeting later.

I patted my fringe down flat. Flatter; flattest. Be wary, Germaine. People are not always as friendly as they seem.

I went to delete the message but another email appeared.

I can go at 12. Or 1? Or 2?
I'll come get you.

He was very eager. Could it be he had an interest in heat loss? Perhaps I'd misrepresented my expertise. Because I wasn't a scientist. I knew very little about it. All I knew was what I'd read in the article. If he wanted to learn more, he would be better off spending the time doing a literature search or trawling the bibliography of the original article in order to identify other articles.

Or did he want fashion advice? But there must be a website that told you when shorts were/were not appropriate.

So . . . perhaps . . . What if it was just an invitation to lunch, nothing more? That was a possibility. Such things must exist. But that in itself brought complications.

I had lunchtime organized. At the start of the week I brought in three tomatoes, a large can of tuna in oil, and 1,000 cubic centimeters of cooked pasta. Each day I put three-fifths of one tomato, 85 grams (undrained weight) of tuna, and 200 cubic centimeters of pasta in a bowl. I microwaved it for one minute, stirred, and then put it back in for an additional thirty seconds. I ate it on the bench near the car park or, if the weather was bad, in my car.

When Jack talked about discussing something over lunch, I was quite sure he wasn't asking to share my tuna pasta. He wasn't envisaging we would sit on the bench together. He meant *go out* for lunch.

And this idea brought with it a multitude of other worries. Was Jack going to pay for lunch and, if so, did this mean I would have to pay another time? What if the lunch I paid for was more expensive than this lunch? Was it wrong to bring a coupon? What about onion and garlic? Because these were appealing items, but problematic.

And what if there was a romantic element to Jack's request? What if "lunch" was in inverted commas? A euphemism for something more?

I wasn't going to . . . Colleagues were off-limits, after what happened with Peter.

It was nice to be asked, though. Assuming it was a sincere invitation. If not for Jack's casual dress sense and what I'd seen of his personality, I might revise him upward, to a 7.2. Perhaps even higher.

A third email arrived:

Hello?
I'm starving.

I checked the clock. Normally I ate at half past, but I could eat at twelve. I could have a cup of tea at three instead of three-thirty and move dinner forward to six o'clock. I might not even notice I'd eaten earlier; I might have dinner at the normal time. Maybe I could even take today's allocation of pasta home and have it for dinner. Jack could pick me up and we could walk to the venue together. I would insist on splitting the bill and make it clear this was a platonic lunch, nothing more. I would eat garlic, and sit at a distance.

The cursor winked. I shut my eyes. *Fine*, I wrote, and hit Send.

– 10 –

Jack was punctual. He came to get me at exactly twelve o'clock. By then I'd decided lunch was a bad idea and if he was even one minute late I'd make an excuse not to go. But there he was: same hiking shorts, same shoes, different top.

"Should we go?" he said.

"Sure." Eva got her wallet from her drawer.

Jack was supposed to say, "You're not invited," but he did nothing of the sort. In fact, it rather seemed he expected she would come.

And so it was a scenario I had not considered: having lunch with *both* of them.

We went to a café over the road. It was not as nice as where I'd been with the mayor. What it gained in proximity it lost in ambience. The woman at the counter did not greet us by name and there were no skinny cappuccinos, only a bain-marie and a sandwich bar.

Eva ordered an assortment of fried goods, Jack, a curry, and I had a roll. We sat in the courtyard outside to eat.

Eva said to Jack, "Did you get the email I sent? The one with the cute cat?"

"Yes."

"Did you like it? Wasn't it great?" She turned to me. "I sent him a photo of a cat riding an invisible bike. That's what it looks like, doesn't it, Jack? Doesn't it?"

"Yeah, I guess. Sort of."

"It does," Eva assured me.

I nodded. "Want to hear some facts about heat loss?" I didn't give her a chance to answer. I didn't know if Jack had explained already—how often did they talk?—but I gave an overview of the article I'd sent. Jack didn't ask for additional information. Neither of them did.

Eva said, "I love cat pictures. Whenever someone sends me one, I print it out and take it home. I have hundreds of them."

"How are you liking the job so far, Germaine?" said Jack.

"It's fine," I said.

"Fine" was the averaged experience. Some parts were > fine, some parts were < fine.

"Just wait until you qualify for long service," said Eva. "Then you'll never want to leave. It's basically five weeks holiday a year. I'm saving mine."

"For what?"

"For if I want to go overseas or something. I might go to Tasmania for a while."

"Tasmania's not overseas," I said.

"Sure it is. *Over*seas. You have to catch a boat to get there. Right, Jack?"

"Well . . . yeah, *over* seas. But it's not international," he said.

"I didn't say it was international. I said it was *over seas*."

Mercifully, the door to the courtyard opened and our food came out.

"How long have you guys been at the council?" I said, as Eva peeled the outside off her dim sum, then ate it, leaving the insides in a squishy ball on her plate. It was hard to watch.

Eva said twelve years, and Jack said sixteen.

"Have you always been in the same positions? Doing the same things?"

The answer was yes, for both of them.

"Where do you think you'll be in five years?" I asked.

Eva said, "Tasmania."

Jack said, "I'd like to move out of home eventually."

"You live with your parents?" I said.

"With my mother, but I'm in a granny flat out the back so it's *like* I live by myself."

I filled my mouth with sandwich.

"Did I say I like pictures of goats, too?" said Eva. "Not as much as cats. But still, more than a lot of other animals."

After lunch the phones were busy. I had little time to work on my spreadsheet; it was all I could do to classify the incoming calls.

There was one for domestic assistance, two for garden maintenance, and then I got my first heavy breather. Some guy, breathing heavily on the phone. I said, "Listen, here. There'll be none of that."

"None of what?" he puffed.

I knew about heavy breathers because, for a brief period, Sharon worked on telephones, too. Different industry, though—sex talk. The good part was she could work from home. The bad part was she was a dominatrix who specialized in ██ and ██.

Actually, no, they were both bad parts. And it wouldn't have been appropriate to tell the current caller to squeal like a pig.

I said, "If you don't start saying something I will have to end the call."

He puffed some more. "I'm . . ."

He was what? I was cringing.

Turned out he wasn't a heavy breather, he was an asthmatic and had run out of Ventolin. I had to call triple zero and say there was an emergency.

I said to Eva, "What happens now? Will they tell me if he dies?"

She said, "You can call the hospital; they'll take him to the Austin. I've sent an ambulance before, but you're not supposed to. Hey—can you recycle tissues?"

After that, the anonymous woman called, the one with the dead husband.

"How was your anniversary?" I said. "Did you go to the Red Emperor?"

"No, I couldn't. I was . . . I didn't even leave the house."

"Was it quiet?"

"It was very quiet."

"You could have put the radio on."

"And listen to some inane rubbish? Prefer the sound of nothing."

For a moment, that's the sound we listened to, the sound of nothing. I knew it well. Sometimes it was loud, and sometimes it was quiet. It wasn't loud right now.

The woman said, "I get so angry since Bernard died."

"That's his name? Your husband?"

"Bernard. Bernard Brown."

So my anonymous caller was a Mrs. Brown. It was a common surname, but it seemed to be extra common of late. I'd met another person quite recently with the same . . .

Oh, wait.

Professor John Douglas would say don't jump to conclusions. Just because it looks like two data points are converging, it doesn't mean they are. But she *did* sound familiar.

"You there?" said the woman.

. . . Said Celia *Brown*.

I couldn't even. If I'd been holding the phone instead of wearing a headset I would have dropped it. How could this nice woman be Celia *Brown*? And vice versa.

"I'm different now. Since he died. Some days I think the old me is gone forever."

"Okay, well—"

"It's true. I never used to be like this."

"I'm sure you have your reasons." I was speaking very quickly.

"How's *your* living situation? You've got a quiet house, too. No partner?"

"No."

"Don't do it. Fine while they're here; terrible when they're gone. Some days I don't think it was worth it."

"Probably not."

"But like you said, keep busy. Which is why I'm calling. Do you know someone who works there called Germaine Johnson?"

I paused, then answered truthfully. "Yes," I said, "I know Germaine."

"What's she like?"

"Very nice. Competent, professional . . . Good with numbers."

"Well, she's not very good with people. I had a letter from her—I'm on a committee," Celia started to explain, though no explanation was necessary.

After my meeting with the mayor I'd sent Celia and the club a letter. At the time I'd enjoyed writing it. It said:

Dear Celia,

This is an official warning. Recently a highly valued staff member visited you and your members regarding an important issue. Your response was less than satisfactory . . .

She read out a different portion. "It says, *The car park at the senior citizens center is classed as 'shared infrastructure'* . . . We've been having problems with the golf club, next door, you see. They're trying to take us over."

"You're not antagonizing them, are you?"

"No!" She was insulted. "What are you insinuating?"

"It's just a question. Sometimes callers mislead us on the phone. Sometimes they say things that aren't true, or they leave out important information." It was on the tip of my tongue to say: *like the fact they put chains on the wheels of other people's cars,* but I exercised restraint.

"I see." The woman on the phone sounded so much like Celia I was surprised I hadn't picked it up earlier. "You lot are all the same, aren't you?" she said, and hung up.

If there's one thing I learned from reading the newspaper article featuring Professor John Douglas, it's that if you can't achieve something one way, it doesn't mean it's not achievable. All it means is you have to identify other potential avenues. He said (quote): "I went down many wrong paths before I found this one."

If I applied this way of thinking—a way of thinking I was genetically disposed to, given he was my father—how else could I make the senior citizens center understand that the car park wasn't for their exclusive use?

One option was to speak to someone other than Celia, someone more receptive. Someone, perhaps, who was also responsible for communicating with the various subcommittees?

I logged off from incoming calls and consulted the handbook to get the number for the senior citizens center. It was under "B" for "Buildings" (i.e., unhelpfully classified).

There was no answer on the first two attempts, but on the third:

"Hello, this is Gladys Watts."

Gladys Watts, the vice president. *And* she remembered having met me. She didn't know my name, but that was easily rectified.

"Sorry, Germaine. I think I missed the phone before," said Gladys. "We're having a bit of a celebration down here."

"Someone won something," I said, remembering.

"Yes, Betsy's going to the CWA final in Sydney. She's representing the state in five categories."

"CWA?" Something to do with clock watching?

"Country Women's Association. It's a baking competition. She won best banana cake, best butter cake, best butter biscuit, best chocolate sponge, and best Monte Carlo."

How boring. Anyone can cook; you just follow a recipe. I didn't waste time with congratulations. There were four calls in the queue, and Eva wasn't doing much to bring the number down. I asked Gladys if she'd got my letter.

She paused. "Yes. Betsy and I were a bit worried about it, actually. But Celia said there was nothing to worry about. She said it was just a formality."

A formality? I felt a familiar prick of irritation. "It wasn't a formality. You were right to be concerned. Concern was entirely the appropriate response."

Suddenly, Eva seemed to sit up. Her ears visibly pricked.

"Is the lease being renegotiated?" said Gladys. "Betsy and I thought it sounded like you might kick us out. But Celia said that would never happen."

Eva's chair moved closer. She was facing forward, but her seat had rolled across.

"I think it's best if I come and speak with you in person," I told Gladys. *"Without Celia."*

"Without Celia?" Gladys sounded nervous. "I don't know if she'd like that."

"Well, don't tell her," I said.

I felt very satisfied when I hung up the phone. Celia might have thought she could ignore me and I'd go away, but that was not the case. Not only was the incident in question to be taken seriously, but I, too, was to be taken seriously. If she wouldn't listen, I'd find someone who would.

11

Francine organized a team meeting. She pushed a chair into our area and the three of us sat in a circle. Eva put the biscuit jars on the floor in the middle so we could all reach.

"How are things going?" said Francine, extracting a cream-filled one. The question was directed at me for first response.

"'Things,'" I said. "What do you mean?"

"Anything and everything," she said. "Work, life; whatever, really."

She made it sound like there were no wrong answers, but that wasn't true. There are always right answers and wrong answers. That's how you know what to say when someone asks you a question.

"Actually," said Francine, as though a thought had just occurred to her. "Here's an idea. We should do some getting-to-know-you activities." She tossed her notebook on the floor behind and wiggled in the chair as though loosening up. The wiggle reminded me of Sharon. She does the same thing when she takes her bra off in the evening. *That's better*, she says.

"Have you ever played the game where you say one thing about yourself that's true and one thing that's not true and everyone has to guess which is which?"

"I *love* that game," said Eva. "Me first. I have seven hundred twenty-three photographs of cats. Or, I have *eight hundred ninety-seven* photos of cats."

"Hmm," said Francine, thinking.

I'd played the game before and this was not a good example of how it worked. I said the two statements were meant to be different.

"They *are* different," said Eva. "How is seven hundred twenty-three not *different* than eight hundred ninety-seven?"

"They're not different *enough*," I said.

"Says who?"

"Okay," said Francine. "Different game . . . Or . . . what if we each say a little about ourselves? Like, where we live and what we like to do on the weekend. I live in Glen Iris, and I like hiking, gardening, and quilting. Now, Eva. Your turn."

Eva turned to face the wall.

"Germaine?" said Francine.

"I'd rather not disclose."

There was a pause.

"We had thirty-seven calls yesterday," I said. "And I answered thirty-three of them."

"Great," said Francine. "Eva, how many did you answer?"

It got worse.

"Five," said Eva.

"Excellent," said Francine, just as enthusiastic as she had been to me.

I had to point out that Eva could not have answered five calls if I had answered thirty-three. "Thirty-three plus five would be thirty-eight. We only got thirty-seven calls."

"You make it sound like a puzzle," said Francine. "If I have six beans and you have seven beans, how many beans are there in total?"

"Thirteen," I said.

"It was just an example," she said.

Eva turned to be part of the circle again. "One of Germaine's calls was from Celia Brown," she said.

"No, it wasn't," I said.

"It was."

"It *wasn't*."

Eva sat on her hands and refused to look at me. Francine tried to sound casual. "Did you get a call from Celia Brown?"

"No, I got a call from *Gladys Watts*, if you must know. But I can't divulge specifics. It's part of my special project."

Eva gave Francine a meaningful look.

Francine brushed biscuit crumbs from her lap, slowly, carefully. "Germaine," she said. "I know the mayor's got you working on something important but . . . How can I say this? Sometimes things are more complicated than they seem."

"And sometimes they are less complicated," I said.

"I suppose."

"And sometimes they are neither more nor less complicated but exactly as complicated as they appear."

Francine put her hand to her chin. "I just hope . . . What I mean is, if you have any questions or if anything seems strange or unusual . . . or if you want some help, just ask."

"Sure." I couldn't imagine that would ever happen.

Confession: After the team meeting I sent an email. It wasn't vindictive. It was simply a series of biscuits-related observations I thought Ralph Garner, the health and safety officer, might be interested in knowing. How was I to know he'd take it so seriously?

Less than an hour later he sent an email of his own:

To: ALL STAFF

From: Ralph Garner, Health and Safety Coordinator

Colleagues,

Recently, biscuit-related signage was erected in the kitchen instructing staff on the use of tongs. I have been made aware that people have flagrantly disregarded this advice. Additionally, in a number of instances individuals have eaten in excess of 2 biscuits/8 rice crackers.

Effective this afternoon, we will *remove all biscuits* to ensure that there is not an outbreak of salmonella or similar. You will recall a recent lunchtime lecture in which I cited incidents of feces in bowls of complimentary bar nuts.

Signage regarding hand washing, etc., has been installed in all bathrooms. We are considering making food-handling training compulsory for all staff.

You will be kept informed.

Regards, Ralph

"Oh," I said to Eva, keeping my voice light. "They're removing the biscuits."

There was no response. Just the curt click of her fingers on the mouse.

"It's probably for the greater good," I said. "Biscuits are very fattening."

The dramatic sipping of Slurpee suggested improved diet was not high on Eva's list of priorities. I went to get a cup of tea.

Upstairs, the space by the urn was empty. The barrels were gone. A printout of Ralph's email was attached to the wall with his signature down at the bottom in black pen, like a medieval edict.

"Did you see this?" said a man holding a Commonwealth Bank mug. "They've taken away the biscuits."

"I *know*," said a woman with a big nose. "They should have warned us. What will I have for lunch?"

"Terrible," I said, and went back downstairs.

"People are very upset," I said to Eva. The words rolled over the top of her computer. We did not speak for the rest of the day.

The weekend came as a welcome respite. Sharon called and said, "What are you doing on Saturday? Why don't you pay your mother a visit?"

"But your birthday's not until next week," I said.

Even if I'd wanted to I couldn't have. The Melbourne Sudoku Forum was on. I got my ticket months ago, when they first went on sale.

I was so excited about going I couldn't eat breakfast. I sat at the kitchen table, staring at a bowl of Weet-Bix, thinking. Not about anyone in particular.

I had my autograph book and a camera and I was just about to leave, but then at the front door I thought to get some extra paper to collect a signature for Sharon and by the time I stepped into the hall I wasn't paying attention. I didn't realize until it was too late.

Jin-Jin was there.

"Germaine," she said.

I told her I couldn't talk. I didn't say where I was going by way of invitation, I only mentioned it so she'd know how important it was and wouldn't hold me up any longer than was necessary. Problem was, Jin-Jin *more* than understood.

"OMG, I *love* sudoku. Can I come?"

"No. You need a ticket."

"I'll buy one."

"I'm pretty sure they're sold out."

"I'll try anyway."

I tried to lose her on the fire escape but though she was short, she was fast. She followed me all the way to the tram stop.

"Do you think Rebecca Li will be there?"

"Maybe."

"Magnus Magnus?"

"I don't know."

On the tram I got out my book. Jin-Jin said, "What are you reading?"

I gave her a stern look and said, *"This."*

Jin-Jin and I got off at Flinders Street and walked along the river to the Convention Center. I thought there'd be more people, a slow-moving mass surging in the same direction, but it was like a normal day.

And Jin-Jin did get a ticket. The lady selling them said they had hundreds left. She even gave Jin-Jin a discount, which seemed unfair. You shouldn't reward people for being disorganized.

I was hoping Jin-Jin and I might separate in the foyer, but she stuck to me like glue. I looked around for familiar faces. I couldn't see Don, but I did see someone else I knew.

Jack might have been at work for what he was wearing: hiking shorts and a hooded jumper. "I knew you'd be here," he said.

I didn't respond. My great day was turning out crappy. While he and Jin-Jin introduced themselves, I kept scanning the area.

When I turned back, a fourth person had appeared in our circle.

She looked like Jack—same hiking shorts, same gap between her teeth—only instead of sandy brown hair, hers was red. I supposed she was his girlfriend. That's what happens with couples. They morph into each other over time, like pets and their owners. Sharon and her Labrador, Barney, were practically identical. I don't know what the redhead's name was. Jack told me, but I didn't listen—that's how uninterested I was.

The bells rang, and we went into the main hall for presentation. Because of the tardiness of our entry we couldn't get a seat for four people in a row. We had to sit in twos, and I got stuck with Jin-Jin. It felt like a short straw, though in truth none of them was very long.

Jin-Jin said, "I love Magnus Magnus."

"I can't stand him."

"How can you not like Magnus Magnus?" she said.

Magnus was Sudoku Australia's golden child. I'd have hated him for that anyway, but I hated him more for what he did to Alan Cosgrove. I scanned the row behind.

Jin-Jin said, "Who are you looking for?"

"No one. I've got a crick in my neck."

As the session was about to start, I had one final glance, which was fortuitous, because it turned out to be the most important one. Don *was* there, standing up in the back. He had a hat on and sunglasses, but the same tan pants he'd worn in the mayor's office.

I saw him, and he saw me. Suddenly, he moved towards the doors. I picked up my bag and walked crab-like over the other people in the row.

In the hall I didn't know what to call out. Alan or Don? I yelled both.

He either didn't hear or didn't want to stop. He went all the way to the other end of the foyer and might have gone out the door, but it was locked. I'd hoped one of us might pursue the other, but not like this. Still, the outcome was the same.

"Hello, Alan," I said.

He tugged on the door handle. When it didn't move he turned around and took his hat off. "Hello, Germaine."

12

Six months ago I'd never have thought I'd be having coffee with Alan Cosgrove. Sharon would say I'd willed it into existence, but I preferred to think of it as an event with a small but not nonexistent likelihood of occurring. Not a coincidence. Don't get me started on those.

We went to a café close by. As luck would have it, we were the only two there. It was as though one of us had hired the place out as a romantic gesture for the other. Only neither of us had.

The waiter got us waters and menus, which he left on the table. Don waited until he was gone and then said, "So you're a sudoku fan?"

"I guess. I mean, isn't everyone?"

This was called "downplaying." You don't want to appear to care too much about things. Caring is a sign of weakness; Peter taught me that. A few people did, actually.

Don seemed different from how he was the other times I'd seen him. Less assured. He fiddled with the corner of his menu and seemed to have trouble making eye contact.

I knew why. He was trying to work out if I knew what had happened. I did, but I didn't believe any of it. Alan Cosgrove was not a cheater.

"I hate Magnus Magnus," I said.

Faces are funny things. You don't know one is not in its most relaxed position until every part of it adjusts a millimeter.

And then he smiled. It could have been a yawn for how contagious it was.

"Are you mad at him?" I said.

Don was like an elder statesman. "A little disappointed."

I knew about being disappointed. "Is that why you changed your name?"

He ran his hand though his hair. "Sometimes you have to start over. Easier than it sounds, of course. But you know Donald Trump lost his fortune three times."

It was six, actually. I'd read Trump's biography. But I didn't correct him. Being right felt like a secondary concern, which was unusual. I couldn't pinpoint my primary concern.

The waiter chose that moment to appear. We flipped the menus open. I ordered quickly—focaccia, chips, drink, a muffin. Don wasn't sure what he wanted. He read over each page slowly, affording me the opportunity to look at him.

He was older than I expected him to be. To me, he was *always*, perpetually, forever, the Alan Cosgrove of my teenage years. But I was thirty-seven now. It was inevitable he'd have faded and shrunk a little.

There was sixteen years' difference in Don's and my ages. When I was fifteen, this had seemed an eternity, like he could have been my father. But now, the difference as a proportion of total age had reduced, and it felt *less* like we were a generation apart and more like we were . . . both adults. I was glad I'd worn my favorite shirt.

Don asked for a cup of coffee. The waiter bowed and backed away.

There was a silence. I should have brought The List. All I could think of were forbidden topics, things I was *not* going to mention:

1. How I had attended every sudoku-related event in the years 1994–2007 in the hope of seeing him.
2. How he'd signed my autograph book at Sudo-Con 2006.
3. Any of the facts I knew about him: birthday, place of birth, which *Guinness Book of Records* titles he'd held.
4. Any of the facts I didn't know but wished I did: current earnings, asset profile, relationship status.

I settled on: "What's been the highlight of your career so far?" I only meant to give him the choice of talking about sudoku *or* something more current, like golf, but Don seemed to have difficulty answering the question.

"Well, 2006 was good for obvious reasons. Being World Champion's an honor and a privilege but . . . I don't know, Germaine. Sometimes life gives you lemonade and other times it gives you lemons. I used to have all the luck. I'd think, *Some idiot out there must be having the roughest time of all* because everything *I* touched turned to gold. And then . . . Well. It didn't last forever." He examined the two hands in his lap, both his. Behind him, the coffee machine gave a dejected sigh.

Don was a shadow of his former self. Once upon a time he was a 9.99999 recurring, now he was a 7. But I didn't mind. There was a kind of beauty in imperfection. A mathematical proof founded on a misconception could still have some elegance. Also, he was more attainable now.

I had half a thought to touch him.

The other half a thought was about Peter. Peter could be inconsistent in his affections, depending on what time it was. If the time was right, he'd say, "Germaine. I'm glad you're here," but if the time was wrong, he'd say, "Stop it. What if someone sees?"

Was this the right time or the wrong time?

Don said, "Sorry, I shouldn't have. I didn't mean to . . ."

I fixed him with my gaze. "Don't worry. You didn't."

I wish it had ended there. That was our best and truest moment. But the food arrived. I didn't mind his watching while I ate; I chewed with thoughtful rigor. But I did mind what happened next.

The waiter brought the bill, and Don said, "I'll pay," and handed over his card. That would have been a fine ending, too. Only the waiter came back and said, "There seems to be a problem."

Don colored and looked through his wallet. The waiter hovered, hands behind his back. Don said, "Oh, dear . . . I've given you the wrong . . . I can't seem to find . . . Germaine, do you mind?"

Don put his hat and sunglasses on, and we walked back to the Convention Center. We didn't hold hands, but I stood close enough so if he decided he wanted to, he'd only have to reach the tiniest amount and mine would be there, waiting.

Just my luck, the session was on a break and Jack, Jin-Jin, and Jack's girlfriend were all hanging around in the foyer. When they saw me, they came over.

I was forced to introduce them. "Don, this is Jack and Jin-Jin and . . . I don't know who she is."

"Germaine," said Jack.

"What?" I couldn't be expected to remember everyone.

Don was very accommodating. He was used to crowds of people vying for his attention. He shook all their unimportant hands and asked how they'd liked the first session.

Jack's girlfriend piped up, but I don't know what she said. Something boring.

Jin-Jin gave Don a funny look. "You know, you look a bit like Alan Cos—"

"*Shh*," I said.

Don, who had kind eyes and the patience of a saint, said, "Can you keep a secret?"

Jin-Jin started hyperventilating. "OMG, OMG."

I translated, as she was a foreigner. "He means shut up about it."

Jin-Jin stopped talking but got her phone out and took a photo.

Jack, who had been quiet up until now, hovering in the background, started talking. "I've seen you before," he said.

"Watch the 2006 final, did you?"

Jack glowered at him. "No, at the town hall . . . With Mayor Bainbridge."

Jack seemed to be in a mood. I knew how it was; sometimes when you come out of a really interesting, really motivating talk it makes you realize how inadequate you are. It can be confronting. But I don't know what he expected. Didn't seem like Jack tried very hard at anything, let alone sudoku.

Don said, "I've known Verity for years."

"They're friends," I told Jack. What I was really saying was, *We all are.* Me, Mayor Bainbridge, and Don Thomas: three vertices of a collegiate triangle.

Jack might have said something more, but the bell began to ding over the loudspeaker. The break was over. Don checked his watch. Then he turned to me—to *me*—and said, "I have to go . . . I'll see you later."

How much later? I wanted to know exactly when, but I was cautious. I could still hear Peter's voice in my ear: *Don't be so needy*, he'd told me a few times. Quite a few times, actually.*

---

*Fourteen, spread over a six-month period.

– 13 –

The afternoon provided an opportunity for people to practice their sudoku and get feedback on how to improve. There were tables set out in the main hall and representatives from the Victorian Sudoku Federation walked around offering assistance. I wasn't an official mentor, but I was helping anyway. And nothing is more helpful than standing behind someone as they fill out their card, whispering tips and insights.

Jack, Jin-Jin, and the mysterious redhead all seemed to get bored. "You can go," I said. But they said they'd wait and went and sat on a line of chairs near the window. I don't know what they were waiting for.

After an hour, the three of them came back, a delegation. Jack asked if I wanted to get dinner when it was over.

I said no. "I have to go home."

"Why?" said Jin-Jin. "Come on. You never go anywhere."

This was not true. I went to work. I visited Sharon once a month, and I walked to a local park at least three times a week.

But Jin-Jin acted like I was some kind of invalid. And invisible. She said to Jack and the redhead, "When I go past Germaine's apartment, I stop and sniff the air to make sure I can't smell a decomposing body. She could easily die and not be found for months."

What rubbish. The Red Emperor would come knocking if I didn't order a meal on a Friday night. And if I failed to pick up my packages from the letter boxes downstairs, Cynthia from the body corporate would notice. I order a *lot* of things online. And what if . . . perhaps . . . Don did, too? If he didn't see me "later," like we'd coordinated, he, too, might concern himself with my whereabouts.

No, my body wouldn't spend more than ten minutes decomposing before it got discovered.

"Come on, Germaine," said Jack.

Despite my misgivings, I agreed to go. Not because I thought it would be fun but because they wouldn't shut up about it. They were practically begging, which was kind of endearing. Even if you don't like someone (or multiple someones), you can't help but be flattered if they like you. You have to admire their good taste, at the very least.

We went to an all-you-can-eat yum cha. It was $36 per person, justifiable only on account of my having a water bottle with a wide neck, which I filled with dumplings to take home. This reduced the price per meal to an acceptable level.

The four of us were discussing the highlights of the convention when the redhead siphoned me off from the general conversation.

"Jack said you just started at the council," she said.

"Did he?" I tried to reel the other two back in. "One of the easiest things to do when you're starting out in sudoku is to concentrate on a single nonet. A nonet is a three by three."

But the redhead turned her body, blocking them from participation. "How do you like it?" she said.

"It's fine," I told her.

"You work in the call center, right?"

"I'm on the Senior Citizens Helpline, but I have other duties as well."

"Helpline, call center. Is there a difference? You answer the phone."

In my lap, the dumpling-filled water bottle got hot. "Who are you?" I said.

She patted her mouth with a serviette. "I'm Marie Curie."

I raised my eyebrows. I wasn't going to fall for that.

"No, it's true. My dad's surname happens to be Curie, and my mum wanted to name me after her mum: Marie."

"How unfortunate," I said.

"I don't mind." She tossed her red hair, which I'd never seen anyone do before, not so assiduously. "Everyone always remembers my name."

"Everyone always remembers my name, too," I said.

"Do they?" she said, with a very negative inflection.

We stared at each other until a new trolley appeared and the waitress removed a bamboo lid. "Chicken feet?"

Marie gave the gelatinous dish a disgusted look.

I picked up my fork. "We'll have two servings," I said.

The conversation returned to a four-way interface. Jack was still in his mood, feeling poorly about his sudoku inadequacies. Or his taste in women. Marie had very little to contribute to the conversation that was even half intelligent. Jack, meanwhile, took his frustrations out on Don.

"I don't like that guy," he said.

"Me either," said Marie, clearly not a free thinker. Lucky we weren't relying on her to discover radium.

Meanwhile, two beers had gone to Jin-Jin's head. She said *again* how she couldn't believe Alan Cosgrove and Don Thomas were the same person, and I said *again* she shouldn't talk so loud.

"I wouldn't worry," said Jack. "I don't think anyone's interested." He said this even after I explained the situation—how big a scandal it had been in the national world of sudoku, which comprised at least fifty people.

Jin-Jin said, "I think Don's very handsome."

"I don't," said Jack, and Marie smirked at me.

Jin-Jin asked what I thought, and they all seemed particularly interested in my answer. It was most unusual. So often I had to repeat myself, and now look: three people hanging on my every word.

"I don't know. I never notice what people look like. I only notice how stimulating they are to talk to."

Marie leaned forward, elbows on the table. "And is he stimulating to talk to?"

"He is, actually."

Jin-Jin held a dumpling in her chopsticks. "If I knew *he* was Don Thomas, I wouldn't have—" She stopped and cast a sidelong glance at me.

I had a dawning realization: Jin-Jin didn't look like a golfer. Her arms were very thin, and she didn't seem like someone who'd have good hand-eye coordination. "How do you know Don?" I said.

She was engrossed in her dumpling. "I don't, I've just heard his name before. I, ahem, go to the senior citizens center next door to the golf club most weekends for a homework group."

It didn't surprise me to hear she needed help with her studies.

"Do you know anything about an incident involving chaining up the wheels of cars?"

"No," she said.

"Are you sure?"

"Yes." Jin-Jin gestured for the waiter. "Excuse me, can we get the bill?"

- 14 -

I kept the receipt from the café with Don, intending to claim it on tax at the end of the financial year. This was not necessary, however, because when I got to work on Monday he'd emailed about paying me back. What a gentleman. And how fiscally responsible.

He said to come by the golf club "any time." He must have wanted to give me the money in person; otherwise, he'd have asked for my bank details.

I was meeting with Gladys at the senior citizens center in the afternoon and resolved to visit Don after. I didn't tell anyone, which was not difficult as Eva was ignoring me—still annoyed about the biscuits. She had the idea it was somehow my fault.

The morning took forever. Jack came to visit before lunch, which provided a minor distraction. He leaned against the wall, his hands behind his back. "How was Sunday?" he said.

"Good. Better than Saturday."

The forum went for two days, but most people (e.g., Jack, Jin-Jin, Marie, even Don) lacked the fortitude for both.

"Dinner was good," said Jack. "We should do that again."

Eva spun around. "You guys went for dinner?" she said. It was the first time she'd talked to me all morning.

I corrected her. "We had dinner in the same group of people."

"*That's* why she's been grinning all morning." Eva waved her annoying Slurpee.

I said Marie was there, too, but Eva didn't appear to hear. She gave a maniacal smile. Was she pretending to be me? If so, it was a terrible impression. I opened my book, wrote her name, and put a black dot against it.

Gladys Watts was not the only one in attendance at our afternoon meeting. The famous "Betsy" was also there. It transpired that in addition to being a cooking "champion" (insofar as you could call it that) she was also the club's treasurer.

Betsy didn't look like a champion; she wasn't wearing a medal or anything. She was wearing exercise clothes, despite being a bit portly, and she had the kind of face that seemed to default into smiling. Some people say it takes fewer muscles to smile than it does to frown, but I have done the research and this is incorrect. She must have trained her mouth to stay like that. I wondered why.

They were in the office when I arrived. I had just put my bag on the table when Betsy asked if I would like a cup of tea and, before I had the chance to answer, announced she'd make a pot and left the room. Gladys said, "Maybe don't say anything until she gets back."

This was a request I was willing to accommodate, sitting in silence even when Gladys changed her mind and said, "How are you, anyway?"

While we waited, I looked out the window. Past the car park and through the wire fence, the golf club's main building was visible. It was long, mostly glass, and it had a grand entrance with pillars.

I tried to imagine where Don's office was. Would it be on the ground floor or upstairs? Would it face this way or look out the other side? I ran my eyes across the building, left to right; up and down.

"It's a nice view, isn't it?" said Gladys.

I was in agreement, but we weren't supposed to be speaking until Betsy got back. I was preoccupied anyway, with the golf club. Fourth window across, ground floor. Don was sitting there now, I was sure of it. He was there and I was here, we were just a few hundred meters apart.

Gladys said, "I don't know what Betsy's doing. How long does it take to make a pot of tea?"

I had a vision: It was a dark night. Don was in his office and I was in the car park, holding a torch. I-L-O-V-E-Y-O-U, I flashed in Morse code.

"Celia will be back at three-thirty," said Gladys.

Don responded using his light switch: I-L-O-V-E-Y-O-U-M-O-R-E.

Then me: N-O, I-L-O-V-E-Y-O-U-M-O-R-E.

"I think we should go and get her," said Gladys.

The kitchen was large, almost industrial in size, but not at all modern. Small brown tiles covered the walls and floors, and the countertops were a mottled peach laminate. There were four white ovens in a row.

Betsy was standing by the sink, talking to an older man. "Sorry," she said when she saw us. "I got sidetracked. Ken says they're short a teacher on Saturday. No one for the mathematics table."

"Tom's sick," said Ken. "Shingles."

"What about Keith?" said Gladys.

"Keith's away. Vacation."

Betsy explained that the senior citizens center ran a homework group for young people on Saturdays. I remembered Jin-Jin mentioning it at dinner.

Betsy said they got students from primary school all the way to university attending. They helped with reading and writing and languages and mathematics. "Maths is always the hardest to find a tutor for. Seems like everyone is terrible at it."

"Does it pay?" I said.

"It's run by volunteers."

There was a long pause.

"You're not any good with numbers, are you?" said Gladys, and I was torn between wanting them to know I was so much more than my current position and the disinclination to participate in something as pointless as "volunteering."

"I wouldn't have time," I said.

"No. Of course not. You've got better things to do."

Then Gladys said that Celia was going to be back soon. Betsy streamlined the tea-making process by using bags instead of a pot. We each carried our own mug back to the office.

The ensuing conversation was very brief.

"The council cannot condone the chaining up of other people's cars," I told them. "If such behavior continues, then . . ." My voice trailed off.

"Then?" said Gladys.

I was evasive, in an ominous way. "Who can say?"

"Celia said the council wants to sell this place," said Betsy. Gladys made a show of admonishing her, but in truth, they both looked interested in the response.

"If I were you," I said, "I'd tell Celia to accept the situation and move on. Hopefully, she'll listen."

"Yes, hopefully," said Gladys.

Unfortunately, Celia returned earlier than expected. I came out the front door and saw her walking along the footpath. I tried to get in my car as quickly as possible, but she spied me and cut across the parking lot.

"Why are you here?" she said.

"Official duties." I still couldn't reconcile Celia with the woman on the phone, who was really quite pleasant.

"We got your letter, and we're not going to do a thing about it."

"I would advise against inaction," I said.

Celia pointed her finger at the golf club. "That lot have been harassing us."

"You've been antagonizing them." It is a great word, *antagonizing*, and very apt in the situation. But it is not a word you hear every day. The last time I'd used it was on the phone. It was unwise to use it again so soon, and with the same person.

Because Celia noticed. Her hand lowered and her pointing finger lost its rigidity. "What did you say?"

"I said you're annoying them."

"You said *antagonizing*."

"I said *annoying*."

"Wait a minute . . ." A slow dawning, a kind of horror spread across her face. She put both hands to her mouth, as if to stop words from coming out. It didn't stop them completely, though, because then she said, "What do you do at the council?"

"This and that . . . I have a very broad skill set." I got in the car and started driving.

I drove for fifteen minutes in a northerly direction. I didn't feel bad; I never lied to her. It was Celia's fault if she didn't realize who I was. She said herself she had a problem with anger. When I spoke to her again, I'd tell her she certainly did.

If I spoke to her again.

The best-case scenario was we'd go on as we did before. That would be my preferred way of dealing with it. If you didn't like how someone was being or wished you hadn't told them your private thoughts or secret hopes and dreams, the best thing to do was pretend you hadn't.

When I was sure Celia would have gone inside, I did a U-turn and drove back, only this time instead of turning into the seniors-center car park, I turned at the adjacent property.

I'd been to the Fitzsimmons Golf Club once before, years ago, when Kimberly had her wedding reception there. Back then it was old and staid. Now, it was much improved. I could see hints of Don everywhere I looked: in the upright pillars out the front, in the bold, red carpet, in the wooden winners panels that lined the walls in the foyer.

I asked at reception for Don, and he appeared almost immediately, a faded vision in a gray suit. He could have been George Clooney if you squinted and got the angle right.

Don said he was *pleased* to see me. Also: *glad* I'd come.

"Pleased" and "glad" were positive emotions, ones I reciprocated.

Don didn't bring his cash tin out, but led me down the hall to his office.

"How was the rest of the convention?" he said.

"It was okay." Coffee with him had been the highlight, but other aspects were pleasant also.

"Did your friends enjoy themselves?"

"They're not friends; they're acquaintances. I hardly even know those people." I had a vacancy in the friendship category, was what I was trying to tell him. I didn't know if he understood the subtlety of my messaging.

Don's office looked on to a rolling swathe of green. Picturesque, I guess. I don't know, I found the view bland, but Don stopped in the doorway and stared out, admiring it in such a way I felt obliged to admire it also.

"Wow," I said.

"I know. I've had this place for eight years and *still* every time I look out that window I can't believe how beautiful it is . . . All those trees. I love trees."

Sharon loved trees. I wasn't mad about them.

"We spend thirty thousand dollars a month on fertilizer," said Don. "And don't get me started on water. It costs a fortune to keep the greens like that."

"Maybe you should concrete some of it," I said.

He laughed, but not unkindly, at this suggestion.

Finally, we could sit down. There was a table. I sat in one chair, and he sat next to me. Next to, not opposite. I couldn't see a cash tin anywhere, only a large brown paper bag, stuffed full. He pushed it towards me. "This is for you," he said.

I was taken aback. A gift? No one ever gave me gifts.

I should have got one when I left Wallace Insurance, but because of the nature of my departure it never happened. I'd thought of sending a card for everyone to sign and write messages—I even pre-filled a return envelope—but every time I went to the postbox I hesitated. Should I be including guidelines on what to say or a pro forma of thoughtful phrases? People don't always know what's appropriate.

I lifted the bottom of the bag, and the contents slid out. Before I could register what was in front of me, Don picked the first thing up.

"This is a signed poster from the State Sudoku Forum in 2004. That's my signature, that's Rebecca Li's and that's Phillip Collins's. He was the—"

"Head adjudicator," I said.

"Yeah, the head adjudicator. That was the first year I qualified for finals. I bombed out in the second semi, though. Put a seven in the second box when it should have been a three."

"Wasn't that 2005?" I said.

He stopped. "You're right. That *was* 2005 . . . What happened in 2004?"

"I don't know." I paused for fake thought, not wanting to seem too enthusiastic, or too much like my actual self. "Um . . . Was that the year you took too long against Janis Woo and got eliminated?"

The way he looked at me was like he'd had eye surgery and was seeing me for the first time.

I made sure my fringe was flat against my forehead. I couldn't believe I was sitting next to him. It was like finding a sock I'd been looking for for ages. Suddenly, I had a pair.

We turned back to the pile.

Don pointed at a gold medal on a ribbon. "Ah, 2006. Now *that* was a good year. You know if you win they give you a trophy at the ceremony, but you have to give it back. They put it on display at the Australian Puzzle Federation's office in Canberra. They let visitors in on the weekends. Get hordes in summer, I'm told."

There were a few seconds of mutual examination, both of us looking at the medal. I didn't ask what happened the following year, in 2007. Did the World Puzzle Federation remove the plaques that had his name on them? Or did they add explanatory cards saying how his titles had been revoked because he'd cheated (allegedly)? I wasn't going to ask; I am not an idiot.

Don picked the medal up by the ribbon and held it out. "I want you to have it," he said.

I said no, I couldn't possibly. Maybe not *never* but certainly *not yet*. Maybe after a period of time, when I was sure he wouldn't change his mind.

"*Go on*," he said.

"No, it's yours. You should put it on your mantelpiece at home. Or on display in a dedicated cabinet."

Don's face changed. His mouth moved in a negative direction. "I can't even give the thing away," he said.

"It's probably worth a lot of money," I said. I was trying to buck him up, same as I'd want someone to buck me up in such a moment.

"Ha. I tried selling it, but no one wants it."

He shifted his hand so the medal swung on its ribbon, like his mood. One minute happy, next minute sad.

I didn't know what to do. Maybe I should change the subject? I'd brought The List. There were lots of interesting topics on it.

Don started mumbling to himself. I don't know what he was saying, but it allowed me to observe him more keenly. This was fortuitous, in a way. Because if I hadn't, I wouldn't have noticed. It was only because I was looking at him so closely that I saw what I *had* seen but hadn't fully taken in:

The crumpled collar on his shirt.

How his tie was faded, and his self.

Why would anyone try to *sell* a medal?

All at once, I realized. I didn't have to do extensive research to quantify the extent of Don's fall. I was abreast of what he'd lost:

- The 2007 World Sudoku title
- Prize money from the 2006 and 2007 world titles, which had to be returned
- $30,000 fine to the World Puzzle Federation
- Undisclosed amounts in legal fees
- His Casio calculator sponsorship deal

But it was only then, in that moment, I understood the true extent of it: Don was broke.

I agreed to take the items only to appease him. At home I set them on the mantelpiece, balancing the medals against the larger trophies and arranging the certificates behind. It was an impressive collection.

I got out my computer and searched to see if what Don said was true. It did appear to be correct. The market for sudoku championship paraphernalia, even when accrued at the national level, *was* limited. I found an old listing for a trophy and emailed the seller, to see if he was a collector. He replied that the listing was a joke.

A joke.

I didn't like to think of Don that way. People weren't jokes. It wasn't funny to laugh at someone.

I kept looking at the collection of items. If they were mine, no way would I ever have given them away. Not even when I died. I'd have asked to be buried with them, like a knight with his sword. But here they were. I touched a medal. I put it on and felt the weight of it against my chest.

I guessed he didn't think any of it was special. Or he *did* think it was special and *I* was special enough to be its keeper. Me. I closed my hand around the metal, hard, so I could feel its edges bite and understand how real it was. It was not imagined. It existed.

- 15 -

As the week went on Eva's thinking regarding the biscuits failed to evolve. When Jack asked if we wanted to go for lunch, she replied, "I'm not going if she does." How strange that she thought her absence would reduce the enjoyment of the situation.

At the café, Jack said, "What's up with Eva?"

I said perhaps, maybe—I was speculating—she blamed me for the removal of the biscuits.

"Why?"

"I have no idea. She has no reason to." Not unless she'd read my emails.

"Oh, well. I wouldn't worry," he said. "She'll get over it."

And she did, eventually. Three days later, when I got to work, she greeted me with the sort of enthusiasm she generally mustered only for leftover sandwich platters.

"Germaine," she said. "How *are* you?"

I was wary. "Good."

"That's good." Her face scrunched upwards. "Hey—would you like a packet of Post-its? I got extra at the stationery cupboard. Noticed you were out."

Normally, Eva hoarded Post-its like they were nuggets of gold. She was always getting more of them and accusing me of stealing the ones she already had. I'd tried explaining that even if I *had* taken them, which I hadn't, it wasn't stealing because they didn't belong to her. They belonged to the council and I worked there, too.

"What's going on?" I said.

"What do you mean, 'What's going on?' Just exchanging pleasant-ries. Let me know if you need any more." She tossed the Post-its over. They landed by the phone; I didn't pick them up.

"Want to know how I am?" she said.

"Not really."

"I'm good. I'm very good. Want to know why?" Without waiting for a response, she rolled towards me. She lowered the volume of her voice. "Because I know how we're going to get the biscuits back. *Yes.* I've started a petition. You'll need to sign. Everyone needs to sign." She shoved a clipboard in my lap. Inside was a wad of paper and on every sheet, the same thing:

We, the undersigned, request the biscuits that were previously made available in three varieties in the staff kitchen be reinstated.

"A petition?" I tried to let her down easy. "Petitions never work."

"It'll work if we get enough people. Frank from Traffic Control reckons we need six hundred signatures. That's our target. Once we hit the target we'll give the petition to the mayor and she'll have to reconsider."

"You'll never get six hundred."

"It'll be easy. I'm going to start with Finance; they're up in arms, apparently. There was talk of a strike." She waggled her hand at the clipboard. "Hurry up. Once you sign, I'll have to get moving. Oh, and—" She coughed. "Frank reckons they've been wanting to get rid of the biscuits all along. Might not be your fault after all."

It was as close to an apology as I could hope for. Perhaps that is why I failed to give it due consideration. With no thought to the long-term implications, I put my name down and handed the clipboard back.

One might argue that my disillusion with petitions had nothing to do with petitions at all. It was their association with something entirely unrelated that triggered my disdain.

The year was 1989. Sharon and I were at the Boronia Mall (Figure 3 depicts our exact locations). She was sitting near the entrance to the supermarket with Jay and Marion from Friends of the Animals.

They were collecting signatures and handing out leaflets. I was on a bench near the toilets, ignoring them and wishing I were elsewhere.

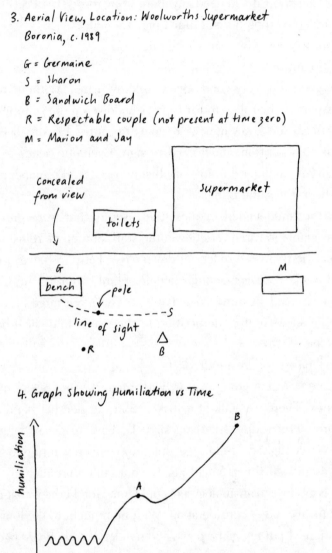

3. Aerial View, Location: Woolworths Supermarket
Boronia, c. 1989

G = Germaine
S = Sharon
B = Sandwich Board
R = Respectable couple (not present at time zero)
M = Marion and Jay

Concealed
from view

Supermarket

toilets

G   M

bench   ⌐pole
            ┄┄┄•┄┄┄┄┄┄ -S
line of sight   △
•R   B

4. Graph Showing Humiliation vs Time

B

A

humiliation

time

Sharon speaks   arrival of
to me   "respectable couple"

It had been a long day, filled with small- and moderate-sized humiliations (see Figure 4).

Sharon was no wallflower. She stood in the middle of the path, the sandwich board beside her. "Sign the petition," she said. "Stand up for animal rights."

In the time we were there I saw, in no particular order: the Eames twins from next door, Nicole Foster and Lucy Daniels from school, and Mrs. Phillips, who taught Italian class. Every time I saw a familiar face my toes curled under and I inched farther away.

To compensate, I told people I was there alone. "Just waiting for my father to pick me up," I said to a family walking past. "He'll be here any minute." Every now and then I went and stood behind a pillar and stared at the bricks.

At the point marked A (Figure 4), Sharon saw me standing there. She nudged Marion. "Germaine. *Germaine.* I know you can hear me. Germaine Johnson, who is standing behind the— See? You *can* hear me. Don't you want to come sit down here with your mother? I saved you a seat." She was laughing too much to keep talking.

The knowledge that she belonged to me and I belonged to her made life difficult enough, but she had to take it further. Not content simply to exist, she was actively committed to undermining my efforts at social advancement to the greatest possible extent. Was it not enough to be the object of ridicule in my own right? Must she continually add to the list of social transgressions I had inadvertently committed? She was very argumentative; it was almost sport with her.

"Meat is murder."

With Sharon, everything was an issue. You couldn't go to the shops and buy a bag of groceries; first you had to endure a commentary on the origin of the milk. Her favorite word was *"Why?"* and everything was a feminist injustice.

"Thanks for your support," said Sharon to a woman with a dog. "Donations are tax deductible."

Her efforts at encouragement were also suboptimal, though on the surface they appeared enthusiastic. At the ceremony for the Victorian Primary Schools Mathematics Competition she gave me a solo standing ovation, which would have been fine if I'd come first. But for a paltry third?

"Don't be so modest, Germaine," she said. "It might be the only thing you ever win."

The peak of the day's humiliation occurred at the point marked B (Figure 4).

A respectable-looking older couple came out of the car park. He was wearing a beige suit, and she was in a pale blue cardigan. They walked down the ramp towards the supermarket. As they approached, Sharon said, "Sign the petition?" as she had a thousand times before. Most people said yes and signed, or no and didn't.

This couple said nothing. They ignored her and kept walking. Sharon, who was used to being ignored and had no problem forcing an issue, made out like she thought they hadn't heard. She stood up, held her clipboard out, and said, louder this time, "Sign the petition?"

Well. The respectable-looking man wasn't as respectable as the suit would have had you believe. He turned around and, in a voice even louder than Sharon's, said, "*Fuck off.*"

Most people would back down if someone started yelling obscenities, but not Sharon. Sharon loves "healthy and informed debate," and if that's not on offer, she'll settle for *un*healthy and *ill*-informed debate. "We're anti-fur," she said, and then everything went downhill (or in fact uphill, if you look at the graph).

Sharon, deciding a picture was worth a thousand words, tried to show the "respectable" man a photograph of some chickens, but he wasn't interested. He was so opposed to seeing it that he covered his eyes with one arm and, with the other, went to rip the photograph in two. But as he lunged forward Sharon stepped back. Neither of them saw the sandwich board set out behind her, and no one expected she'd roll over the top of it, but that's what happened, and she landed heavily on the concrete.

By this time, a crowd had formed. There must have been fifty people standing there. They all saw the manager come out of the supermarket and, without asking what happened or questioning anyone, tell Sharon, Jay, and Marion they had to leave. *"We* have to leave?" said Sharon, still on the ground. *"Us?"*

"Yes, *you,*" said the manager. The respectable man smirked, and not one person standing there watching said anything.

Sharon was angry, but Marion started packing up. "It's fine," she said. "Sharon—stop." Jay put the leaflets back in the milk crate and folded up the tablecloth.

"Germaine," Sharon called. *"Germaine.* We're going home."

The crowd turned in a single unit to gawk at me as I broke cover and oh, the humanity. I wished a sinkhole could have formed in that exact location and swallowed me up. Even if respectability was a veneer, an illusion, I wanted it. At that moment I'd have given anything to be on *their* side.

- 16 -

One of the most annoying things about the helpline was when someone called and you helped them and then they called back saying
whatever you'd done hadn't been any help. This was the "repeat
caller" category in my spreadsheet. It was the least efficient category.
Second and third calls always took longer than a first call because the
caller was more argumentative.

"James" said he'd called previously about his pension payment. He
said someone told him they'd sort it out and all they did was send him
information about government processes and areas of responsibility.

I asked if he'd read it. He claimed he had, but when I asked which
level of government had oversight of income support payments, he
had no idea.

"Here's a hint . . . It's not council."

"Okay," said James. "But can you help me anyway?"

I *was* helping, wasn't I? I was directing his call. I swear I spent
half my time saying the same thing over and over. The only thing
that stopped me going mad was the fact I'd worked out what to do
about it.

It was Professor John Douglas's belief that you shouldn't collect
data unless you were going to use it. I had a use now, a higher purpose:

To automate the helpline.

It was going to make my job a lot easier. Calls like this proved
we didn't need *people* answering the phone; we needed recorded
messages, a voice that said, *Press 2 if your call relates to pension pay-*

ments. Then we could send the call straight through to the Department of Social Services or—even more expedient—have the phone ring out.

All the data and information I'd been collecting was going to be pivotal in making it happen. I couldn't wait to present the idea to Francine. She was going to be so pleased.

"It's very stressful," said James.

"It's basic common sense. Just call the department and speak to them."

"But they don't answer."

Sounded like they'd adopted my system already.

"I just want to talk to a real person," James went on.

"What if we speak for ten minutes and *then* you call them. Would that work?" Didn't matter how long my conversation with James went on for; I was removing the repeat caller category when calculating average call times anyway.

"So you *can* help me?" said James.

"No, but we can talk. What do you want to talk about?"

James must have inadvertently hung up.

He rang back straightaway, though. "Helpline," I said.*

But it wasn't James.

It was Celia.

I'd been wondering if she'd call. Either she was going to or she wasn't. This wasn't a case in which identifying potential outcomes helped to work out which was more likely.

"I have something to say to you," she said.

If only Eva had answered the phone. The stupid petition, she was off getting signatures again. Maybe I should pretend there was a problem with the line.

But I didn't have to worry. Celia said, in her normal voice, as

---

*I'd stopped saying "Senior Citizens Helpline" and was just saying "Helpline." One day I might even reduce it to "Help." It was a small efficiency, but a couple of words here and there and that's ten seconds. Ten seconds times a hundred calls is a thousand seconds (16.666667 minutes).

though we had never met in real life, "Beds. They're so big when there's only one of you in it."

I relaxed. "Maybe that's how they're meant to be. Maybe people aren't meant to sleep in the same bed." The times Peter and I shared a bed he created a big dent in the middle and rolled into it. I was on the edge, trying not to fall out.

"I still sleep on my side," said Celia. "Next to the window."

"I don't have *a* side. I sleep on one side for a week and then the other for a week and then I don't have to wash the sheets as much."

"Does it work like that?"

"Yeah, I read it somewhere. *Australian Journal of Domestic Chemistry*, I think."

Later in the week the mayor called. She said, "Germaine, do you feel like a coffee?"

I said, "Don't you mean a skinny cappuccino?"

"That's exactly what I mean."

In the café, we sat at our usual table. The mayor waited until the drinks arrived before telling me she'd spoken to Don.

My eye twitched when his name was mentioned; I couldn't help it. I even turned around to look behind me, half hoping, half dreading he'd be there, but he wasn't: just a void his exact size and shape. Much like the one in my apartment.

"He said he saw you. At a . . . convention?"

"Sudoku," I said. "He used to be the world champion."

"Poor Don," she said. "He's paid the price ten times over."

"And he didn't even do it," I said.

The mayor drank her coffee.

"Don and I are planning the mayoral ball at the moment. This year it's at the golf club. We're trying to sort out the catering. Don wants to do something special. He's very particular about things, you know."

He was particular; I was particular. It seemed like we were meant to be. "I really enjoyed seeing him," I said. This was code for: *You can tell him I'm interested.*

She said, "I'm sure he did, too." Was she also speaking in code?

It was hard to tell; that is the problem with codes that have not been previously agreed on. And even if it was code, she might have been speculating, she might not know for sure he'd enjoyed my company. She patted her lips with a napkin.

"The ball's a big deal, Germaine. A lot of important people attend."

I asked if staff were allowed to come, and she said occasionally a staff member would attend.

"As a reward?" I said.

She bobbed her head from side to side. She said, "I'm not sure everyone would see it that way. I guess some people might think it was boring," and we laughed together at the idea.

It would have been good if we'd gone back to talking about Don, but the mayor wanted to know how the senior citizens had responded to the letter I'd sent. I was pleased to tell her their response was as it should be: They were taking it very seriously.

"Even Celia?" she said.

I conceded Celia's attitude was less than satisfactory, but said the rest of them appeared to understand. The mayor was pleased, which made me pleased also. In numeric form it would have been: Pleased^2.

Saturday morning. I had no intention of going to the senior citizens center, but I happened to be driving past with, coincidentally, a couple of textbooks and a calculator in my bag, and on a whim decided to do something different.

Gladys and Betsy were sitting on the chairs in the foyer. Gladys was wearing normal clothes, but Betsy was in her exercise outfit again. Gladys looked worried when she saw me. "Germaine? What's wrong?"

"Nothing, I was just in the neighborhood." I glanced down the hall. Where was the homework club? Where were the troubled youth? I'd imagined more loitering.

"Do you live nearby?" said Betsy.

"Not really. You going for a run?"

"I'm teaching aerobics after homework club."

"Oh yeah. Homework club. Forgot that was on." I hitched the bag of textbooks on my shoulder.

"It'd be great if you could help," said Betsy. "We'd really appreciate it."

"I suppose I could stay for a bit. Not long, though. Hour, hour and a half tops."

A book slid off Betsy's lap as she got up and waved at me to follow.

Homework club was held in the main hall. There were tables in clusters with students of various sizes—little ones, medium-sized ones, ones of university age—grouped around them. Some of the tutors were sitting down; others were wandering around helping. I was the youngest tutor by multiple decades; the others were all ancient.

"Germaine," called a voice from up the back. It wasn't until it giggled that I realized who it was. Jin-Jin. She was being so loud and friendly I had no choice but to go over.

"Hi, Jin-Jin," I said, still standing.

"Are you here for the homework club?"

"They asked me to come down and tutor people in mathematics."

"Are you good at mathematics?"

"I'd want to be, given I studied it for five years."

"Great," she said. "I need some help, please."

I cursed myself and contemplated the empty seat. How annoying. Here I was, making a voluntary contribution to the betterment of society, and Jin-Jin was going to be the beneficiary. I'd have preferred to help someone more deserving. Underprivileged but obviously intelligent, a child preferably, with untapped genius that only I was able to unlock.

Helping Jin-Jin was only going to encourage her. What if she started visiting?

We could get stuck talking in the hallway at the apartment block or, worse, stuck *not* talking. I'd be trapped in my own home, living in absolute silence in case she came past. What if she knocked? What if she wanted to come in? What if she knocked and wanted to come in regularly? My mouth went dry.

Jin-Jin patted the chair and I lowered myself into it. "I can only give you fifteen minutes of my time."

She giggled. "How are you getting home?"

"I'm not going home after. I'm going . . . elsewhere."

"Okay." Jin-Jin opened her book. She was doing a basic mathematics subject, part of a business degree, she said. The problem was a probability equation:

The following table gives a set of outcomes and their probabilities.
Let A be the event "the outcome is greater than 1."
Find:
Outcome = 1, Probability = 0.1
Outcome = 2, Probability = 0.6
Outcome = 3, Probability = 0.3

Easy.

But Jin-Jin didn't think so. She didn't understand what an event was, and she didn't understand what an outcome was. She was having difficulty working out where the numbers went.

"I hate maths," she said. "I'm never going to use it. I want to do Human Resources."

"Human Resources?" I said. "Oh, Jin-Jin."

"I like people. I'm good at relationships," she said, but she wasn't giggling now. In fact, she looked sad. She did a halfhearted pencil scribble in her book.

I was encouraging. "Mathematics is all about relationships, Jin-Jin. *Relationships between numbers.*"

"Are you in a relationship?" she said.

"No." *Not yet,* my heart fluttered.

Jin-Jin rested her elbow on the table, cupping her chin in her hand. "My boyfriend Lee and I had a fight."

"Oh, well."

"Yeah." Jin-Jin wasn't smiling anymore, and I realized I'd never seen Jin-Jin not smiling. It was an uncomfortable experience. I shifted her exercise book closer and started working on the problem.

"It's complicated," she said.

"Relationships between numbers are much simpler than relationships between people," I told her. "People are unpredictable; you never know what they're going to do, you never know what they're going to say. But numbers? Numbers are reliable."

"He thinks I study too much."

"No one can study too much. It's an oxymoron."

"I don't want to break up."

"It's quite probable you will. Most relationships end eventually."

"How probable?" she said, and then, perking up: "You said you can estimate the probability of anything. What is the probability Lee and I will break up?"

I hesitated. This was not the most appropriate application of the theory in question, but perhaps I could use it as an example, a way of demonstrating the theory's underlying essence.

"Let's see. What's his name? Lee? Right. The probability that you, Jin-Jin, and Lee will break up is equal to the probability that you break up with him *plus* the probability that he breaks up with you."

I turned her exercise book to a clean page. "*Or* we could say that the probability of you breaking up is 1 *minus* the probability you stay together. If we assign breaking up the letter 'B' and staying together the letter 'S'—"

Jin-Jin interrupted. "Can we make staying together the letter 'L'?"

"L?"

"For *Love*."

"We can assign any letter value; the letter is just a stand-in."

Together we worked through the rest of the problem. It was simple, really. We assigned likelihoods to each scenario and multiplied the numbers out. We even adjusted the likelihoods to understand the effect of different values. Reduce the likelihood of Jin-Jin breaking up with Lee and the probability of them staying together increased.

Conversely, increase the likelihood of Jin-Jin breaking up with Lee and the probability decreased.

"This is good," said Jin-Jin. "They never did it this way in class."

I covered my mouth with my hand and grinned behind it.

"One day I might tell you about the golden ratio," I whispered, too quiet for her to hear.

After Jin-Jin (twenty-five minutes) I stayed on to help Jake and after Jake I helped Penny and after Penny there was Charlie.

Charlie was six. He sidled up with a pair of plastic glasses on. "Who am I?" he said.

"I don't know. Who are you?"

He pushed the glasses up his nose. "It's for Book Day. This is my costume."

I guessed Harry Potter (no) and Albert Einstein.

"Einstein's not a book," said Charlie.

"There are books about Einstein," I said.

"I'm Encyclopedia Brown. The boy detective?"

My lack of familiarity was a cause of exasperation.

"No one ever guesses. This is *exactly* what he wears—pants, a T-shirt, and glasses—but no one ever guesses."

"You should carry an encyclopedia around."

"But he doesn't carry an encyclopedia around," said Charlie.

I said it might assist others in recognition, but Charlie said he couldn't dumb things down just so people understood. He was unwilling to compromise or present an inaccurate portrayal of the truth. I fell a little bit in love with Charlie when he told me that.

And so the day went. Three hours passed, and I didn't even notice. When it was time to leave, Betsy came into the hall and asked everyone to put the tables away because aerobics was about to start, and they all did, really quickly. I heard a man say, "That's Betsy, she won the CWA," like it was a big deal, on a par with a sudoku final, for example.

While Jin-Jin was preoccupied with folding the legs on a trestle,

I slunk over to the door. Betsy saw me. "You don't want to stay?" she said. "It's free."

I told her the literature indicated aerobic activity was less important for well-being than other lifestyle factors.

Betsy didn't contest this. "How'd you like the homework club?"

I said it was pretty boring.

"Can you come next week?"

I sighed. "I'll probably have to. Not like those idiots are going to work that stuff out for themselves."

- 17 -

Getting in the car and putting on my seat belt, I wondered if I should rethink my attitude towards exercise. A lot of people had turned up at the aerobics class and, though I had never found popularity to be an indicator of merit, it did suggest the activity might have some value. I wondered what Professor Douglas would have thought: The newspaper article in which he'd been featured was silent on the issue. That said, I knew he was in favor of experimentation.

I had an understanding of the impacts of doing *no* activity, but what about the impacts of doing *some*?

Aerobics didn't sound that interesting, nor did running or swimming, and I definitely didn't want to do any team sports. But perhaps . . . golf?

I turned in at the entrance to the car park.

I wasn't looking for Don. I went in only to ask about membership prices. Golf is notoriously expensive, even if you don't live in Japan. But in doing so, I happened to mention to the woman on reception that I was a friend of his. "Is he in?" I asked. There was a line of numbers in my stomach, wiggling in anticipation.

"He's around . . . but he's pretty busy." The receptionist slipped a flyer under the window. "Here's the price list. If you'd like me to call Daisy, our membership manager, she can show you around. Or if this is not a convenient time, I can book something in during the week."

I looked down the hall. Don's door was open. If only he'd come out. If only I could go in. I was worried I hadn't thanked him properly for his gift. Maybe he'd like to see a photo of it all, set out on the mantelpiece. I had several, mostly landscape but a couple in panoramic view. It would take only a minute.

"Daisy is free at half past," said the receptionist.

Plus, if Don knew I was here and *hadn't* gone to see him, it was likely he'd be upset. He'd said, *Don't be a stranger*; I didn't want him to think I was trying to be one.

I started walking down the hall.

The woman on reception called out, but I waved my hand at her. "It's okay. I know where I'm going."

Don *did* look busy. He was squinting at his computer screen and typing madly, sheets of paper all across the desk. When I said, "Hello there," his first facial expression was one of irritation, but it softened when he saw it was me.

"Hello, Germaine."

There is nothing better than the sound of one's name. Nothing, except the sound of one's name on the lips of someone you are grateful *knows* your name.

"To what do I owe this pleasure?" he said.

I turned into an irrational number. I couldn't express myself. "I was just . . . Which is to say . . ." I stopped and held up the flyer. "I'm thinking about joining."

"Wouldn't have picked you for a golfer," he said.

"Golf and sudoku. That's two things we have in common." Or *would* have if I joined.

Don didn't say to come in but the chair opposite him was empty so I filled it. "I really liked your gift," I said.

The way his face lifted, I had a flash of the old Alan Cosgrove.

"Suppose you've put it in a drawer somewhere," he said.

"Oh no. It's on display."

"Ha. Yes, I'm sure."

I got my phone out. Don protested and said he didn't need to see, he didn't mind what I did with *all that crap*, but he took the phone eagerly when offered. Zoomed in, even.

"That's very flattering," he said.

"I'm going to have to increase my insurance premium, though. What if someone tries to steal it?"

He laughed and handed the phone back. "Verity said you were funny."

"Did she?"

"She did."

So they had talked about me, and positively. If only I'd been privy to their entire conversation. "Are you nearly finished for today?"

"No, we've got another dinner this evening. Be a big day and a late night."

He was tireless. That was another thing we had in common. I should be documenting them, in case he hadn't noticed.

"Daisy going to give you a tour?" said Don.

"Yes, but not today. During the week, I think." I'd have to come back.

"I'll speak to her. Make sure she gives you a good deal."

I made a time with the receptionist on the way out.

On Sunday it was Sharon's birthday. In the morning I went shopping for a present. I got her six vegan cupcakes and a book on financial planning for people in their fifties and sixties. She better get on top of it. No way is she living with me when she gets dementia and forgets to feed herself.

But even if she didn't get dementia, our living together was not a good idea. We were not great housemates. This wasn't because of differences in cleanliness or because one of us was late in paying bills. (Sharon paid all the bills. Eventually.) It was more the disappointment.

It took me a while to realize about Sharon's disappointment. It was only when I had her approval, albeit fleetingly, that I understood it was there.

When I was in grade five, Sharon came home from parent-teacher interviews and said, "Ms. Phillips thinks you might be gifted."

I wasn't surprised, but Sharon was. She was surprised to an almost offensive degree. First thing she did was drag the phone from the dining room into her bedroom. Then she called Aunt Caroline. "Germaine's teacher thinks she's gifted," she said. "I know . . . It explains *everything*."

The test was expensive, but Ms. Phillips said the school would pay. The morning of, Sharon called in sick and the two of us walked to the bus stop. It took ages to get from Boronia to the city, but I didn't care. I'd been waiting forever for something like this to happen.

I thought the testing place would be modern and new age, like something out of *The Jetsons*, but it was a dark and dingy office at the top of three flights of stairs, the kind of place you'd find Scientologists lurking. That was something I knew all about, thanks to Sharon.

The receptionist led me to a room and handed me a booklet. She said, "You've got ninety minutes." She didn't click a stopwatch; maybe it was back at her desk. Sharon, standing behind, held up a crystal and mouthed the words, "Do you want this? For good luck?"

I ignored her, like I always did.

The test was easy. I didn't even use a calculator or make notes in the margins of the paper, and after, Sharon asked how it went and I told her it was a cinch.

We had to wait two weeks for the results to come in. That whole time, Sharon bragged to anyone who'd listen and to a bunch of people for whom listening wasn't their strong suit, *Germaine might be gifted, Germaine might be gifted*. It was unlike Sharon to do that. Insofar as she ever talked about me to other people, normally it was to roll her eyes and say, "Try living with her."

Those two weeks were the most pleasant in my primary school career. I don't know if Ms. Phillips told the class, but they seemed to sense it. Instead of tripping me up in the queue for tuckshop or hiding my lunch, they ignored me. It was a satisfactory outcome for all involved.

I knew the results had come back because Ms. Phillips sent the class to lunch and asked me to stay behind.

I walked to her desk, a fluttering feeling in my chest. It was like being in the final round of a game show. I was about to find out if I'd answered the million-dollar question correctly.

"The letter came from the testing facility," said Ms. Phillips.

I could see a scoreboard all lit up; the name GERMAINE was flashing.

"I was wrong," she said. Ms. Phillips didn't even wince. "You're not gifted."

At home, Sharon told me she knew she shouldn't have got her hopes up. Then she swept me into a hug, her curly hair irritating the skin on my cheek, and said, "But I'm probably not gifted either, if that helps."

"No," I said. "It doesn't help."

In the afternoon I drove to the house I grew up in. On a straight street with shaved lawns and concrete driveways, ours was the one with the long grass and the multicolored fence.

Sharon was on the verandah out front, looking at her laptop. The dogs were lying on their sides at her feet. When they saw me, they started barking. All four of them ran down the steps and wiped their snotty noses on my pants as I got out.

"Get off. Sharon, make them go away. These pants are dry-clean only. Ugh, it's licking my hand."

"He's just being affectionate, Germaine. He's trying to give you some attention. Ooh, he *does* like you. Are you premenstrual? Barney is very attuned to pheromones."

How annoying. Just my luck to be wasting pheromones on an old black Labrador. I should have been at the golf club.

Inside, Sharon put the kettle on. I dumped the present and the cupcakes on the table and fished in my handbag for the antibacterial gel, rubbing it on my hands while we waited for the water to boil.

"What were you doing on the computer?" I said.

"Why?"

"Just asking."

"Never know with you. Wouldn't be surprised if you were in a thing with the government. Suppose I can't do much about it if you are. Just remember, there'll be a lot of dead chickens on your head if Friends of the Animals goes down for tax fraud."

"It won't be my fault if Friends of the Animals goes down for tax fraud. It'll be yours for not complying with the legislation. Everyone has to pay taxes, Sharon. It's part of being in a civilized society."

"Oh, God, I shouldn't have said anything. You'd sell your own mother down the river, wouldn't you? Done it before."

"Rules are rules," I said. I didn't regret turning Sharon in to Greenpeace. If you're going to collect money for a charity, the least you can do is give it to them.

"You're a monster, Germaine." Sharon always said that.

The kettle boiled, and Sharon made the tea. She got the cups from the cupboard and came and sat down.

I slid the present across the table. "Happy birthday."

She undid the wrapping. "A book." She turned it over. "About superannuation. Gee, thanks. This going to make me a millionaire, is it?" She flicked through a couple of pages and set it aside. "I suppose I should ask about the new job."

"I got a promotion," I said. "They've expanded my role." I threw the pattypan from the cake at the bin. It went straight in but Sharon didn't notice. "I'm working for the mayor now. Do you know Mayor Bainbridge? She's Kimberly's friend, but she's very intelligent. She was a 'Woman of Influence' last year. They only picked a hundred."

"Speaking of Kimberly." Sharon screwed her nose up. "Did you get her invitation?"

"What invitation?" I picked the icing off a second cupcake.

"Germaine."

"What? I'm going to be really busy with my new job. I'll probably be working most weekends."

"She's your only cousin. Family's important, no matter how unlikable they are. Plus, I already said you'd go. It's okay, you don't have to buy a present. I'm getting them a Ugandan goat. Well, not them. I'm getting a Ugandan village a goat, and I'll give Kimberly the certificate."

"Sure you're not just printing a certificate and pocketing the money?"

"Shut up, Germaine." She gave me a look. "That was a one-off thing."

18

The opportunity to help Don arose quicker than I'd imagined. On Monday the mayor sent an email to Francine and me. It read like a wartime telegram:

HAVE RECEIVED ANOTHER COMPLAINT RE CELIA BROWN. (Stop.)
PLEASE EXPLAIN. (Stop.)

Francine came by five minutes later, her hair looking more frazzled than usual. "Are you busy?" she said. "The mayor wants to see us."

Stacey grimaced as we entered. She mouthed the words *Not happy* and waved us through. Francine pushed her glasses up on her nose, though they hadn't fallen down.

In her office the mayor was glaring at her computer. "I thought we'd addressed this," she said, without looking over.

Francine hurried to sit down. "Has there been another complaint?"

"Yes, there has been another complaint." The mayor turned the monitor so Francine and I could see the screen.

It was a photograph, taken from the front steps of the golf club, looking towards the senior citizens center and the car park in front of it. Normally, both were visible through the tall wire fence—but not now. The fence was covered in banners. There were dozens of them. They had black capital letters and ran for meters in each direction. **CAR PARK FOR SENIOR CITIZENS CENTER ACTIVITIES ONLY**, said one. **TRESPASSERS WILL BE PROSECUTED**, said another.

"Not sure how she plans to prosecute trespassers, given it's a public car park." The mayor pressed her lips together.

I shook my head, incensed. All I could think about was Don—indignant on his behalf.

"Don's been very good about it," said the mayor, as though she could hear my thoughts, "but it's more than a little embarrassing." She said she'd had the banners removed, but they'd been there since at least Sunday morning. I didn't say I was there on Saturday morning. Was that relevant? I didn't think so.

When the mayor said, "This cannot continue," I was in complete agreement.

"Rules are rules," I said.

"We'll have to think about our approach. If the papers get wind of it, they'll put some ridiculous spin on things and there'll be hell to pay."

Francine made a comment, something about waiting or giving them another chance—I don't know, I was too busy working out how to tell Celia. It would have to be person-to-person, face-to-face. "You're fired," I'd say, pretty much the way Peter said it to me. This was different, of course: She deserved it.

The mayor picked up a pen and clicked it down. "Francine, you're going to have to help with the communications. What's the nicest way of saying, *We're shutting you down*?"

Wait, what? Shutting them down?

It took a minute for the mayor's words to sink in.

"We've spoken about this before," said the mayor. "Haven't we, Francine?"

Francine's jaw had dropped. She was struggling to respond. "I'm not sure that's what we've said, exactly."

Unbidden, an image of the homework club came into my head. What about Gladys and Betsy? And, to a lesser extent, Jin-Jin? The little boy Charlie whispered in my ear: *I have so much potential, Germaine.*

What were they doing, invading my private thoughts? I bit my lip. Concentrate on Don, I told myself.

"We *can* shut it down." The mayor was firm. "And we will."

Out the window, it began to rain. Drops of water made their way down the glass.

Francine was talking, but I couldn't listen. I shifted in the chair, crossing and uncrossing my legs, deeply uncomfortable. What was wrong with me? I'd known this was a possibility. I resolved not to care. No, I *didn't* care. Caring wasn't part of the Douglas genome.

And yet.

Francine suggested perhaps I write them another letter. "Or we could give them another warning?"

"We've written letters," said the mayor. "And we've given warnings."

That was true. At some point, warnings had to have consequences; otherwise, they were suggestions. But the consequence seemed disproportionate. The ratio was wrong. *One* person was the problem, but *multiple* people were being affected by the outcome.

"Can't you just get rid of Celia?" I said, interrupting Francine, who was now talking about a warning *system*, in which one warning escalated to another different type of warning.

"No." Francine tried to sound firm. "We couldn't do that."

But the mayor did not dismiss the idea out of hand. "Go on," she said.

"Kick Celia out. Get someone else to be president of the committee."

"But she's been there for *years*," said Francine.

I ignored her, imploring the mayor. "It'd be much quicker. Same outcome, less negative publicity." I could tell she was taking in what I had to say. It was as though a spotlight was shining on my person.

The mayor drummed her fingers on the desk. I had her full attention. It might have been just her and me in the room. Francine had all but disappeared.

"Gladys would be good. She's the current vice president," I said.

[Francine, a tiny voice in the background: *I really think this is a bad idea.*]

The mayor began to nod. "You know, there is some merit to that approach."

[Francine, not nodding: *Maybe we should . . .*]

The mayor announced we would proceed as I had suggested. "Germaine, get rid of Celia," she said. She didn't care how I did it, so long as it was done. She was—I quote—"leaving it in your capable hands."

NOTE: She did not say anything about the capability of Francine's hands.

I called Gladys straightaway. "We need to talk."

"What about?" As though she didn't know.

"About Celia. Is she there?"

Gladys's voice took on a theatrical quality. "Why don't you come back at seven o'clock this evening, *Norma*? After the aerobics class? We could discuss the matter then."

"Aerobics? Is Betsy teaching?"

"Yes, Norma. Betsy will be there."

When the workday concluded, instead of going home and having dinner, I went home and got changed. I put on running shoes and a pair of old leggings. I still wasn't sure about aerobics, but I was curious about Betsy. Winners have an aura, even if their category of endeavor isn't a very useful one.

The class was being held in the main room, where the homework club was. The tables had all been cleared away, but chairs were set out in a half circle. They all faced in the direction of, and were equal distance from, a single chair in the middle. That's where Betsy was sitting.

She was smiling as always. "Gladys said you were coming."

I did not smile back. Betsy's attitude was hard to interpret. To the outside observer she seemed "friendly" and "affectionate," but this could be part of a plan to disarm me. I had to be wary.

Betsy didn't say anything about Celia or the signs; rather, she gestured at the chairs. "Did Gladys tell you it's *chair* aerobics? We do it sitting down."

"That's fine." I assumed the position directly in front of her. Her face did not falter.

"I heard you won a competition," I said.

Betsy nodded. "CWA."

"You're famous."

Unlike Don, who would have perked up visibly if someone said that, Betsy responded by changing the subject.

"Do you have hobbies?" she said.

"Yes." I did not elaborate.

The room began to fill, very slowly. One of the last to arrive was a man in a green tracksuit that said "La America." Though a number of chairs were vacant, he had his sights on mine. He came and stood next to me, looking down. "You're in my spot," he said.

"Am I?"

"*Yes*. I always sit there."

I'd been in situations like this before; if you acquiesce, the demands will only escalate. I stared at him and clutched the sides of the chair. "Not always," I said.

Usually bystanders pretended not to notice what was going on, but Betsy came straight over. "James, sit somewhere else."

James? I narrowed my eyes at him. "Did you ring the council helpline?"

He was taken aback. "How do you know? Who *are* you?"

"That's Germaine." Betsy gestured for him to shuffle over. "Now *move*."

After class Betsy, Gladys, and I convened in the office. I had to lean forward to stretch my back, feeling the surprising effects of the workout. The difficulty of raising one leg and tapping it on the floor many times in quick succession would not have occurred to me. My heart rate was *still* elevated, and I could feel muscles I knew existed intellectually but hadn't ever learned the precise location of.

Betsy told Gladys I was great at chair aerobics. "Germaine's a natural."

"I believe it," said Gladys.

"You know, we do normal aerobics as well." Betsy got a timetable off the top of the filing cabinet near the window and handed it to me. "Maybe next time you'd like to do that instead?"

I glanced at the sheet of paper. "Why? Because of James?"

"Oh, James." Betsy told Gladys James was being a pain.

"James *is* a pain" was Gladys's response. She was quite insightful.

"Ignore him," said Betsy to me.

This was a clue. It showed she wasn't friendly to everyone. Either I had been singled out as more deserving or, more likely, they were trying to get close to me for reasons undisclosed.

"It doesn't matter, I don't care." Whichever it was, I wasn't going to thank her for sticking up for me. Just because she told him to move, I wouldn't let it cloud my judgment. I wasn't dazzled by her fame.

"I only said that because people who go to *chair* aerobics usually have mobility issues," said Betsy.

"Maybe *some* people go because they have mobility issues and *some* people go because they like sitting down."

"Maybe." Betsy didn't sound convinced.

But I was there for a reason. "We need to talk about Celia," I said.

They knew, of course. I didn't have to explain.

They tried to absolve themselves of responsibility, saying they'd told Celia not to do it and Celia hadn't listened.

"She never listens," said Betsy. "We said it would cause trouble, but she did it anyway."

Gladys began to describe a bus trip in which people had arrived early but the car park was already full—it was irrelevant, whatever she said.

"We weren't there when she put the signs up," said Betsy. "If we had been, we'd have said something."

"We were on the bus," said Gladys.

I recalled some training I'd done at Wallace Insurance:

When advising someone their claim has been denied, you may find they react with emotion. It's important to show you're listening to what they have to say, even when it has no bearing on the situation in question. It gives them the feeling of "being heard."

"I understand," I said. And: "That's difficult." And when the blow had been sufficiently cushioned, I crushed a piece of paper into a ball and tossed it in the bin. "*However*, you will have to get rid of her."

"What?" said Betsy. Gladys didn't seem to catch what I said either. She squinted, as though her eyes—as well as her ears—were having trouble listening.

"*You will have to get rid of her,*" I repeated, louder this time.

"Oh no. We can't do that." Betsy was adamant.

"Never," said Gladys with equal vigor.

They seemed to think it was just an idea and they had the option of rejecting it. I really had to spell it out, in such specific terms it began to sound harsh. Less inevitable, more vindictive. I decided not to say it was my idea. Let them think it was a directive from . . . somewhere.

Gladys's eyes went watery.

"But why?" said Betsy, even after I patiently listed all the reasons, counting them off on my fingers: the current complaint, previous complaints; the current warning, previous warnings.

"But it's been going on for ages," she said.

"Yes. And now it's reached a tipping point."

Once they understood they both went quiet. Gladys said she didn't know how to break the news to Celia.

I offered to help but Betsy said no, they'd prefer to do it. "It's the least we can do," she said. She was very serious, like she was a doctor telling a patient they were about to die.

Betsy touched my shoulder as I went to leave. "We know you're only doing your job."

"I'm doing *more* than my job," I said. "I've been picking up extra duties."

The three of us said a strained goodbye.

19

Francine's office was small and tidy. It had a large window, though given it faced the photocopy room, this wasn't quite the coup it might have been. Her desk was empty aside from three stress balls with cracked foam and a silver insulated cup.

"I feel very uncomfortable about all of this," she said. "It's giving me a stomach ulcer, I nearly didn't come in today." Francine was worried after our conversation with the mayor, but I wasn't. For two reasons: (1) Francine worried about everything, and (2) she didn't understand the underlying factors that were at work, whereas I did.

This was the sort of problem that looked complicated on the surface, but once you realized that Celia and Don had an inverse relationship, it was very straightforward:

$$f(C) = D/C$$

Where:

C = Celia
D = Don

Difficult, eh? But if you got rid of Celia by making $C = 0$, then the whole thing resolved itself. Also, if $C = 0$, then D for Don = infinity and that's the biggest "number" there is.

And helping Don had its own rewards. They were hard to quantify at this point in time, but appreciation seemed like a good foundation for a relationship. Particularly where it was complemented by a strong sexual attraction.

Thirdly, and this was the most important point, it's opportunities like this that can change everything. You solve a problem for someone important and they'll ask you to solve another one, and another. Before you know it, you're their chief problem solver. That's an indispensable role, one that requires an office, a personal assistant, and a team of staff. Maybe even a dedicated page on the company website.

"I think the best thing would be if we got everyone in a room and talked about it," said Francine. "We could put on a morning tea and get Donna from HR to facilitate. She's very good with conflict."

"Francine." Sometimes I felt like I was her boss, not the other way around.

"Germaine, we're not meant to meddle in the appointment of committee positions. They're supposed to be independent. I'm ninety-nine percent sure there's a policy that prevents our being involved."

But we *were* involved, regardless of the policy. I told her I'd already sorted it with Gladys and Betsy. It was done and dusted.

"What do you mean, 'sorted it'?" said Francine.

"Gladys and Betsy are going to speak to Celia," I said. "They completely understood our point of view and were happy to work it out for us. It's not an issue." This was meant to make Francine calmer and less worried, but it didn't seem to work. If anything, she looked *less* calm and *more* worried.

"But what if Celia won't go? What if she calls the paper? What if they print a story saying we tried to get rid of her?"

While Francine generated scenarios, I looked around her office. If it were mine, there were a number of improvements I would have made. I'd have put the desk on the other side so I could see people as they went past, maybe monitor their use of the photocopier. Nothing too onerous, just a tally, not times of day or duration or anything like that.

I'd also take down those family photographs and not just because it would be weird having a cluster of strangers, someone else's partner and kids, staring at me all the time. Too many personal items suggests competing interests. If it's five p.m. on Friday and there's something that needs to be done, your superiors want to be able to rely on you. They want to know you're not going to nick off because Suzie has a ballet concert or little Archibald's got a birthday party.

Francine picked up a stress ball and started squishing it. "What if someone sues? What if we end up in court? I couldn't lie under oath."

I'd put up motivational quotes and a picture of Isaac Newton. No, Carl Gauss. Less obvious, and I could assume a knowledge base of zero when telling people about him.

"What about Celia? She's done a lot for that club. She's its life force."

Celia, Celia, Celia. It was as though Francine, Gladys, and Betsy all had Stockholm syndrome. That's where kidnapped people start to sympathize with their tormentors. "They're really very nice," they say from their makeshift dungeon beneath the stairs. "If only you got to know them."

"She really *is* very nice," said Francine. "If only you got to know her."

Later in the week, when Jack mentioned going for lunch, I said instead of going to the café, we should eat on the bench outside. "I will provide food for both of us," I said. I had my pasta-tomato-tuna combination left over from the previous week and didn't want to waste it. Jack was very pleased, though if I am honest, it was less an act of generosity and more a reflection of how much there was and how old it was. Three days is just a guideline.

When Jack came to get me, Frank from Traffic Control was sitting with Eva at her desk. They were discussing the biscuit petition. The two of them, Frank and Eva, had begun to meet daily to bark motivational phrases at each other and set targets for their subordinates. Yes, subordinates. They'd managed to recruit six unfortunates from Planning and Building as collection officers. They were to be set up in "strategic locations" at the town hall and elsewhere to coerce staff into signing the petition. Not that people needed much coercion, mind you.

"Ed and Lucy will have to sit in the canteen from nine to five. I don't care if they have work to do. If we want to get these signatures, that's where we'll get them," said Eva.

Frank, a short, round man with a lot of hair on his arms and not much on his head, agreed. "Means we can send Wendy and Fred back down to the Aquatic Center. If we get that lot on board, we'll be almost there."

"Sounds like you two are working hard," said Jack.

"We've got four hundred thirty-two signatures so far," said Eva. "We'd be nearer five hundred, but those arseholes at the pool have been holding out. Reckon they don't want biscuits; they want protein bars."

Frank flicked his tie, correcting its position against his shirt. "It's an ambit claim. We can talk 'em down."

"Well, we all appreciate your dedication," said Jack. "Don't we, Germaine?"

I was noncommittal. Eva's dedication meant she was no longer answering the phone or responding to routine inquiries. I was doing her job *and* mine and still getting paid the same amount. I'd also begun to question if it had been wise of me to sign the petition. What if the mayor frowned upon it? What if my involvement had negative implications for my career?

Eva's eyes narrowed at Jack. "You've signed, haven't you?"

"Of course I've signed. I was one of the first, remember? Jesus, Eva. If there's one thing I'm about it's free biscuits."

Jack and I went up to the tearoom to get our lunches ready. He had his own bowl and I scooped a sizable serve of noodles in. It was quite a large serving, more than three hundred cubic centimeters, but he wasn't very grateful.

"Are these okay?" he said, scrunching up his nose and sniffing them, which I did not appreciate.

"They're fine, Jack."

"They look a bit hard."

I had half a mind to say, *Well, don't have any then*, but I bit my tongue. I picked up the bowls and put them in the microwave. They both fitted if you didn't mind that the platter couldn't spin, which I didn't.

While my back was turned and I was preoccupied with determining the appropriate cooking time, Jack moved swiftly.

There were two tomatoes. *Two.* Two × three-fifths of a tomato meant our total tomato requirement should have been one and one-fifth. That was all we needed. Perhaps a little more given the volume of pasta, but wasn't that my decision to make? So far as I could see we did not need a whole tomato each.

But Jack had cut them both up into a giant mound of tiny little pieces. When I saw what he'd done I looked at him.

He lowered the knife and took a step back. "What? Was I not supposed to do that?"

My eye twitched, but otherwise I was very calm when I asked if he thought this would be too much tomato.

"I think the question is," said Jack, "do *you* think it's too much tomato?"

"I don't normally do that much." I didn't immediately cite the usual allocation, but he got it out of me.

"You eat three-fifths of a tomato?"

"Give or take." Exactly three-fifths or as close I could get without weighing.

Jack seemed amused by this. "That's very precise."

I didn't rise to his baiting of me, but when the microwave went off, I took out his bowl and stabbed his pasta with a fork several times.

"Germaine," said Jack. "There were two tomatoes, and they were both quite squishy."

"I don't mind. Honestly, I don't care."

"They were *very* squishy, Germaine."

"Squishy, were they?" I put his bowl back in the microwave. "I'm never doing this again," I said. "Next time *you* cook."

"Next time I will," he said.

I left work early for my membership tour with Daisy at the golf club and immediately wished I'd looked at the price list before organizing it. The joining fee was more than $7,000 and there were annual fees on top. Daisy better, as Don had promised, give me a good deal. No matter how strapped for cash he was, I wasn't that altruistic. Or that interested in health and fitness.

Daisy was maybe twenty-five, with long blond hair and lots of freckles. She was very enthusiastic about golf. "It's a great sport if you want to meet people," she said.

"What sort of people?" I asked.

"People" were everywhere. If my only requirement for relationships was *to have some*, I'd hang around at the homework club. I'd go for lunch with Jack and Eva, or I'd invite Jin-Jin around for dinner. But having observed Sharon all these years, I knew there was such a thing as being *too* inclusive. It was probably what drove my father away.

Daisy assured me the club was very selective. "We don't take just anyone," she said. She didn't say *but we will take you*, but that was her meaning. It wasn't the high school chess club, after all.

Or the Year 7 debating team.

Or Brownies, circa 1987.

I'd found where I belonged. Or would belong, if I could find the money and present myself appropriately.

Daisy took me the long way around the building. We walked through the bistro, past the poker machines, and out the glass doors onto the first tee for a view of the course.

Clipped lawn was bordered by trees—one variety—planted at precise intervals. There was a body of water, its edges so crisp and so sharp it was like a piece of blue cellophane had been cut out with scissors.

"Isn't the air fresh?" said Daisy, breathing it in in a way that reminded me of Sharon, meditating. I looked the other way, running what must have appeared to be a knowledgeable eye across the fairway.

Daisy said, "Have you played for long?"

"A little while." Very little. Technically, never.

"Okay. Well, the course is eighteen holes, fully couched and—"

I tuned out.

Had Don remembered I was coming? I hoped he was okay. He'd had a hard enough time of it already without being harassed by a bunch of senior citizens. Had the mayor told him we were getting rid of Celia Brown, or would I be the one to reveal the news? How exciting it would be, to witness his reaction firsthand.

Daisy pointed vaguely to the east. "That's Box Hill. We have reciprocal relationships with them and four other clubs in the region. We also offer formal coaching, from the course professional, and informal, from some of our more experienced members."

I asked if Don did any coaching. It was an innocent question, but Daisy gave me a knowing look. "He does, actually. He's quite popular among a certain set."

I didn't like her implication.

We went back inside, this time walking towards the hall that led to Don's office and back to reception. Before we got to Don, Daisy opened a set of doors.

"This is the main function room. We do weddings and corporate dinners for up to three hundred people. Members get a ten percent discount on hall hire and catering."

We paused, looking. Then she said, "Let's go find a room and we can discuss membership options."

We walked towards Don's office. As we got closer the electricity in the air intensified. I could feel charged particles moving around.

I held my bag; how solid it was. If only emotions or ways of being were so concrete, and I could pick up *happy* or *content* or *easy to love* and put it in my pocket.

"This is a good time of year to join," said Daisy. "We've got some great deals at the moment. There are a number of different options."

We got to Don's door, which was open. I glanced in and saw him sitting at his desk.

"We also have packs for new members. You get two free coaching sessions and a T-shirt if you join before Saturday."

Daisy kept walking but I didn't. I called out, "Hi, Don."

He looked up. We shared a long, glorious moment. Then Don shuffled some paper around. "Germaine . . . What are you doing here?"

"I'm doing the membership tour."

"Right, the tour. How's it going?"

Daisy, who was up ahead, came back. He wasn't talking to her but she said, "Great. The weather out there's lovely."

Don said, "Make sure you give Germaine a good deal."

Daisy said, "I will, I will."* Then she started to move off, but I didn't follow. I asked Don if he had a minute and, when he said he had several, felt a small pang of excitement.

Daisy's voice moved into reevaluation mode, upgrading its initial perception of me. "I'll meet you back at reception," she said.

A certain set indeed.

When she was out of earshot, I told Don I was sorry to hear what had happened with the car park.

"Thanks, Germaine. That means a lot."

I lowered my voice. "Don't worry. You won't have any more problems there. Celia Brown's leaving."

If he hadn't known what was happening he would have asked *why* she was leaving or how I knew, but he didn't, which meant he knew already. The mayor *had* told him.

I didn't mind, I wasn't jealous of their relationship, but I would have liked some acknowledgment of my personal contribution, a sign that he knew how much effort I'd put in.

He exceeded my wildest hopes in this regard.

"They must love you at the council," he said.

Did he say this because he thought I was eminently lovable, or was it an offhand remark? I couldn't tell by looking at him. I went to leave.

"Wait." Don fossicked through his drawer. "I forgot to give you this." When he put his hand out he was holding a certificate. It said:

---

*Daisy did not give me a good deal. It was a terrible offering. Four thousand dollars in start-up fees plus another $150 to pay by the month. Also, the much-lauded free T-shirt came only in an XL. I said I'd think about it.

EASTERN REGION SUDOKU CONTEST 2004
THIRD PLACE
PRESENTED TO Alan Cosgrove

"You can add it to the shrine," he said.

It wasn't a shrine, it was a display, but I didn't tell him that. And I wasn't disappointed. "Thanks. I love certificates. I've got fourteen of my own, you know."

I would have loved to tell him what they were for. But all he said was, "Now you've got fifteen." He didn't realize the fourteen were ones I'd earned myself: a different category from ones that belonged to him. Maybe I should have clarified.

- 20 -

That night Jack messaged saying he was going to bring me lunch tomorrow and was there anything I didn't eat. I said I ate everything, though this wasn't strictly true. There were lots of things I didn't like. But I decided to see if they happened to appear. See if he'd allocated portions and I happened to inadvertently stuff them up.

I was sick of answering the phone. Talking to people all the time took a lot of energy. What kept me from complaining about it was my spreadsheet. Whenever I opened it up, I remembered I wasn't only answering calls, I was collecting evidence. Professor John Douglas said everything in life should be based on evidence.

Every time I got a call I logged it, recording a number of relevant characteristics. It wasn't just a basic classification anymore. I'd created a series of meta-categories and subcategories and was developing a coding system, which would help in the future, when we had to branch the calls. For example:

Press 1 if you're calling about home nursing. [Code: 1]
Press 1 if you're calling about personal care. [Code: 1, 1]
Press 2 if you're calling about doctors' visits, including transport. [Code: 1, 2]

I wanted to make sure the line items that got their own numbers were the highest demand requests. That way I'd minimize the number of staff required—conversations were time-consuming. If it was a recorded message, the caller would *listen*, but if it was a person that answered the call, the caller felt the need to *talk* as well. This introduced a layer of inefficiency.

I told Francine that, a couple of times, but she was not concerned. She said, "I know, Germaine, but it's nice for people to have human contact sometimes, don't you think?"

It might have been nice for them. It wasn't particularly nice for me.

Repeat callers were *still* the worst-performing category. If I had my way, we'd limit the number of times the same person could call over a set time period.

Like James. He kept calling about his pension payment, and when I didn't change my position on what he had to do, he got Betsy to ring.

"I'm calling on behalf of a friend," she said.

"Betsy, it's Germaine. Tell James to call the Department of Social Services. It's got nothing to do with council."

"But Eva's fixed it for us before."

"Eva? Eva who works here?" Betsy must have got the names wrong. I couldn't know for sure because Eva was off with Frank, making sure the signature collection officers were doing their jobs correctly. "Some of them are real slackers," she'd said.

"Eva *has* fixed it before," said Betsy.

Maybe that's why James kept calling? Because he wanted to speak to Eva?

Yet another reason automation was going to be a big success.

When Jack came to get me for lunch, he was holding a picnic basket. I hate picnics, so that was a black dot. We went outside. I thought we'd sit near the bench we sat at last time, when we had the pasta, but Jack said he knew somewhere better, which I thought hinted at an unpleasant competitive streak. We cut through the car park and down a laneway and there, on the other side of the road, was a park. We walked over to sit beneath a large tree.

Jack told me to wait and opened up his basket. Inside was a picnic rug, which he unfolded and laid flat on the grass. Then he got out two food containers, fogged with steam, and a large bottle of orange

juice—*Ha*, I thought to myself. I hate orange juice. I couldn't wait to
tell him. But by the time he'd put out two cloth napkins, folded in the
shape of paper planes, two checkered plastic cups, two checkered
plastic plates and knives and forks with checkered plastic handles, I
found I didn't feel like saying it.

Jack stood up. "What do you think?"

I shrugged. "It's okay. I prefer chairs to sitting on the ground."

Jack ignored this. "Please," he said, gesturing.

I sat on the lower right-hand quartile of the rug and Jack sat on the
upper left. He clicked the lid off a food container and put some on
my plate. It was lasagna, store-bought, like from a café.

"I couldn't get anything with tuna and tomato," he said.

"That's okay. I had enough yesterday." Actually, if anyone had
enough of the tuna-tomato-pasta combination yesterday, it was Jack.
When we'd started eating it, I'd admitted, largely in fear of salmonella—the tuna was a funny color—that the pasta was a little hard
and maybe even rubbery, but Jack insisted he didn't mind. "It's nice to
be cooked for," he said, and finished every piece. Marie mustn't have
been very good at cooking. I wondered if she was good at anything.

Now, on the picnic rug, Jack picked up his container of food. We
sat and ate. It was quiet in the park; there were no visual stimuli.

Jack asked how the helpline was.

"Busy. We had fourteen calls today, and Eva only answered one."

"Do you have a favorite caller?"

I did, but it was complicated and I didn't want to say. "No. They're
all equally painful."

Jack did a half laugh; it was a sort of snort, really, but not an unpleasant sound. I wouldn't have minded hearing it again.

"I don't get too attached," I said. "I'm like a robot." That's what Peter
said—not to me, to other people. *"I-am-Germaine, I-am-Germaine,"* I
added, in the automated-sounding voice that Peter used.

But Jack didn't think this was as funny as the staff at Wallace Insurance had. "You're not a robot," he said.

"It's a joke, Jack. I'm being funny."

"Well, it's not funny." Suddenly, he was very serious.

I rolled my eyes. But I sort of wished he'd been there, when Peter did his original impression.

On Saturday morning I left for the homework club ten minutes earlier than necessary and *still* ran into Jin-Jin. She was loitering by the fire escape with her backpack on. Her face lit up when she saw me.

"Hi, Germaine." She followed me to the car, opened the passenger's-side door, and got in. She wriggled out of her backpack, dumped it on the seat behind, and started fiddling with the dial for the heating.

I took a deep breath. "Jin-Jin," I said. "You can come with me this week, but don't get any ideas. I'm not giving you a ride every week. Nothing against you—it's just easier. I don't want to have to wait if you're running late, and I don't want to have to tell you if I want to leave early. It's better for both of us if we go separately."

She giggled. That inane, perplexing giggle. It was as though she was immune to discouragement. "Okay, Germaine." And then, as though she had heard none of it: "What d'you do last night? No, wait, let me guess: You ate Chinese takeaway and watched murder mysteries on TV."

Sometimes I wondered if Jin-Jin was spying on me. Did she stand on her side of the wall with her ear to a glass, straining to hear? Did she hang around her front door, looking through the peeper, waiting for me to appear?

"You must have the Red Emperor on speed dial. They see your number and start cooking. *It's Germaine from number twenty-three. Quick, get the fried rice on, ha-ha.*"

I turned the heating off and pushed the button so the windows went down.

"And you're always alone in there, Germaine. No one ever comes to visit you. Don't you get lonely?"

"Lonely? I don't get lonely, Jin-Jin. I don't have time to get lonely."

"I get lonely," she said. "Lee works at night and I don't know so many people here."

She sounded sad. I was glad we were both facing forward and I couldn't see her face. I might have been required to do something. Instead, I pointed out how bad the traffic was. "You'll have to remember that next week when you're taking the bus. Might want to leave early."

"You know"—Jin-Jin perked up—"you should come for dinner some time, Germaine. One Friday night we could eat together. Instead of takeaway you come over and I'll cook. I'll make you katsu curry. Proper katsu curry, my mother's secret recipe. You won't guess what's in it."

"If it's MSG, I'm allergic. I get headaches. Anyway, I'm too busy."

When we arrived at the senior center, I would have liked to sit in the car for a bit, sending Don telepathic messages across the lot, but I couldn't because of Jin-Jin. We got out and went inside.

Charlie was in the foyer, pinning posters on the noticeboard. He seemed happy until I asked how the Book Day parade went, and then his face clouded over. He didn't win. Some kid rented a Hulk costume and got first prize. We agreed this was unfair. Leaving aside the fact that renting a costume is cheating, the Hulk is a comic, not a book. "You were robbed," I told him.

"I appreciate your support," he said. Charlie is very articulate for a six-year-old.

Gladys and Betsy were in the office. I left Jin-Jin and Charlie to go speak to them. The three of us had just sat down when Celia appeared in the doorway. She had on the same mean face as usual.

"What are *you* doing here?" she said.

I was going to say the same to her, only Betsy interrupted.

"Germaine's helping with the homework club," she said. "She's the new mathematics tutor. She's great with the young people."

I had never met anyone as consistently friendly as Betsy. It continued to arouse my suspicions. I didn't know what she was trying to do, but whatever it was, Gladys was in on it.

"Better than great," said Gladys. "Germaine's fantastic. I don't know what we've done without her all these years."

Celia was still glaring, only now it was at the three of us. It was a very confusing situation. I had to stay alert, observing what was happening so as not to be tricked or made a fool of.

When Celia was gone, Betsy apologized on her behalf. "Sorry about that. She's a bit out of sorts these days."

"Yes," Gladys agreed. "You get a glimpse of the old girl every now and then, but most of the time she's in hiding."

"Don't worry." I stayed positive. "She'll be gone soon anyway." This was their moment to say everything was organized, there was a new committee and Celia was not a feature of it. But they were strangely silent.

I repeated myself. "She'll be gone soon anyway."

Betsy picked up an empty cup. "Would you like a cup of tea? I made some jam drops . . ."

"What I would like is a status report and an ETD. That's Estimated Time of Departure. I say 'soon' but I'd like to know *how* soon. A week? Two weeks?" The mayor wanted Celia gone by the end of the month, but anything earlier would be a bonus, for her and me. I wondered when she decided on Employee of the Year. Because it didn't say on the council website.

The room was quiet. Gladys examined the palm of her hand and Betsy looked out the window. My stomach began to sink. "You have told her?" I said.

Gladys made a long "mmm" sound, which was difficult to interpret but didn't sound positive.

"We were going to." For once, Betsy was not smiling. "*I* was going to. But it's not that easy. Celia's bark is worse than her bite, you know. She's . . . sensitive."

"We haven't found the right moment," said Gladys. "And then we thought it's probably better coming from you, Germaine. If *you* say it, she'll know it's official. If we say it, she'll only get mad at us."

I started to panic. I'd told Don it was sorted, and it wasn't, not nearly. I fanned my face.

"That's not a problem, is it?" said Betsy.

"Should we have mentioned it earlier?" said Gladys.

- 21 -

I was standing by the printer when I saw the mayor. She was wandering the building. Every now and then she did that, walked through the office and talked to people or photocopied something. It was unnecessary, Stacey could just as easily set up a meeting or make copies of whatever it was, but that's why everybody loved it.

She stopped to talk to one of the cleaners. "Hi, Bob," she said. She knew everyone's name, even the names of people who didn't really matter.

Mayor Bainbridge, in short, was a charismatic person. Charisma is an important attribute to have if you want to be successful. It's even more important than height or appearance, and those things are very important. CEOs and leaders of big companies (and, incidentally, psychopaths and serial killers) are always charismatic. Charisma is a way of getting people to like you, and because they like you, they suppress other emotions like jealousy or skepticism or even distrust. I had a bit of charisma already, I knew, but it was something I was keen to cultivate.

The printer beeped: paper jam. I flicked the side panel open and peered in, moving slowly, waiting for her to see me.

Which she did. "Germaine, I was hoping to run into you."

"Mayor Bainbridge." I freed a piece of crumpled paper and shut the printer flap.

"How's that cousin of yours?" she said. "I believe she's renewing her vows."

It was unfortunate Mayor Bainbridge knew Kimberly. Having her in common meant we often ended up talking about her, and since I didn't like Kimberly, I didn't want to do that.

I'd have preferred to talk about myself. I wanted to tell the mayor *my* hopes and dreams and hear *her* talk about how she got to where she was. It would be exciting to be her protégé, to have the sort of relationship I could mention if I ever had to make an award acceptance speech. I wouldn't attribute everything to her, but I could point out it was she who'd seen how special I was when others were being shortsighted.

"It was a beautiful invitation, wasn't it?" said the mayor. "And the Park Hyatt is a lovely venue."

It hadn't occurred to me that Kimberly would invite Mayor Bainbridge to her party. Maybe I'd ask if I could sit at the mayor's table. It would mean Sharon would have to sit on her own, but I could have dinner with her any old time. And we could always talk or text in the breaks between courses.

But alas:

"I'm so sorry Christos and I won't be there. We're taking a little holiday in Fiji before everything ramps up for the state elections. You know how it is." The mayor checked behind her before moving closer. "Germaine . . . How's our special project coming along? Has Celia *moved on*?" The way she said "moved on," it sounded like a euphemism for "passed away."

I was annoyed. I'd been hoping to give her good news, but Gladys and Betsy's incompetence meant I couldn't. Yet. "There's been a small setback," I said. I told her it was no big deal, nothing I couldn't sort out. I was quite sure it would be all tied up by the end of next week.

She was disappointed, I could tell by her face.

"Could Francine help?" she said.

Francine? What possible help would Francine provide?

"I doubt it," I said.

"Okay, so long as things are moving. Don will be happy when it's sorted. You know he really likes you, Germaine."

"Does he?" I willed her to elaborate. Willed it with all my person.

But she continued at a tangent. "I shouldn't say this, but the golf club is not doing very well at the moment."

"Oh. That's unfortunate." It was as I'd suspected—Don was broke. He needed help. *My* help; help only *I* could provide.

"Look, I only mention it so you know how important it is. How much he—and I—appreciate everything you're doing."

And so getting rid of Celia Brown had fallen to me. The more I looked into it, the more complicated it seemed. The committees and leases had been deliberately set up to ensure they were independent of the governing body—they were *meant* to sit outside the mayor's sphere of influence. Achieving the desired result would require "creative" thinking. Luckily, this type of thinking was second nature to me.

To start, I identified the variables of interest:

C = Celia

M = The mayor

E = Election

As an afterthought, I added G = Gladys, because she was the one who was going to replace Celia, but in fact the G could just as easily have been B (Betsy) or O (some other person).

Next, I worked out which were the "known" variables and which were the "unknowns."

The "knowns" were E and M. This was because I knew what I wanted E (the election result) to be and I knew what the mayor (M) wanted the election result to be. Given these were the same, I assigned E and M the same values.

This left G and C as unknowns or unpredictable variables. They were the ones I had to worry about. One thing I learned at Wallace Insurance was when it comes to complex equations, unpredictable variables can wreak havoc on your overall result. Low likelihood does not take things out of the realm of possibility: One in a thousand doesn't sound like much, but it's a whole lot more than zero.

I fiddled around for ages, trying to identify the best- and worst-case scenarios. I focused on optimization, which involved:

1. Making the worst-case scenario so unlikely it was essentially impossible;

and/or:

2. Reducing the impact of the worst-case scenario. That is, making the worst thing that could happen not that bad.

I was shuffling C, M, and E around to get G on its own when I had a revelation. I'd been looking at things the wrong way. Instead of trying to convince Celia her time was up, I should *make* it so her time was up; I should engineer the up-ness of her time. If she wasn't going to walk, she'd have to be pushed. Once I worked that out, it was easy. Barely an hour later, I'd created:

The Deepdene Policy on Committees Occupying Council Buildings.

Specifically bylaw 1.2:

Members are prohibited from serving as president for a period of more than five years. Individuals who have served five years are deemed ineligible for reelection for a minimum of seven years thereafter.

I added a fictitious date and put the whole thing in typewriter font to make it look older and more legitimate. Then, with the satisfaction of one who has devised an elegant solution to a difficult problem, I sat back to envisage the precise nature and magnitude of Don's appreciation.

Next time we had lunch Jack and I went to the café. I got a sandwich, and he got a vegetable pasty. While he was eating, a bit of pastry broke off and got stuck on his cheek. I could have told him, but he was being weird about Don, and thinking about his future embarrassment made me feel better.

He kept calling Don "Greg Norman." "How's Greg Norman?" he said. And: "What's his handicap?" He pressed me for information about our relationship, but I didn't say much. You might say there wasn't much to say. Or you could say, and this was my preferred way of thinking, that Don and I were taking things slow. We were letting our relationship evolve organically. The mayor's words kept running through my head, *He likes you, Germaine,* and for now they were sufficient. It was almost more convenient this way than if we had been in an actual relationship. Not only more expedient but less irritating. This way he was everything I wanted him to be. Aspects of his personality I didn't like—I hadn't identified any of these yet, but inevitably I would—couldn't get in the way.

Jack squeezed tomato sauce onto his plate. "What's Greg doing today? Still whining about those little old ladies?"

"He wasn't whining, Jack. He had a perfectly valid complaint. But anyway, that particular issue is close to being resolved." Though it was too short to do properly, I swished my hair over my shoulder.

Jack gave me a funny look. "What do you mean, *that particular issue is close to being resolved?*"

I shrugged. I hadn't told Jack about my special project, but perhaps I should.

Trying not to sound smug, I explained what I'd been working on. The gist. I glossed over some of the detail, and he may have thought the policy I'd created was preexisting.

"Germaine," he said, "be careful." He sounded serious.

"Yes, Jack."

"I mean it. Be careful of the mayor. She's . . . self-interested."

"Everyone's self-interested, Jack. Just because you do something that's good for you personally doesn't mean it's not good for other people."

"Doesn't mean it is."

That was the problem with Jack in a nutshell. It wasn't that he was stupid, he was just easily satisfied. He'd cultivated a kind of contentment, a satisfaction with mediocrity. He was happy to plod along, to lead a small life filled with small things.

I had been living a small life, too, but now I was outgrowing it; my life was expanding rapidly. Like the big bang.

"All I'm saying is, be careful." Jack raised his eyebrows in a knowing way and took a bite of his pasty. I watched with irritation as the flake of pastry fell from his cheek and landed on the plate.

- 22 -

Jack's misgivings didn't deter me. The opposite: They reminded me that it's important to have vision in life, and if that vision requires a little manipulation or creativity, if you need to operate in the gray area instead of the black (or the white, as the case might be)—so be it. Utilitarianism dictates the greatest good for the many; people don't realize that invariably involves a fair amount of bad for the few. If you need to upset a small number of people (sometimes as small a number as one) to get something done, it's not the worst thing. What's important is the final result:

A lot of happy old people, one happy mayor, one happy Don >>> a single, sad Celia.

I wrote Celia a letter, informing her about the policy and what it meant for the current committee. I outlined the key provisions and advised that we would require records outlining who had held what position across the previous five-year period. If she herself had been president for that period of time or longer, she would, in accordance with the policy, have to stand down.

Celia responded a week later saying she had received my correspondence and determined it did not apply.

I filed her letter and drafted another.

This acknowledged the committee's efforts in previous years but repeated: The council had a policy. I said I was happy to attend the next committee meeting and explain it further. This would also be an opportune time to check records. *Best*, I signed, *Germaine Johnson*.

One final letter arrived. It said my presence at the next committee meeting, much less my involvement in the selection of said committee constituted a—quote—"ridiculous waste of time." If I needed things to do, Celia suggested I start by picking up the rubbish at the train station, there was plenty of that. Or culling stray dogs, she knew of a few mangy mutts (mangy owners, too). *Regards*, the letter concluded, *Celia Brown*.

Our correspondence ceased after that.

In addition to progressing the mayor's special project, I'd organized to meet with Francine to show her my spreadsheet. She was skeptical when it came to the idea of automating the helpline, but according to Professor John Douglas (as per the article), once someone had the facts in front of them, it was much harder to dispute what was really going on.

Normally we would have met in Francine's office, but they were installing software on her computer, so she came to me. She sat in Eva's seat, which was vacant at the time.

When I opened the spreadsheet, I took a good bit of delight in hearing Francine gasp. Yes, there was a lot of information. I'd recorded everything.

I went to the first tab. "This is where I input the data. These are *all* the calls I've answered. If you want to know how many Eva's answered, you could go to the centralized data set and deduct my calls from the total number. You could also deduct my total call time from the total call time for the helpline overall. That might be an interesting thing to do."

Interesting *and* enlightening. But Francine wasn't jumping at this suggestion. Hopefully, she'd be more proactive about other items.

I clicked a different tab. "This is where I've done trend analysis to work out what most of the calls are about. And this"—another tab—"is where I've matched call time with category, so you can tell what categories are most time-intensive to talk about."

Francine said, "It's a lot of work you've put in, Germaine."

"I spend all my time working when I'm in the office." I looked pointedly at Eva, who'd just walked in holding a Slurpee.

Francine had to stand up to give her back her seat. "Maybe we should talk about this later."

But I had only one other major point to make. "If we *did* automate the helpline, we could probably cut back on staff."

"Automate? Do you mean recorded messages?" Eva had not been invited to participate in the conversation but was offering her opinion anyway. "I hate those things. Lucky I know how to get around them."

I'd been holding a pencil to point things out to Francine on the screen. Now I wanted to snap it in two. "You can't get around them, Eva. That's the whole idea."

"*I* can. I know how to bypass all recorded messages and go straight to an operator."

"How?" I was humoring her.

"You just press star four times, followed by the number seven."

"Yeah, okay." I made a face at Francine in the hope she'd make a face back, but hers stayed straight. I wished the mayor were here.

"Sounds like everyone is doing a great job around here," said Francine.

"Seriously." Eva swished her plastic cup around. "It works for any phone line."

The senior citizens club committee meeting was being held on a Tuesday, straight after one of Betsy's chair aerobics classes. I decided to attend both. The night before I packed my runners and five copies of the policy I'd created (stained with tea to give it an air of age and credibility) into my wheeling briefcase.

Chair aerobics was full again, but I was early enough to get the best position. This pleased Betsy ("I'm glad you came") but it did not please James ("La America").

He came and stood in front of me, in front of the chair he used to sit in. "You," he said.

"Hello, James."

He took a different seat but frowned through the whole class. This used some muscles but not the ones we were primarily concerned with.

After class I changed out of my runners and put on work shoes. As I went to leave the room Betsy said, "Wait. I'll walk with you."

"No," I said. "I'll walk alone." I didn't want to send the wrong message.

We had to walk quite close anyway, the office being down the hall, but Betsy stayed a step behind.

Five people attended the committee meeting: me, Celia, Gladys, Betsy, and a man in a check shirt called Tom. He was the club secretary. "Sorry," he said when he saw me. "I didn't know you were coming; there's only four copies of the agenda." He got up to print one more, but Celia stopped him.

"We're out of paper," she said.

"There's some in the—"

"None there either."

I had to share with Gladys. She didn't put her copy in the middle, she kept it more on her side, making it clear I was the outsider.

First order of business was the minutes from the previous meeting. Tom embarked on a detailed account of a trivia night long past, but mercifully Celia cut him off. She said the minutes appeared to be in order and did someone want to "move" them? Betsy moved the minutes and Gladys seconded. Tom made careful notes.

Second order of business was the treasurer's report. Betsy began to read. "We have fourteen thousand six hundred and fifty-seven dollars in the bank and another sixty-seven dollars in petty cash. We need to buy some chessboards next month, and the Italians have requested a new bocce set."

"A new bocce set? *Pass*. There's nothing wrong with the old one," said Celia. She added, "Tom, don't minute that. Write: *The committee is considering this request*."

We went through the moving and the seconding rigmarole again and then it was time for other business.

I raised a hand. "I have other business."

Celia ignored me. "No? Let's move on, then. Next item on the agenda is use of the communal cupboard in the hall."

I talked over the top of her. "This is regarding the council's Policy on Committees Occupying Council Buildings." Not wanting to dwell on specific details, I turned and unzipped the front pocket on my briefcase. I got out the copies I'd brought and handed them around. There was a sufficient number; no one was left out. "You should have this already," I said. "I sent a letter about it."

"And I sent a letter back," said Celia.

I offered to read the policy aloud, but Tom thought it was better if we all read it to ourselves. That was fine with me. I was flexible and accommodating.

Tom began to read, Gladys began to read, and Betsy began to read.

Celia did not begin to read. She didn't pick up the policy; she didn't put her glasses on to see it better; she didn't cast her eyes in its direction. Instead, she clicked her pen. Then she looked around the room; then she pushed her chair away from the table. "It really has nothing to do with us," she said.

"It says it's for 'occupants of council buildings,'" said Tom. "We're occupants of a council building."

"I've never heard of it before." Celia clicked the pen again; the sound began to grate.

"It says you can't be president for more than five years."

"No one's ever mentioned that."

"Sounds like they only just rediscovered the policy," said Betsy. "Is that right, Germaine?"

Was this part of her act? I wasn't sure if her friendliness extended to willful naivety. But she, and Gladys, who was also nodding, really did seem to believe the policy existed. I took this as a positive reflection on my writing skills.

"It was filed incorrectly. Once we realized its existence, we notified the committees affected as soon as was practicable." I shuffled some papers around. "According to our records, Celia, you've been president for fifteen years."

"This is the most ridiculous thing I've ever heard."

"Ten years in excess of the maximum of five."

"It's discrimination. I absolutely refuse—"

"According to the policy, you need to stand down."

Celia folded her arms across her chest. "I'm not going anywhere."

"If you fail to step aside, then—and I'm quoting bylaw two point seven here—"

"Next order of business is the cupboard in the hall."

My voice got louder. "The committee will be null and void—"

Hers also got louder. "Tom, I want you to make a sign."

"No committee means the Deepdene Senior Citizens Club will cease to exist."

"The sign should say 'Groups are not permitted to store items in this cupboard.'"

The two of us were standing now, leaning across the table, yelling. Little globules of spit flew through the air like tiny angry bullets. My blood was so elevated in temperature it was in danger of turning gaseous.

"THE MAYOR SAYS YOU HAVE TO," I said.

"I DON'T CARE."

All at once there was a great *crack!* as Betsy slammed a book down on the table. The sound cut through the air and echoed all around.

Everything was still.

Then Betsy reached out and put her hand on Celia's hand. Celia flinched, but she didn't flick it off. "Celia" was all that Betsy said.

And so a glorious smell, that of victory, began to fill the room.

Celia didn't move, but something in her shifted. She could smell the victory, too.

Very slowly, she stepped backwards. Without saying anything she moved towards the door, opened it, and disappeared down the hall. Her footsteps faded as she went into the car park, leaving the four of us behind.

It was strange. I didn't expect them to release streamers or start singing and dancing around, but I did think there'd be an undercurrent of happiness or excitement on their part. A sense of relief—not necessarily expressed, but still evident.

There was none of that. In fact, if I had to graph the mood of the room with time on the x axis and joy on the y, at this point the line would have dipped below the horizontal. It was not just a *reduction* in the level of joy. We were in deficit.

"That was awful," said Gladys. "How depressing."

Tom agreed. "I've known her for thirty-seven years, and I've never seen her so upset."

There was silence in the room. A lot of silence, and no gratitude at all.

Eva wasn't there when Mayor Bainbridge came by the next morning. She appeared at the entrance to our area, her pastel pink shirt bright against the gray walls. "Germaine," she said. *"Well done."*

"What for?" I feigned confusion. I could feel an accolade coming, and such things are best drawn out. Most people say "thanks" when they get a compliment, I always say, "Pardon?"

"You did it. No more Celia Brown, eh?"

"Oh, that." I was nonchalant, like it was just another thing, no more remarkable than anything else I'd achieved of late.

The mayor came forward. It appeared she was seeking some form of physical contact. A hug? Another glorious shoulder squeeze? I got up in readiness, but at the exact moment I reached my full height she stopped short, pulled out Eva's chair, and leaned against the back of it. I lowered myself back down, slowly, so she wouldn't notice.

"Tell me everything. How did you tell her? What did she say? Was she angry?" The mayor was gripping Eva's chair in anticipation.

I could easily have provided a thorough account, only . . .

When the mayor had said, "Do what you have to do," she hadn't specified the boundaries of acceptable action. Was "create a fictitious policy" permissible or not permissible?

"It was fine," I said. "Celia was a bit . . . annoyed, but she saw reason in the end."

"Annoyed? Not at you, I hope. I hope she could see she brought it upon herself."

"Yes. I mean, I think so."

"What's wrong, Germaine?" The mayor's face softened. "Oh, dear. It was awful, wasn't it? It was awful, of course it was. If it's any consolation, we've had more complaints about Celia Brown than we've had about anyone, ever. I don't like to speak ill of my constituents, *but*—" She lowered her voice. "I think she might have an undiagnosed mental health problem. Don't say I said that; I'm just thinking out loud. It's Chatham House Rules between you and me, you know."

And just like that, my uncertainty disappeared. If I'd doubted any aspect of our relationship up until now, this proved it: I was part of the inner sanctum.

"So? Was it awful?" She was cringing on my behalf.

"It wasn't great. But I have to tell you . . . My, ah, approach was a bit . . . inventive."

"Oh?" She listened in silence while I explained. I made it sound simple and straightforward and only ever called my creation a policy once, thereafter referring to it as "the document."

"You know what I should say, don't you?" said the mayor when I was finished. "I should say, *That's not the way we do things around here, Germaine* and *There's a policy about policies*, but let's be honest. Sometimes you have to be a little . . . creative to get things done."

I didn't know how tense I was until I relaxed. Of course it was fine. Of *course* she understood. She and I were friends. We were better friends than she and Kimberly, probably. We had more in common.

"Don is thrilled, as you can imagine." The mayor adjusted her hair so it was sitting better. "He wanted to come down and thank you himself."

"Did he?" My voice was a squeak.

"He did. Only they had some disaster at the club. Something to do with the kitchen. He said he might call instead."

I fiddled with the button on my cuff. "Does he have my number?"

"No, but he can go through the switch. Or maybe he'll call the helpline, I don't know."

"Okay, I'm here all day. If you speak to him." I wasn't going to go to lunch or the toilet or anything. I was going to stay where I was, in the chair, by the phone, waiting.

There was an annoying sound, loud and shrill, and then Eva came around the corner. She was whistling. You would have thought the mayor loved whistling, how enthusiastic she was in greeting her. "Good morning, Eva," she said.

"Good morning." Eva was less enthusiastic. Curious, as she was the whistler.

The mayor shifted her weight off Eva's chair. "Right, I'd better go. Thanks again, Germaine."

When the mayor was out of earshot, Eva said, "What was she doing here?"

"She just came by."

"She's never come by before."

I shrugged.

Eva folded her arms and leaned back. "It was about the biscuits, wasn't it? Go on, admit it. She was snooping, wasn't she? Trying to get more information."

"Okay, sure. Yes, it was about the biscuits."

"I knew it. That's why I've been taking the petition home every single night, for this exact reason." Eva unzipped her jacket and pulled a fat wad of paper from the inner pocket. She unfolded it and smoothed it flat. Then she picked up the phone. "Wait until Frank hears about this."

To an outside observer, it would have seemed like my performance that day was the same as always, but in fact it was well below par. I scheduled cleaning for Mrs. Harris on a Sunday, which meant we had to pay penalty rates (double time and a half, plus a break allowance) and told Bob Jones he qualified for a Meals on Wheels discount when he didn't. My mind was on Don. Specifically, his calling—or lack of calling.

Celia called before he did.

I knew it was her because I was stuck doing a Meals on Wheels order and Eva kept getting hang-ups. When I finally finished, I picked up a new call and a voice said, "About time."

She didn't say who *she* was, but she asked, in a pointed fashion, who *I* was.

I said I couldn't say. When pressed, I said the council had a policy of anonymity.

"A policy." She got quite snarky. "You've got an awful lot of policies over there."

"Do we? I wouldn't know, I haven't been here that long."

That's when Celia snapped, like a rubber band pulled in two directions. "For crying out loud, Germaine. That was not a real policy. What the hell's happening over there? That man next door's a con artist."

"He's not."

"He is, actually. Didn't you read the paper?"

"If you don't stop yelling, I will end the call."

The phone went silent. It was the sound of nothing again, but this time so loud it seemed to echo.

"Are you there?" I said. I wasn't nice about it, which I regretted because then I thought I heard a sob.

Celia said in a wobbly voice, "Germaine, I don't have anything to do tomorrow."

I wished she hadn't told me that. I hated trying to find the calendar of upcoming events on the council website. It was hidden under a succession of tabs that were not at all intuitive.

I also knew how time could slow. After what happened at Wallace Insurance, it went at a glacial pace. Instead of seconds making up minutes and minutes making up hours, seconds seemed to go for minutes and minutes went for hours: i.e., there was quite a lot of day to fill and not a lot to fill it with.

"I miss Bernard," said Celia.

I closed my eyes. On the phone she was harder to dislike; I don't know why. Maybe her face made her more irritating.

I turned to see if Eva was listening. She was oblivious, on the phone herself. How unusual.

I cupped my hand around the microphone to make double sure Eva wouldn't hear. Then I whispered, "You can always call me. I'll answer."

Don didn't call all day. He must have been busy. Or maybe he'd tried to call but had trouble getting through. Maybe there was an issue with the phones? Some glitch in our system that was blocking his number. Or maybe the problem was at *his* end and he wasn't able to diagnose it.

I should conduct a test to see.

When Eva went to meet Frank, I dialed the golf club. It was four rings before someone answered: a Charlene.

"Charlene, are your phones working?"

"Excuse me?"

"Are the phones working at the golf club?"

"I believe so. Who is this?"

"No one." I hung up.

They did seem to be working. So it was a mystery why Don hadn't called, given how much he wanted to.

When he didn't call the next day—or the one after—I decided to solve the mystery and went down to the golf club during lunch.

Don was in his office. He didn't notice me at first, staring from the doorway. I knocked, but he didn't hear.

"Must be pretty important," I said. That got his attention.

"Germaine. What a nice surprise." After a bit, he added, "Come in."

I went in and sat down. Neither one of us spoke straightaway. I had the sense he was waiting for me at the same time as I was waiting for him. I guessed he was nervous. I tried to help him relax.

"I watched a clip of you and Rebecca Li on YouTube last night," I said.

"Did you?"

"It was the one where you put the seven and three in the wrong order. It gets me every time. I yelled at the screen, *Don't do it!*"

"I remember that. I don't know what I was thinking." He made a funny face. A face *I* found funny. Not everyone would have found it so humorous.

"We all make mistakes," I said, not thinking.

The face dissolved. "We do."

It wasn't going very well. I was making conversation only until he remembered what he was supposed to tell me.

But it wasn't coming to him. He must have had a lot on his mind.

I gave him a hint. "So . . . Celia's gone."

His face sprang into action now he understood. "Right, yes. Sorry, I forgot. *Thank you*. Thank you, Germaine. Great job."

"The mayor said you were pleased. I think she thought you were going to call me."

"I *was* going to . . . I forgot. We had some issues. I did mean to."

"I thought your phones might be down."

"No, they're working."

"Unlike your kitchen."

"Ha—yes."

I wasn't disappointed at how he was being. I wasn't.

"The seniors center's got a kitchen," I said, conversationally. "It's very big. I'm sure they'd let you use it if you wanted to." Maybe they would, maybe they wouldn't. I enjoyed offering, though.

"That's good to know."

"Yes. It's huge. But old. They keep talking about fixing it up. Like everything else over there . . . That whole building is in a state of disrepair. It's practically falling down."

Don was very interested. He really seemed very engaged in this topic of conversation. "Pretty bad, is it?" he said.

"Oh, it's terrible. They keep talking about doing a fund-raiser . . . Hey, Mayor Bainbridge said you're good at raising money. Any ideas I can pass along?"

He was thoughtful. "I guess it depends how much you need."

"Oh, a lot. A *lot*."

"Well . . . We usually go to businesses, or we have a dinner and charge people a premium to attend. But that's for campaign finances. There are different, er, *incentives* involved."

Incentives . . . What incentives were there for improving the state of a senior center? It was a shame they weren't all younger and perter.

Don and I had a bout of quiet thinking time. Then he said he should "let me go," when I hadn't even realized he was holding me up. How thoughtful of him to notice.

- 24 -

Less than a week later the mayor asked to meet with Francine and me again. She didn't disclose what it was about, but I surmised it related to the senior center.

I was correct. Once Stacey had shut the door, the mayor mentioned it almost immediately. "I've got news for you, ladies. Good news, I think. But first, the seniors. How are they faring without their illustrious president?"

"Good." I'd been at the homework club on Saturday, and though everyone said, "Where's Celia?" and "I miss Celia," it was essentially the same as always. Better, in relation to some criteria—e.g., the car park. It had been unusually full, and multiple vehicles had the Fitzsimmons Golf Club sticker in their front window, but no one got upset about it. No complaints, no incidents, no strongly worded signs. And if there were other criteria that weren't performing as well now Celia was gone, they hadn't yet revealed themselves.

"Good," said the mayor. "I knew if we got rid of that woman everything would calm down."

I'd known as well, but I hadn't had a chance to mention it.

"Now, the reason I've got you both here is I'm afraid the work down there is not entirely finished. I've got another special project that needs doing."

Francine pushed her glasses up on her nose. She looked worried.

"I've been thinking," said the mayor. "I'm concerned that the senior citizens center might not be compliant with the building regulations. I drove past last night, and the fence was falling over and there was a broken picnic table and junk everywhere."

"The disabled toilet is also broken," I said. "It doesn't flush properly. And when it rains the floor in the kitchen gets wet."

"Exactly. If something went wrong, we'd be in all sorts of trouble. Some old duck slips on a faulty floorboard and breaks her hip? My God, I hate to think."

Francine removed her glasses. "We've known this for ages. Celia wrote every year and asked for money to undertake repairs and . . . we . . . said no every time."

The mayor did not find this helpful. No one did. Sometimes I couldn't believe Francine was a team leader, as she didn't seem to understand basic human interactions. The mayor didn't want to hear what she should or could have done.

The mayor had been sitting forward. but now she leaned back in the chair. The additional distance seemed to give her a better view of Francine and me. Her eyes flicked from one of us to the other and back again.

Then she made an announcement, selecting her words carefully. It was a shame there wasn't a larger audience; her diction was excellent. "We can't have anybody getting hurt. Germaine, I want you to go down there. And take Ralph from Risk Management and Health and Safety. Do you know Ralph? He's very good, isn't he? Take Ralph down there and do a safety audit, the two of you. Have a look around and see what needs fixing. Everything. No matter how small, I don't care if it's a light bulb that needs changing, I want it on record."

This was unexpected. It was more work for me, and Ralph wouldn't be much fun to hang around with, but it was good news. My first thought was, *Celia will be pleased*. My second was, *Celia might never know*. There was something disappointing about the latter.

I would have thought Francine's response would be more straightforward, but her reactions seemed to be on a time delay. "A safety audit?" she said.

"You're worried about resourcing," said the mayor. "You'll be pleased to know I've already thought about that. It'll be a big job, coordinating a redevelopment, and I want Germaine to do it. I know your team's at capacity. I'll allocate money to backfill her position. You can hire a temp."

Privately, I thought they might need more than one and made a note to mention this to Francine later. Francine, meanwhile, had stopped taking notes and was just sitting there with her mouth open.

The mayor kept talking. She wanted me to take on the seniors club exclusively. Even better, rather than report to Francine, I'd be reporting to her direct. I was also—*ta-da!*—getting my own office.

Francine managed a question. "What about the budget?"

When the mayor said they'd find the money, Francine didn't stop frowning. I felt a pang of sympathy for her. Here I was, hardly there any time at all and I was on the fast track. Francine might not even have realized before that she was the slow one.

"I don't need to remind you both that this is a confidential project, ladies. We don't want word getting out. Germaine, you'll need to speak to Stacey about the office arrangements. She knows what's happening."

Francine and I were getting up to leave when the mayor stopped us and asked to speak to me alone. Francine flipped her book shut and walked out.

"Germaine, I've arranged for you to receive a pay raise. Just a small one, to recognize your increase in seniority."

I couldn't have been happier if this had represented a career trajectory I was actually invested in.

"It's *so* good helping out those less fortunate, isn't it?" The mayor beamed.

"Personally, I find it very satisfying," I agreed.

It took Stacey a week to set up my new office and it took me less than ten minutes to pack everything up, ready to move in.

"Can't believe you've got an office," said Eva. "And I can't believe they moved my couch to put you there."

"Eva's couch" was a thinning gray sofa kept in the upstairs storeroom that had been repurposed as my new office.

"You could always take it home, Eva," said Jack, his voice muffled. He was bent down, under the desk, trying to disconnect the monitor.

"That's not really the point, is it?" said Eva. "Where am I going to lie down when I'm tired? What am I meant to do when I need time out?"

"You could always come visit." I was feeling charitable. It wasn't only getting an office (and a computer) that had me in a good mood. It was the unmistakable feeling that things were changing and life was getting better. I was fulfilling my destiny.

"Why?" said Eva. "Are you keeping the couch in there?"

"No. But I do have three chairs."

"That's ridiculous." Eva kicked her footrest over. "I'm going to get Francine to give me an extra chair. We should all ask for extra chairs, Jack. They should give everyone two chairs. Two chairs or an office."

I put a packet of Post-its and a bottle of hand sanitizer in my moving box.

"I don't want my own office," said Jack, still under the desk.

"*Are you listening?*" said Eva. "Two chairs *or* an office. One or the other."

Jack stood up and brushed the dust off his shorts. "I've got a chair, Eva. And I don't want an office."

Eva said, "Well, you can give me yours. I'll have both."

Jack didn't agree to her proposal. Instead, he changed the subject altogether. "How are the biscuits going? Any news?"

Eva said she hadn't heard.

"I wouldn't hold your breath," I said, helpfully. "Budget's pretty tight, you know. Can't see biscuits being a priority."

"Oh, *can't see biscuits being a priority*? Suppose not, now we're spending all our money on new offices and surplus chairs."

I swallowed my indignation. While I expected it from Eva, I didn't expect it from Jack. He should have said something supportive but instead he just stood there, winding the computer cord around his hand and his elbow so it made a series of loops.

I put the last of my office supplies in the moving box and held it up. "I have to take this upstairs."

They didn't even say goodbye.

- 25 -

I was excited to tell Gladys and Betsy about the safety audit, more excited than I'd been about anything in a long time. That Saturday at the homework club was hell on earth, trying to keep it to myself. I was bursting; it was like having diarrhea. Every time I stood up I thought something might slip out.

Once Ralph and I had finalized the logistics I called Gladys on the sly from my new office. Feet on the desk, I said, "Gladys. I've some important news. Can't say it over the phone, though. Have to tell you in person." I was being secretive, so as to maximize the surprise.

"You've got me worried, Germaine. Is everything okay?"

"I'll be there in an hour."

My mysteriousness worked. The two of them were standing at the front of the building when I arrived. I parked the car and strolled over. I held my hand up like a stop sign when they started asking.

"You might want to sit down," I said, and we went inside.

It felt weird being back in their office. I'd been at the center a number of times for the homework club, but I hadn't been in the *office* since the day we got rid of Celia. That was two whole months ago now, but being back there, it felt as if it had happened yesterday.

It should have been a good memory, a thing I reflected back on in the aftermath of other triumphs as I catalogued all my achievements. But somewhere along the line the memory had morphed. The facts hadn't changed, but the way I felt about them was more ambiguous. Sometimes, when I wasn't even thinking about it, I'd remember the look on Celia's face or how no one had clapped or cheered like I thought they might. I knew it didn't matter: The mayor was happy and I had my promotion and those were the most important things. But occasionally—hardly ever really, but maybe once or twice—the thought manifested:

Maybe it did matter. Maybe my promotion *wasn't* the most important thing.

Then I realized how stupid I was being.

Gladys and Betsy were sitting stiffly, waiting for me to speak.

"Are we going to have a cup of tea?" I said. "Or a snack? I'm a bit hungry."

"Just tell us, Germaine," said Gladys.

I confess I was enjoying stringing them along. It was funny how they really believed it was bad news.

"This is harder for me to say than it is for you to hear," I said. "I shouldn't be telling you this; it's not meant to be publicly known yet."

Betsy made a motion with her hand—yes, yes, hurry up—and then put her arm around Gladys because Gladys was going to cry.

"It pains me, it really does," I said, giggling on the inside, and when I couldn't do it anymore, I cried, "*Surprise! Surprise!*"

They flinched.

"The council's going to fix this place up."

It took a minute for the news to sink in.

"I just nearly had a heart attack," said Gladys.

"Was that really necessary?" said Betsy.

Betsy walked me out. Gladys, who shed a few residual tears even after I said there was nothing to worry about, stayed in the office. As we made our way through the foyer, I commented to Betsy that the place was looking good. She said, "We did a cleanup. There was a lot of junk around. Celia didn't like throwing things out."

"Didn't she?" I felt a twitch when I heard her name, almost like a guilty spasm.

"Celia's a real hoarder. I kept telling her we didn't need the VCR, everyone uses DVDs now, but it didn't make a difference. You know what she's like." Betsy held the door and we went outside. We stood on the top step, looking out across the car park. There were more cars than there used to be.

"How is Celia?" I said.

I hadn't heard from her. Every time I picked up the phone and said, "Helpline," I'd wonder if she might be calling.

But she never was.

"Don't know, haven't seen her. She hasn't been back since . . . Well, you know. Tom doesn't think she'll come back."

"Oh."

"Yeah . . . I don't think she will either."

We started down the steps, towards the car. "Does she have family?" I asked.

"Not now Bernard's gone."

Betsy mistook my silence for me feeling bad and patted me on the back. "Don't blame yourself, Germaine. We're responsible, too. We should have done something sooner. People had complained many times, and we just brushed it under the carpet."

"I don't feel bad," I said.

"Celia rubbed people the wrong way all the time," said Betsy. "I remember the day she threw the Genealogical Society's family trees out. I'm not sure who was madder, her or Norman. I thought he was going to have a hernia. And the parking. My God. You should have seen her when the Photographic Society wanted to use the loading bay." Betsy laughed to show amusement, but her laughter had a funny, empty sound.

She glanced at me. "Look, maybe I'm wrong. Maybe she will come back. And you know, she might not have family, but she does have people. There's Charlie and Vera. Celia looks after Charlie all the time."

"Charlie?" The little boy?"

"Yes, Vera's a single mother. You wouldn't think it, but Celia's actually very good with children. In fact, she's probably enjoying having a break from this place."

"Yeah, probably . . . She's probably writing a letter *right now* to say thank you."

"Mmm . . ." said Betsy. "No, probably not."

The following week Ralph and I went to the senior citizens center together. He made me wear a fluorescent safety vest, even when we were in the car, and spent the fifteen-minute drive emphasizing the importance of thoroughness. It was critical, he stressed, that we identify absolutely everything.

Before commencing, we stopped by the office to let Gladys and Betsy know we were there. Unfortunately, the two of them insisted on walking around with us, even when I insisted they didn't have to. I'd have pinched one of them if they'd been standing closer.

We started outside. "I'm glad you're all in covered footwear," said Ralph. "This paving is very uneven."

Betsy scoffed. "You think that's bad? When the floor in the John Stanley Room gets mopped, it's like a skating rink. Trish Bobbet slipped over last year during choir practice, and the whole alto section went down like dominos."

Ralph made a note on his clipboard.

"The kitchen's not much better," added Gladys.

We walked down the side of the building, around the vegetable garden, and past the old outhouse to the shed in the back. Ralph looked at all the cracks and measured how big they were using a tape measure attached to his belt. He shook the fence palings and poked sticks in parts of the weatherboards where the paint had peeled.

"See that?"

"What?"

"*That.* Could be termites. Might not be, but I'll write it down. And have a look at that." He pointed at the guttering and sucked his teeth. He was very good at his job. He was a walking, talking, glass-half-empty-and-about-to-fall-on-you-and-shatter kind of guy.

When we'd completed a loop, Ralph gave us a hint of his overall assessment. "I can't believe they've let this place go for so long . . . I mean, look at it."

"Yes," said Gladys. "There's quite a lot to do. If we were to repaint the outhouse, do you think we could change the color?"

Ralph gave her a funny look. "Biggest problem here is your roof." He pointed with his pen. "The rest needs work, but it's not going to fall down tomorrow. That roofing, though—one big gust of wind and woof. Slice someone's head off."

"That'd be top priority, then." Betsy gestured at me to write it down.

Ralph checked the clock on his phone and said he had to get back. Betsy asked when he was planning to audit the inside of the building, but Ralph said that wasn't necessary. Then he ducked off to the bathroom, leaving the three of us standing under the entrance.

"I still can't believe this is happening," said Gladys. "Celia's been trying to get the council to fix things up for years but . . . Well, they've never been very interested."

"It's Germaine. She's done it, hasn't she?" said Betsy, patting me on the back. "Don't know where we'd be without you."

"Probably somewhere pretty crap" was my suggestion.

That night I stayed back and worked into the evening. I couldn't see much from where I sat, but by the time I finished up, I was pretty sure everyone had gone home. When I came downstairs, the side door was shut and I had to go out through reception.

I expected it would be empty, but it wasn't. Someone was waiting for me.

"How come you're here?" I said, and he got all flustered, which was a glorious thing to witness.

Don had come to see me. He denied this, but I knew. It was a game we were playing, like cat and mouse. Peter used to play that, too, only he was the cat and I was the mouse. They were fixed roles. If I tried to be the cat, Peter got annoyed. Like when I turned up at his brother's birthday party that one time.

With Don I was bold. "Want to see my office?" I said.

Don rubbed across his mouth and cheeks, feeling his whiskers. His perfect whiskers. Each one was like the head of a very sharp gray-lead pencil.

Don wasn't supposed to come in without signing the visitor book, but it was late and though they'd been awarded Employee of the Year two years running, no representatives from Customer Service were around—I am only stating what is fact.

All I did was use my pass to open the door. Could I help it if Don followed?

Two people could walk side by side down the corridor, but I walked in the middle so he would have to go behind and follow me.

"It's just up here," I said in a husky voice.

"Is there a toilet I could use? I need to pee." Don's voice was high and kind of squeaky. And *pee*? I would have said urinate, or not disclosed.

The women's toilets were right there, but they'd had to move the men's for the renovations. I told Don they were out of order.

He went into the women's bathroom; I went in after him.

We were only a meter or two apart, just the toilet door between us, and that didn't touch the floor or the ceiling. I was aware of Don standing on his side, holding himself or sitting down semi-naked, if that was his preference. His being so exposed and so *close* felt pretty intimate, and pretty incredible, if I thought about it, which, as the minutes dragged on, I had ample time to do.

"Are you on your phone?" I said.

He didn't answer but began to urinate. It didn't last long, but while he was going I thought perhaps I heard him get a text message. I didn't ask about this; people get prickly if you question their private lives, even if you think you're part of their private lives. Because you might not be, you know. That can happen. Anyway, I was being laid-back, a desirable character trait, one that comes naturally to me.

Don came out and put his hands under the tap.

"You forgot to use the soap," I said.

I was glad my office was so small. With the two of us in it, we had to stand quite close. Don was being mindful of my personal space and kept inching closer to the wall, but I inched with him, to let him know I wasn't going anywhere. So that was how we moved, first his feet and then mine, all the way to the wall, where we had to stop.

We weren't so close as touching but we were breathing the same air—it seemed to come out of his mouth straight into mine—which probably altered the balance of oxygen and carbon dioxide. Maybe that was why I felt so giddy. Don seemed more giddy, though. His face was a funny color.

"Are you okay?" I said.

"I'm fine."

The way he said it, the way we were standing . . .

I had a sudden flash of Peter and me, after we left the Wallace Insurance Christmas party two years ago. But where Don and I were vertical–parallel, Peter and I had been horizontal–parallel—we were in my bed, him on top and me lying on the mattress. The weight of his body pressed against me, pinning me down. He was like a human stapler.

I took a step back from Don so he could decide what he wanted to do. If he wanted to continue along this path or if he'd made a mistake and no matter how much I tried to convince him, he wasn't interested anymore.

Don was feeling uncertain. He slipped out from where he was standing, but he didn't leave; he just stood farther away. A confusing distance. Especially as he said, "Germaine, you're great."

"You're great, too, Alan," I said.

"I'm not—"

"I meant to say Don."

But I'd ruined it by then. He stepped around the back of me, returning to the door, where he hovered. "I shouldn't be here," he said.

"It's okay, *Don*," I stressed his name. "Don't worry about it."

We had plenty of time, anyway. It wasn't like Susan Reynolds was going to swoop in and steal him off me. Sharon says people can't steal things if you don't have them to begin with, but she doesn't know what we had. No one does, except for Peter and the fourteen staff members I heard him telling in the canteen a few days before the Incident, and that was very edited.

26

The homework club was on the weekend. I'd given up telling Jin-Jin she couldn't get a ride with me; it was like talking to a brick wall. I had to accept how it was or change living situations.

Charlie was arriving just as we were, in a beat-up old bomb, yellow with a dent in the side. There was a woman with him. His mother, I supposed. Jin-Jin and I walked to the front door, and the two of them ran to catch up.

Charlie said, "Germaine, you look like a man from behind."

"Charlie," said his companion—it *was* his mother. Vera. She introduced herself, but even if she hadn't, I would have known. Her eyes were not only the same color and shape as Charlie's (i.e., blue and round), they were inset the same amount (i.e., very deep). Their noses were unusually thin to compensate.

Jin-Jin already knew Vera, or knew her enough to know who normally rode in her car. "No Celia this week?" said Jin-Jin. Celia must have been a bludger for rides, too. No wonder she and Jin-Jin got on.

"No Celia again," said Vera.

"Have you seen her? How is she?" For someone who had no interest in maths or anything else important, Jin-Jin could be very inquisitive.

"The same." Vera put her hand in her pockets, her dress stretched down. "You know something's up when she's not even writing letters."

This was worrying. As I'd told Celia once before, it was important to keep busy. Counterintuitive as it might sound, there was such a thing as too much thinking time. But it was obvious she wasn't following my advice.

"She's not really doing anything," said Vera. "I don't know why the council had to get rid of her. Seems petty if you ask me."

Jin-Jin nodded, the pink fluff on her headband bobbing up and down. "Very petty."

"What does petty mean?" said Charlie.

"It means *mean*," Jin-Jin said.

This was an incorrect translation. "It doesn't mean *mean*."

"It means *very* mean," said Jin-Jin.

"It does *not*. Can you move?" She was hovering around the door in the most infuriating fashion. "Some of us would like to go inside, you know." I stepped around Jin-Jin, to the door, and opened it with such force I nearly bowled the three of them over.

Later, Charlie and I were practicing multiplication using flash cards. We were halfway through the pile when Charlie said, "Celia isn't very good, Germaine."

"Isn't she?"

"She's not doing anything. She just sits there most of the time."

"Maybe she's meditating." I picked up the next card. "What's four eights?"

"Celia told Mum that she didn't think she had to leave this place. She thinks someone *made up* the reason she had to go. Why would someone do that, Germaine?"

I dropped the card on the floor. I had to go under the table to pick it up. Blood rushed to my head due to gravity.

"Jin-Jin's right," said Charlie. "It's very mean."

Celia was being dramatic. Even if she wasn't club president, she was still allowed to attend the center, and if she didn't want to attend the center, she should do something else. Like knit, or walk somewhere. At the very least she should spend her time *allocating* time. She should make a plan for the day: fifteen minutes for breakfast, ten minutes for a shower, ten minutes to get dressed. If you didn't keep yourself occupied, it was a problem.

At home, I thought about what had helped me after I got . . . after I resigned.

Sharon calling was one thing, but there's only so much you can rely on other people for. What had pulled me out of the funk?

I looked around the room. The TV was there, but I didn't think footage of Alan Cosgrove would help in this particular situation. But what about . . . My sudoku book was on the coffee table. I picked it up.

The whole first section was level ones. They were so easy anyone could do them. It would take me five seconds but someone else up to thirty minutes, maybe even more. If you had a lot of time on your hands, you might welcome suggestions for how to fill it.

I copied the sudoku onto a sheet of paper, put it in an envelope, and held the envelope in my hand. One envelope was very light. In order to increase the weight, I repeated the above six more times with six different sudoku, producing six more envelopes, seven in total. Seven envelopes for seven days.

On the front of each I wrote: MRS. CELIA BROWN.

On the back I put: ANON.

In the morning, at the office, I checked the files and found an address for Celia, on the very first letter the council had received.

I copied it out seven times. Then I walked out through reception and deposited the first envelope in the red postbox in the front of the town hall.

The rest of that month passed quickly and so did the next. I didn't see Don, either by chance or by organized visit. But that didn't mean I didn't think about him. I wondered what it meant that he'd come to see me. It had to mean something, but did it mean more than the fact that he'd left before anything had happened? Or less? I had no way of knowing.

In the meantime, Ralph and I worked hard on the safety audit report, a process that was every bit as excruciating as any other exercise in teamwork I had ever experienced. There were a lot of meetings, a lot of emails, and many hours spent haggling. Ralph talked more than he listened, which meant I had to talk more and louder to compensate.

Together, though me more than him, we produced a forty-four-page report. It listed all the hazards and risks and ranked them in order of importance. Everything was costed, from new carpet to re-wiring and retiling. I spent a weekend working out if it was more economical to buy cheap incandescent light bulbs that didn't last or expensive halogen ones that did, before realizing the council had a policy on lighting in its buildings, rendering the whole question redundant.

The finished product was a masterpiece. If he could have, Michelangelo would have wallpapered the Sistine Chapel with it. Instead, I paid for it to be professionally printed and bound with my own money, one copy for my office, one copy for my bookshelf at home, one copy for Stacey to give to the mayor. *With compliments*, said the slip paper-clipped to the cover. And then:

Nothing.

Not a word.

It was like waiting for Christmas or World Maths Day to arrive. I kept walking past the mayor's office, but Stacey asked me to leave. "You're weirding me out," she said, and "Don't you have somewhere to be?"

Three weeks later, on a Wednesday:

It was only nine a.m., but I'd been at work for ages. Team leaders and coordinators (even just prospective ones) have to be seen doing extra hours. It's motivational for others. The only problem is that when you have your own office, it's possible this will go unnoticed. That's why you need to document it via email. I'd sent:

A scanned Dimmeys catalogue with cheap safety vests to Ralph.

A link to an article I'd read on ergonomic workstations (*Attention: All Staff*).

A memo letting people know I had found an earring in the ladies' toilet.

Just as I was penning a follow-up, *Earring owner found*, my in-box pinged. Stacey. The mayor wanted to see me *immediately*.

I dropped everything. My heart started thumping, and my palms got sweaty. I took a deep breath, picked up my notebook, and power walked to see her.

I hoped the mayor and I were going to discuss the report in detail. I had a dream in which she pointed out which parts were particularly insightful and asked questions about my methodology—when I woke, I brainstormed questions and thought about the answers in case it came true. But there was none of that.

The mayor's face was serious. "Take a seat, Germaine," she said.

The blinds were drawn on the windows, and the room felt dark. The vase by the cabinet was empty.

She held up a copy of my report and for the first time ever I started to second-guess the work I'd done. Had the costing spreadsheet included GST? Had I factored in CPI for longer-term projections? Did I misunderstand the level of detail that was required?

"Thanks for this," she said. "And well done. It's very comprehensive."

A compliment; but I didn't relax. I was uneasy. I shut my eyes and opened them. Blinking, I suppose you'd call it.

The mayor put her glasses on and flicked through the document, scanning the pages. "It's not in very good shape, is it?" she said. "I knew the old place needed work but not this much work."

The feeling of uncertainty deepened, even as I explained the prioritization system. "The criteria are outlined on page three," I said. "I've come up with multiple scenarios: short, medium, and long term. Ralph's satisfied that the short-term scenario meets the minimum safety requirements. He says in the next year doing the roof and a couple of small things is critical, but we can hold off on the rest for a little while. Three to five years, perhaps."

A pause.

The mayor glanced down at the document. Though the expensive thermal cover was flat, she pressed at the top corners with the palm of her hand, as though they'd curled up.

"Germaine," she said. "Some people are dismissive of this position.

They think the mayor is just an idiot in a ceremonial robe who's here to cut ribbons and get her photo taken for the local paper. But that's not true. It's more than that. I have to make tough decisions sometimes."

Oh, I knew, I knew, I said. People were so naive.

"You know how tight the budget is. Things aren't getting any better. We have less money now than we did five years ago and more things we need to do with it.

"Do you know how many buildings we have? We have one hundred and four buildings. *A hundred and four*. That's not including public toilets. Some of them are new, of course, but some of them are quite old and the senior citizens center isn't even the worst."

The back of the chair was digging into me. I moved around, trying to find a more comfortable position.

"We can't have people using a building that's not sound. As you can imagine, this is a difficult decision . . . But."

All at once, I was very still. I knew what she was going to say before she said it. I watched her mouth move and heard the words in disjointed phrases.

Not a decision I take lightly . . . Safety is of the utmost concern . . . And you've seen the figures, Germaine; the budget is already so tight . . .

It seemed important to maintain the idea that this was not in any way unexpected. That I had known it was coming. But it *was* unexpected, and I had *not* known it was coming. I felt like an invisible belt had been looped around my chest. It was being pulled very tight.

The mayor pointed at the criteria in my report. It was a matter of capital investment versus usage, she said, nothing more than that.

And I agreed. I knew how it was, I said. When I worked at Wallace Insurance, I made decisions like this all the time. "The numbers never lie," I told her, and she brightened.

"*Yes*," she said. "Exactly."

I wasn't pleased. I was the opposite of pleased. I felt light-headed.

And then she said his name. *Don*. And that one word seemed to change everything. It brought clarity: *Don*. I was helping Don.

More than I'd realized.

"He's interested in buying it," she said.

I kept nodding. What an excellent idea, I said. He could expand his portfolio; add additional holes to the course, and perhaps, at last, a car park.

"I knew you'd understand, Germaine. Now, whatever you do, don't tell anyone. There are a few ducks we have to line up before this goes live." She rubbed her hands together. "Funny how things turn out, isn't it? I bet you're glad you got rid of Celia Brown now. Otherwise, we'd have a real riot on our hands, wouldn't we?"

27

I went back to my office and stared at the computer. I hadn't wanted to say this to the mayor, especially as I wasn't an expert, but this sounded . . . unusual. If one was playing devil's advocate, it might have been construed as . . .

But no, they wouldn't be doing anything untoward. Because if anyone understood how the system worked, it was the mayor herself. And I had to be careful in my thinking regarding Don. Just because he'd been accused of cheating, one time, many years ago, didn't mean anything. It was never proven. It was a rumor, and rumors were not facts. People don't do PhDs or even undergraduate degrees on rumors, do they? No, because it would be irrational.

In any case, it was out of my control. I was a cog in a wheel. A clever and productive cog, but a cog nonetheless. That was how I'd explain it to the senior citizens.

The senior citizens.

My heart slumped a little at the sides. I didn't want to think about them.

I tried to focus on my computer instead. What was I meant to be doing? Something with a spreadsheet.

But they were insistent. Celia, Betsy, Gladys. I found myself visualizing their faces, their exact expressions when they heard the news. I was glad I wasn't on the helpline. Celia would be angry. She'd call and ask questions, things that were impossible to answer. Call times would be terrible. Perhaps I should tell Eva to switch the "out of office" on.

I got up to walk around the desk.

What if I ended up in prison? You don't have to knowingly engage in criminal behavior to get caught up in something bad. There's a hundred examples of innocent people going to jail because they were doing things for other people. Things that seemed perfectly accept-able on the surface, maybe even expressions of appreciation or admi-ration or even love, but weren't altogether strictly legal underneath.

But Don would never. Or the mayor—she was far too intelligent. Intelligence had to be a protective factor.

I didn't have to *call* the senior citizens; I could send a letter.

I rolled up my sleeves and started typing.

Dear Gladys Watts, President of the Senior Citizens Club,
   This is to advise . . .
   Due to unforeseen circumstances . . . beyond our control . . .

In the morning I didn't feel well. I emailed Francine and said I wasn't coming in. Then I dragged myself to Dr. Smithfield. She asked what was wrong, and I described my symptoms: a feeling of restlessness, agitation, difficulty sleeping.

She was quick to reach a diagnosis. "How's your work life? Any-thing making you anxious? Sometimes anxiety can manifest physi-cally. It might be worth taking a few days out."

That wouldn't be it. "It's probably just my hemoglobin," I said, and held my finger out. Hb was in the healthy range, though, so it was hard to say.

At home, I put the TV on and sat on the couch with a blanket. I knew I was unwell because I found myself listening out for Jin-Jin, hoping she might knock on the door. I even looked out the peephole when I heard the elevator. It was the guy from number 24 walking past. I felt so sick I went to visit Sharon. If I was dying, the least she could do was look after me.

"You look fine to me," she said. "Want to stay for lunch?"

She microwaved two bowls of soup, and we sat in the lounge with them like we used to. Only difference was, back then I'd have eaten quickly and gone to my room to study. I studied a lot in high school. Your grades in high school determined where you went to university and *that* determined where you got a job and how much you got paid and pretty much the rest of your life.

Or so the theory went.

While we ate, Sharon got the newspaper out and opened it up to the quiz. She read the questions aloud and we wrote our answers down and compared them at the end. It was seventeen to twenty-seven in her favor.

"That was rigged," I said. "You must have cheated."

"Feeling better, then?" Sharon took my bowl and put it with hers on the coffee table. "How's work?"

"Fine." I don't know why everyone was so obsessed with my job.

"Just fine? What are you working on?"

"Nothing."

"Nothing at all?"

It was too long and involved to go into, I told her. And complicated, she wouldn't have understood all the intricacies. I tried to change the subject, but she persisted. She kept asking until I told her about the seniors center. Then of course she got on her high horse.

"That's exactly what happened in ninety-seven with the wetlands. Paul Dibbley said the council couldn't restore them because they didn't have the money. But you can't sign an international convention to save waterfowl and then just change your mind. You can't tell the orange-bellied parrot they didn't make it through the budget subcommittee."

The problem with Sharon was she wasn't rational. She got way too emotional about things.

"No wonder you feel sick," she went on. "I'd feel sick, too, if I was responsible for evicting all those old people."

"It's not my fault," I said. "Don't shoot the messenger."

"You've let all your friends down," she said.

"They're not my friends, they're acquaintances. I was only there for my CV."

"And here I was thinking you'd changed."

"People don't change, Sharon. It takes thousands of years for a species to evolve."

She lay back on the couch. "I don't know what I did wrong with you. I was a very present parent."

I can't imagine why I then told Sharon that Don might buy the senior citizens center. I suppose I was trying to show that the situation had an upside. I should have known how she'd respond.

"Let me get this right . . . The mayor is selling the senior citizens center *to a friend of hers.*"

"A friend of *mine.*"

"And this 'friend' just happens to own the golf club next door? What a coincidence."

"*Yes.* It's a coincidence." I didn't believe in coincidences normally, but this did seem to be one: two events, apparently related, actually completely independent.

I could prove it, too. All I had to do was demonstrate the conditional probability of (A) the seniors center having to be sold and (B) Don wanting to buy it was the same as the probability of B occurring on its own.

$$\Pr(A \gg B) = \Pr(A)\,\Pr(B)$$

I explained this to Sharon, writing the equation on a sheet of paper, but her mathematical skills weren't up to it.

"What's A again?" she said, frowning.

"A is the center being sold."

"Oh. So A is one? And what's B? No, wait. B is seven."

She didn't understand that it didn't matter what A and B were numerically, it was the relationship between them that mattered. "Think of it as a Venn diagram with two circles and no overlap."

There was a long pause.

"Doesn't matter anyway." I took the sheet of paper back. "The center's unsafe, and there's no budget for fixing it. Who cares who buys it."

"If it looks like a rat and smells like a rat . . ."

"You don't know Don like I do. He would never do anything untoward." I smoothed the cushion on the couch. "Don's the most upstanding person I've ever met." Maybe not the *most*, but he was fairly upstanding. I mean, there was no formal scale.

"Oh, Germaine." Sharon sat up. "You're not doing it again, are you?"

I picked up a cushion and plucked an invisible hair from it. "I don't know what you're talking about."

"You're not . . . *overly invested* in this Don person, are you?"

I raised my chin. "We're invested in each other."

"Does he know?"

I put the cushion aside and went to get up.

Sharon tried to stop me. "Don't get your knickers in a knot. I'm only asking. Germaine, come on. Don't be like that. It's only that you do have a history of reading things into things that aren't there. You have a way of latching on."

This was why I didn't tell Sharon anything. She made me sound like a piece of unwanted Velcro.

"Germaine, I don't want you to be disappointed, that's all. Come on, sit down. It's not worth getting upset about . . . You're right, it doesn't matter. Who cares? Those old people sound boring anyway. And they'll be dead soon. Or incapacitated."

Typical Sharon, always being negative. "They're very nice people, actually. They're interesting, I quite like them."

"Oh, for fuck's sake. I can't win."

- 28 -

I was back at Sharon's house the next day to pick her up for Kimberly's vow-renewal ceremony. I got there ten minutes late just to spite her. Unfortunately, she didn't notice. I ignored her in the car. She didn't notice that either.

Kimberly's vow-renewal ceremony went for an hour and forty-five minutes and differed from her wedding only by orders of magnitude: It was bigger, longer, and more elaborate. There were two ring bearers, four flower girls, and a dozen doves, which Uncle Barry released when the priest said, "You may kiss the bride."

Afterwards, everyone stood in the courtyard eating hors d'oeuvres and having drinks while we waited for the dinner to start. Kimberly flitted around in a dress made of taffeta and lace with 817 glittering diamantes hand-sewn across the bodice. She whispered the precise number to us when we congratulated her at the end of the ceremony.

"I bet it came from a sweatshop in China. That would be just like Kimberly. They work in appalling conditions, the Chinese. Sometimes they can't even see what they're doing, the room is so dim."

I looked around for a waiter.

"Germaine, are you going to talk to me?"

"Sure. What do you want to talk about?"

"Look. I'm sorry if I implied that Don wasn't *invested* in you."

"You didn't imply, you *said* he wasn't invested in me."

"Fine. Sorry if I *said* he wasn't invested in you." She moved her face in front of mine so I had to look at her. "I'd like to meet him," she said.

"I don't know if he wants to meet you."

"Perhaps you could ask."

I swished my drink. Some of the ice thawed. "I'll think about it."

At that point Kimberly swanned over to say hello and tell us she was glad we could make it. Channeling the mayor, but not completely, I muttered a perfunctory *Thanks for having us*.

Sharon told Kimberly she looked nice, which was diplomatic of her.

"I'd hope so," said Kimberly. "I've been working out with a PT for the past twelve weeks. That's a personal trainer, Auntie Sharon. Dropped three kilos and toned up. You wouldn't have thought I'd have three kilos to lose, would you? Well, I did. It was carbs. No carbs after five and the weight just fell off. That's how you do it— carbs. Most effective way to lose weight."

Being around Kimberly brought out my corrective instinct.

"*Wrong*," I said. "Quitting carbs wouldn't be the *most* effective way to lose weight. *Most* effective would be starvation. Don't eat anything. That would make you lose the most weight."

"Yeah, fasting works. Gastro's pretty good, too," said Kimberly. "I got gastro last time I went to Bali and I was like a Czech gymnast when I got back."

"Great," said Sharon as a cool breeze blew across the courtyard. The three of us were standing in front of the glass wall that looked into the dining room. All the tables and chairs were covered in white linen and the centerpiece of each was a glass bowl with goldfish in it. Sharon asked what was happening to the fish when the reception was over.

"Don't worry about them, Auntie Sharon," said Kimberly. "Those fish are only worth about eighty cents each. The pebbles and seaweed probably cost more than that."

Sharon's knuckles went white around her wineglass. "Is that a joke?"

"No, seriously. Eighty cents." Kimberly picked up a savory mini-Cronut as the waiter went past. "Eating all the carbs I can now. Yeah, we'll chuck the fish out at the end of the night. Staff can take them home if they want, but I'm not going to."

Sharon's corrective instinct also began to surface. "Kimberly. You can't do that, they're living things."

"What? Oh, I forgot. You're a vegetarian, aren't you? Vegetarian? Vegan. That's where you don't wear leather, isn't it? God, I could never not wear leather. Can you imagine only owning synthetic shoes? Well, I suppose you can."

I thought Sharon would have something more to say, but suddenly she was incapable of speech. Not that Kimberly noticed. She turned to me. "How's work, Germaine? Hope you're not embarrassing me."

"I got a promotion," I told her.

"Verity says she likes you. She's very polite, though. She'd never say anything bad. I just hope you're not, you know . . . I hope you're not overthinking things."

"What do you mean by 'overthinking'?" I said. "It's all just thinking, isn't it?"

"I'm not saying don't think, I'm just saying . . . You can't think about everything, can you? If everyone thought about everything all the time, then nothing would ever happen, would it?" She finished the Cronut and wiped her hands on a napkin. "It's like those goldfish. It's not my problem what happens to them, is it? All I want is a few beautiful centerpieces for my big day. If I thought about what happened to the goldfish afterwards, then I probably wouldn't have got them, and if I hadn't got them, then I wouldn't have all those beautiful centerpieces. You see? Point is sometimes it's better not to think too much."

All of a sudden I felt sorry for the goldfish. They were only a few stupid guppies, but it didn't seem fair. It wasn't their fault they'd ended up at Kimberly's reception.

I looked across at Sharon. Something seemed to pass between us. Not only a shared defiance; it had a noble quality to it, too. I felt lighter inside.

Kimberly was still talking. "There's sorbet for dessert, ladies. You'd be happy about that, Auntie Sharon. No animals died in the making of it."

Kimberly said later we made a big song and dance about nothing, but I thought we were quite discreet. During the bridal waltz I asked a waiter for two garbage bags. We put one inside the other and walked from table to table, pouring the fish in. We tied the bags at the top, and they sat on my lap during the speeches. Then Sharon held them in the car on the way home. The water sloshed when we went around the corners.

We opened the front door, and Sharon went into her bathroom and put the plug in the bath. The water rose and the fish went in, plink-plonk, plink-plonk, thirty-seven times.

I peered down at them. "Are they still alive?"

"There's two dead ones." She fished the bodies out with a tea strainer. "But the rest seem okay. Poor little things. Your cousin's an idiot. I mean, please." She swished the water with her hand. "I'll have to get them some plants in the morning . . . I think Marion's got a spare tank. She used to have fish."

"A tank?" I looked at them dubiously. There were an awful lot of them.

"You might be right. Maybe I should dig a pond? Give them some room."

We stared at the golden blobs swimming around. They had no idea we were there. I felt benevolent, like a parent wanting the best for them. Like some parents.

I looked at Sharon, kneeling on the floor, one hand trailing through the water, the other resting on the side of the bath.

Photographs had long revealed that Sharon and I possessed a similar side profile. But that was the only thing we had in common. Other than nose shape, we were opposites. She had blond hair, and mine was brown. She tanned easily; I burned. She liked fish, but, to be honest, I didn't. All they did was blink and swim around. Nothing would change in my life if they all died. And yet, their presence at this moment seemed to expand it somehow.

Sharon touched my leg. "That one reminds me of you."

An orange one with brown splotches was hanging back on its own at the tap end. "Because none of the others likes it?"

"No." Sharon gave me a look. "Because it's got a big head. Lots of brains."

Yes, lots of brains. Not much of anything else. That's how I was. Even if I did save a few fish one time, it didn't mean it was going to become a pattern.

"It's eleven o'clock," said Sharon. "You probably have to get home."

But it was late, and I was tired. "Maybe I'll stay over. For safety reasons. It's very dark."

Sharon was pleased with my risk-averse behavior. "I'd like that. You could help me dig the pond in the morning."

We never did things together. It never seemed to work out when I spent too much time with Sharon. But maybe . . . for the fish?

I wasn't what you'd call an ichthyophile, but perhaps, deep inside, I had the *capacity* for loving fish. Or liking them. Even just noticing they were there. Maybe a fish had something to offer, inherently, without trying.

In bed, I thought about Don. I was having second thoughts about him, which are generally the opposite of first thoughts. If a first thought was *black*, a second thought might be *white*. Or if a first thought was: *Don wouldn't do anything wrong*. A second thought might be: *He has before*.

But this was different. In this instance, Don would have known there was a chance *I* might be implicated if things got found out; I could get in trouble. He wouldn't sacrifice our relationship, a relationship he personally had progressed by coming to see me, for his own personal profit.

Would he?

Talking to Sharon had made me paranoid. I reminded myself Don thought I was—quote—"great." He wouldn't have said that unless he meant it, and he wouldn't have come to see me if he didn't want to.

But then . . .

He hadn't come back.

I had this sticky memory, one I was trying to let go of . . . I'd told Don the center was run-down. It was just a passing comment, and everyone knew already; however, the audit had been announced quite quickly afterwards. Was this also a coincidence? Did I really believe in them? Professor Douglas didn't.

I rolled onto my back and started counting the cracks on the ceiling. One, two . . .

I kept trying to focus on the cracks and, when I couldn't focus on them, on the weight of the blanket, and on the goldfish. When this didn't work, I tried to identify the positives in the situation.

Once the senior center was closed, I'd have all my spare time back. Not going to the homework club meant I could do other things, like sudoku or tidy my apartment. I wouldn't have to talk to Jin-Jin all the time or let Charlie win at Trivial Pursuit anymore. With all this new time, maybe I really would take up golf? I wasn't sure if I'd like golf, but I was willing to try. If Don was involved.

Don . . .

What would Sharon think of Don? She hadn't liked Peter, the one time they met. She tried, though. She wore a brown suit without my even asking, and her hair in a bun. I was touched. She eyed his unusually dark hair and said to him, "I've often wondered what sort of person Germaine would end up with."

"Well, keep wondering," he said.

- 29 -

Sharon and I got up the next morning feeling enthusiastic. About everything: breakfast, putting on old clothes, getting the shovels out of the shed. It was just unfortunate our enthusiasm didn't assist us with an effective digging technique. Also, we were both better at bossing than we were at being bossed.

"Sharon, you need to put your body weight into it. You have to really push it in."

"If you'd managed to remove more than a cubic centimeter of soil, I might take on board what you had to say, but I don't see a lot of anything happening over there."

We persevered for a while, but it was very difficult.

Midmorning we decided a tank with regulated temperature would be better for the fish.

Marion said she'd come over and drop it off in the afternoon.

Sharon and I made tea, and we sat on the porch to drink it. "That was fun," she said, and I agreed. We hadn't achieved anything at all, but I felt better than I had in days. Somewhere between the wedding and digging (not-digging) the pond, the feeling of restlessness and anxiety had dissipated.

Sharon patted Barney. "Hope Kimberly likes her goat."

"She'll hate it."

"*I know.*" Sharon gave a gleeful laugh. It reminded me of Celia.

Sharon would have liked Celia. She would have liked Betsy and Gladys, too. And Jin-Jin, and Charlie and Jack. Maybe even Eva.

"I don't *want* them to sell the senior citizens center," I said, not looking at her. "But I understand why they have to." Once you understood something you couldn't suddenly not understand.

"Okay," said Sharon.

"There are incoming expenses and outgoing expenses, and they have to balance. It's got nothing to do with people."

"You really are a monster—" She went to laugh, but I cut her off.

"Stop saying that."

Sharon recoiled. "Fine, I won't say anything. I won't talk. I'll just sit here and be quiet." She crossed her arms and pouted.

I should have known that brief period of companionship wouldn't last. We were too different; I put it down to the Douglas in me. The Douglas was the dominant gene pool. Hers were all recessive—like the hair.

"The Douglas?" said Sharon. I hadn't realized I'd spoken aloud. "You're not going on about the Douglas genes again, are you?"

I shrugged. The truth of it was, I'd long since given up caring about Professor John Douglas. He was most likely deceased, and anyway, one-sided caring isn't very satisfying; you're better off forming a relationship with a plank of wood. At least you can touch it if you want to, or make a bookcase.

But I couldn't deny Professor Douglas had had an influence on me. There was part of him *in* me; I was how I was because of him. A leopard can't change its spots; a prime number's always indivisible.

"Oh, Germaine." Sharon looked at me with a mixture of pity and condescension. "I probably should have said this a while ago . . . John Douglas isn't your father."

"Yeah, yeah."

"No." She looked uncharacteristically grave. "He's not."

I stared at her. The dog was still.

"He's not your father. I know, I know. I should have told you sooner. Look, it was a joke, and it got out of hand."

"No . . . wait . . . my father, he's Professor John Douglas. He *is*."

"No. Douglas is just some guy you saw in the paper when you were little. You were the one who decided he was your father; I just went along with it. Wasn't until later I realized it had kind of set. What's it matter anyway?"

I couldn't compute what she was saying. I felt like an Excel sheet with an error code, a loop where the summation of the loop mistakenly includes the cell doing the summing.

"So who is my father?"

"Sperm donor. Don't know much about him, to be honest."

"Don't know . . . He could be *anyone*?"

My father was an unknown variable.

And I was . . . I wasn't sure what I was. Right now I was aghast. "What is *wrong* with you?" I said.

"My therapist says—"

"*You're* the monster. *You* are."

"I won't do it again." Sharon didn't look at all contrite. "I don't know why you're so upset. You're a bit old to have daddy issues."

I realized there were noises coming out of my mouth. It was opening and closing; I felt like the rescue guppies in the bath.

IF (Germaine [did not] = [descent of] John Douglas), then what did Germaine = ?

I had no idea what I felt, but I didn't like it one bit.

"Germaine?" said Sharon in a small voice.

"What."

"You're not a monster. You're just a bit unusual. Which is good. I wouldn't want you to be the same as everyone else."

"Okay."

"I mean it."

"Sure."

I drove home, a quiet drive through quiet streets. Numb. There was no Douglas in me. No Douglas, none at all.

Who was I?

Everything had changed, and nothing had. I felt like the medieval people must have felt, living their whole lives thinking the world was flat and then being told it wasn't. It must have been hard to accept the idea, even when the proof was explained.

How could I not be the scion of John Douglas? What about our similarities? He was a mathematics professor and I was good at math. And . . .

There were others, surely. I couldn't think of them. Was that all? The list did not seem comprehensive.

I was intending to drive home but, distracted, made a wrong turn and by chance ended up near the town hall. Then I found myself going down the side street by the oval and turning and before I knew it I was at the golf club.

Don seemed extra enthusiastic to see me. I wished Sharon was there to witness his excitement. "Look who it is," he said. "My favorite council worker."

Was I, though? Was I?

I stood in front of him, looking at his innocent face. I was one hundred percent sure I trusted him. I didn't think he'd do anything illegal or that might compromise our relationship.

Ninety-five percent sure.

It used to be, if there was a degree of uncertainty about something, I'd say to myself: *What would Professor John Douglas do in this situation? I only meant: Would he be satisfied with the level of proof?* But now that was irrelevant. What did it matter what he thought? I only had to answer to myself. Was *I* satisfied?

I'd proved it to Sharon using probability statements, but I could reduce the level of uncertainty further by asking questions.

"Did you have anything to do with next door getting shut down?"

Don put his hand to his mouth, like a fence being hastily erected. "Me? Do what?"

His response suggested he knew it was happening. This wasn't necessarily an indication of guilt, but I had hoped the news would surprise him. If Don was surprised, then it seemed more plausible this was all a big coincidence.

"What could *I* have done?" said Don. "I'm not the mayor of the city."

"But you could have told her what I said."

"About what?"

"About how it's run-down."

"Did we talk?" said Don. "You and I?"

"Yes, here."

"In this office?"

"Yes."

I wasn't hurt. Anyone could forget a casual meeting; it didn't mean anything.

"What do you think I told her?" said Don.

"Nothing. It doesn't matter, forget about it."

"You think I told the mayor something you said. Something private."

"No, I—"

"It's okay. I don't blame you. But I would have hoped you of all people would give me a second chance." Don hung his head, the way he did every time Alan was mentioned.

I told Don he didn't need a second chance. He was still on his first chance so far as I was concerned. Don said, "Thanks, Germaine," but the way he said it was sad and disbelieving.

Poor Don, poor Alan Cosgrove. I understood so completely how he felt. His insides had holes in them, deep voids that were just empty.

But I could fill them.

I had the letter advising the senior citizens of the outcome of the safety audit and the center's pending closure in the glove box of the car. With all that had happened, I hadn't had a chance to put it in the outgoing mail. Given how close I was and the necessity for cutting costs, I thought maybe I should hand deliver it.

I should have thought again. The timing was terrible.

As I walked to the front door, meaning to slip it underneath, the door opened. And—what were the chances?—there was Gladys, with Betsy right behind her. When they saw it was me, they were stepping over themselves with excitement.

"Goodness me. How about that? We were just talking about you," said Gladys.

I should have spent the 50 cents on postage. The best way to deliver bad news is not in person: When Sharon dies I hope to learn about it in the obituaries.

"I didn't think you'd be here," I admitted.

"We've been working out how to spend the money we get allocated. You said to prioritize and that's what we've been doing," said Betsy.

The space available in my neck to enable breathing seemed to shrink. "There is some news," I said in a tight voice.

The worst part was how understanding they were. "It's not your fault," said Gladys a total of nine times, all the while dabbing her eyes. Nine is a lot of times to say the same thing.

Around the fifth time, it stops being reassuring.

Suffice to say I wanted to get out of there. That's why, when Betsy said, "James is still worried about his pension payment," an issue that was entirely unrelated, I agreed to help.

Betsy went inside to get his forms. Gladys continued to snort into a tissue.

When Betsy reappeared, she was holding a thick wad of sheets. There must have been fifty pages. "Here they are," she said, giving them to me. "Are you sure you don't mind calling?"

I took them all and backed away. "Yeah, yeah, fine. Whatever."

- 30 -

I was glad I offered to help James. It gave me something to do in the morning, something that wasn't related to the closure of the senior center.

I spread his forms across my desk and dialed the number for the Department of Social Services. The voice at the other end said, *Press 1 for family payments . . . Press 2 for income reporting.*

It was quite calming actually, having someone tell me what to do. I didn't have to think; I just had to follow their instructions. I pushed 3 for pension payments, 2 for outstanding payments, and then 4 to speak to an operator. Easy.

Only, no operator. Just hold music, and the occasional voice that said: Did you know that for certain requests (not yours) you can log on to our website?

I was on hold for a long time. Four hours in total, and it would have been longer, only the mayor came to see me.

She was standing in the doorway, holding a small plant in a gold pot. Her expression was very serious—she must have known how unproductive I was being.

I put the phone down, expecting her to say, "Germaine, we need to discuss your performance." That would have been fair.

But instead, she said, "How are you feeling?"

I wished she hadn't.

There was a churning mass of unfamiliar emotions in my stomach, and I was trying to keep it there using the time-honored technique of pretending it didn't exist. I didn't want the mayor to know about it.

I was confused. Confusion, I had discovered, was not a simple, singular entity; it had multiple facets. It was possible for a person to be confused about a lot of things simultaneously.

Fortunately, before I could answer, detailing the ways, the mayor reframed her inquiry. "You didn't come in on Friday."

No, I'd called in sick. What had I told Francine? A migraine. I pressed a palm to my forehead and coughed. "I'm much better. Almost fully recovered."

"Good." She came in and sat opposite me. "I was thinking about you all weekend, Germaine. I kept going over our conversation. I hope you're okay. You know it's not your fault we have to shut the center down, don't you?"

I said yes. It was, after all, what I had been telling myself, what I had told myself a hundred times.

"And you know it's not Don's fault either."

No, it wasn't Don's fault, although he *was* the primary beneficiary. I wondered if the mayor benefited in some way, then I felt guilty for wondering that.

There were things I didn't know, of course. Of these things I didn't know, only some of them were things I *wanted* to know; there were others I had no interest in learning about (as shown in Figure 5).

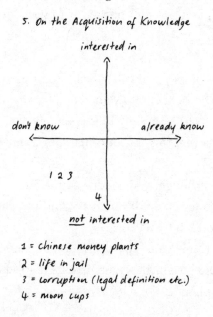

5. On the Acquisition of Knowledge

interested in

don't know   already know

1 2 3

4

<u>not</u> interested in

1 = chinese money plants
2 = life in jail
3 = corruption (legal definition etc.)
4 = moon cups

The mayor seemed to sense my uncertainty. She put the plant on the desk and leaned forward. "What's the problem, Germaine?"

"It's just . . . Is Don rich now?"

"No."

"Then how can he afford . . . ?" This information was supposed to sit in the lower left-hand quadrant of Figure 5, but it seemed to be shifting upwards.

The mayor listened, as she always did.

"He's not rich *now*, but maybe his situation will improve. You know what it's like. Things change; nothing's set in stone. Maybe, perhaps, in the future . . . When he has a little more land, he might be able to expand the golf club's facilities."

"Like he could have a coffee cart?"

"Yeah, a coffee cart. Or"—she was very casual about this, as though she was just tossing it out there—"some kind of gaming machine?"

Gaming machines. I blinked. That was controversial. I knew how Sharon would react to that. She'd be pretty upset; a lot of people would.

"But I thought—"

"There's a lot of wheeling and dealing in politics," said the mayor in a way that discouraged further inquiry. Then she put her hand around the gold plant pot and pushed it forward. A trail of dirt led across the desk directly to me. "This is for you," she said.

"Okay."

"It's a Chinese money plant. It's meant to bring you luck, but you have to put it in the right spot. I've had one for years."

"Thank you." I wasn't sure if Chinese money plants helped accrue income; I wasn't sure if this was information I *wanted* to know, either (see also Figure 5).

"My pleasure. I thought you needed a little pat on the back. You're doing a great job, Germaine. It's not easy, and you can't please everyone. But don't worry. It'll blow over."

That was true. Time would pass. The senior center, the homework club, all of it would be a distant memory one day—if everything went according to her plan.

"Hey." She brightened now. "What are you doing the last weekend in November? You know the mayoral ball's on at the golf club. Christos can't come, and I thought maybe *you* could be my plus one. You'd have to sit at my table . . . and Don's."

"Great." It *was* great. It was.

What was wrong with me?

"I'm going to make the announcement about the closure of the center that night. I know it's sooner than we thought, but time is of the essence. I need to get things moving before . . ." She glanced behind her. "Just between you and me, Germaine, I might be moving on. Or *up* might be a better way of putting it. Looks like I might just have the numbers this year."

She explained that while the council had been a "wonderful place to work" and she'd "loved being mayor," she'd achieved all she was able to. There were bigger things, better things on the horizon. Her voice was a whisper: *state government.*

She was leaving me. I picked up the plant and held it tight.

"It's where I can make the biggest difference. Mind you, it won't be easy. It's not *what* you know, is it? Unfortunately. But lucky for me, and thanks to Don, the 'who' seem to be on my side."

"Congratulations," I said.

"Here's the best bit: Where I'm going, I'll need a reliable advisor." She waited for my reaction.

"I'll need *you*," she added, when I failed to respond.

If this had happened a few months ago when I first started, I would have been pleased. And a bit relieved—finally. About time Figure 1 (Career Trajectory) came to fruition. But a lot had happened since then, and while I felt some of these emotions, they were tempered by others.

The mayor patted the desk, like it was an obedient dog. "You're with us now."

So we were tethered. Which was fine so long as we were headed in an upwards direction, but what if there was an unexpected vertex? What if one of them fell?

When the mayor was gone, I dialed the department again. The hold music was soothing, and as long as I was listening to it I didn't have to do anything else.

I'd been waiting only ten minutes when a call came through on the other line. I picked it up but didn't speak into the receiver. I was keeping open the possibility of hanging up.

The voice at the end was unexpected: male, and very young. "Germaine?" said the voice. "It's Charlie."

Charlie? "What's wrong?" I said. He sounded serious, like something bad had happened. What else could go wrong?

"I'm calling about," he hesitated. "It's just . . . Well. We didn't get today's sudoku. Celia was worried."

"I wasn't worried. I hate those stupid things," said Celia, in the background.

I was glad to hear her muffled voice, even if she wasn't talking to me. Even if she was saying she hated sudokus.

The sudokus. I'd sent a total of twenty-two, one per day for twenty-two days and then nothing the past three. In all that had been happening I'd forgotten.

I never knew if she was getting them, there'd been no indication, and the audit report had taken up so much time that I hadn't been to the homework club and hadn't seen Charlie. I liked to think she'd been doing them, or if she hadn't she'd seen the envelope and knew that I was thinking of her. Maybe she even imagined I was sorry.

"Can you put her on?" I asked Charlie.

Charlie said to Celia, "Germaine wants to speak to you," but Celia didn't want to speak to me, not even when I told Charlie how important it was. She refused to get on the phone—she seemed to be in a recriminatory mood, which I supposed was a step up from listless.

But I had to tell her. "Say she's not the only one that's going to miss the place . . . They're shutting the center down, Charlie."

There was a kind of echo as this was conveyed, then: "What the hell?" and then Celia was shouting in my ear at a volume that suggested she was worried her voice might not carry. But it was carrying: I could hear her loud and clear.

"There have been some unexpected developments since you left," I said.

"Unexpected developments? What have you done?"

"It wasn't me. I didn't do anything."

Celia did a slow breath in, the kind that seemed to be for my benefit. I hate breaths like that, shows of patience. She kept doing it while I told her what had happened, how hard I'd worked and how things had changed with no prior warning.

When I was finished, she did a last patient breath and said, "Well? What are you planning to do about it?"

"Nothing."

Why would I try to do something about it? It was what's called a "foregone conclusion." That's when the end is a fixed point and there's no way of changing it.

She didn't like that. She handed the phone back to Charlie.

"You okay, Charlie?" I said.

"I'm okay."

There was a pause.

"Ask me if I'm okay."

"Are you okay, Germaine?"

"Not really."

I had twenty-four hours of respite, and then the phone rang. This time it was Gladys.

"Can you come to the club tomorrow? We're holding an emergency committee meeting to work out what to do."

I coiled the phone cord around my finger.

"Germaine?" she said, after a bit.

"It's too late, Gladys. There's nothing we can do."

"Celia thinks there is."

"Celia? She's not on the committee."

"It's the committee plus her. Plus you, if you come. How's nine a.m.?"

I pulled the phone cord so it squeezed my finger. It was like a noose, getting tighter.

This was the problem with getting close to people: They started to rely on you. If you did something nice, you got a reputation; they expected you'd do other nice things. And I didn't want to. The feeling was . . . It was fear. I was afraid of what might happen.

But then Gladys said, "Come on, Germaine," and I felt myself waver.

I liked to think I was self-sufficient. I was an island with pristine waters and enough edible plants and animals that I didn't have to import supplies. I mean, it was nice when boats came to visit, but it would ruin everything if I turned into a major tourist destination.

And I had to be pragmatic. I had bills to pay and a career to think of. "I can't, Gladys."

"Okay." One word, but so full of disappointment. "Sorry, Germaine . . . I shouldn't have asked."

Click.

The phone went dead.

- 31 -

I continued on my unproductive downward spiral. My mood was like a vortex, feeding on its own negative energy. The only time I felt a prick of relief was when I saw Jack in the empty tearoom. And then he opened his mouth.

"Guess what?" he said.

"What?"

"Marie sent me something she thought *you* might be interested in."

"Marie Curie? What is it?"

"You'll see. Wait here, I'll go get it."

"No, don't—"

But he was gone, out the door and down the stairs, and quite slow in coming back, which didn't help my disposition.

On his return, he handed me a document, about twenty pages. I glanced at the top sheet, but the print was small and hard to read.

"Remember how we talked about heat loss that time?" said Jack. "And you sent me an article, breaking it down by body part?" He had a bemused expression on his face, as though this was a "joke" I was going to enjoy.

"Yes . . ."

"Well, I showed Marie, and she was very skeptical. She said she'd never heard of the *Journal for Scientific Medical Studies of Australian Sciences*. And she pointed out the research wasn't peer-reviewed."

"Really? Did she?" My disdain for Marie multiplied.

"So she went looking for herself and found this. If you look on page seven"—Jack pointed at the document—"it says, *thirty-four percent of temperature regulation is attributable to legs*." He started to laugh but only for a moment. Then he stopped.

"What?" he said.

"Nothing."

Jack exhibited a dawning realization that this hadn't gone how he'd expected. "Don't you want to read it? What's the matter? Come on, Germaine. It's a joke."

"Yes, it's very funny. Bet you both laughed about it for ages."

"*No*. We didn't." His head fell to one side. "*Germaine*."

"Ha-ha-ha-ha." I was very forceful in my amusement, so he could see what a sense of humor I had, how lighthearted I was. Then I wrung out the paper, like it was a tea towel, or an arm getting a so-called "Chinese burn," and I threw it to him.

Or *at* him, whichever.

The best thing about coming home was I didn't have to talk to anyone. I was going to lie on the couch in complete silence, doing nothing. I parked the car on the street and was dawdling along the footpath when I ran into Jin-Jin.

"Have you heard?" she said. "They want to shut the senior citizens center down."

"Yeah, I've heard. I was the first to know."

"It's so sad. That's how I've met all my friends . . . Except for you. It's lucky we live so close, isn't it? We can easily keep in touch."

Jin-Jin and I walked towards the entrance of our apartment block and then, as though things weren't bad enough already, there was Sharon, loitering by the front door.

She was wearing a lurid purple dress and holding a Tupperware container. If I'd known she was coming, I would have worked late. I had half a mind to go back to the office right then, but I didn't get a chance; she'd seen me.

"Surprise," she said.

I stepped away from Jin-Jin in what might have been a seamless transfer of irritations had Jin-Jin not put her oar in. "Are you Germaine's mum? You look exactly like her. I'm her neighbor, Jin-Jin."

Sharon said, "The girl from number twenty-two? You do exist."

"You've heard of me?"

It was annoying how excited they were.

Sharon held the container up. "I've got something for you," she said, raising it in the air. And then to Jin-Jin, "Would you like to come in for a cup of tea?"

"Jin-Jin's busy," I said.

"I'd love to," said Jin-Jin.

I frowned at the elevator buttons the whole way up. There was a column of takeaway containers in the kitchen, near the sink. Jin-Jin was going to have a field day. *You have Red Emperor on speed dial, Germaine . . . Red Emperor on speed dial . . . All you do is be alone.*

I don't know why Jin-Jin was so interested in seeing my apartment. It was the same as hers—same layout, same fixtures, same everything.

The two of them stopped in the lounge room. I snuck into the kitchen and tipped the containers in the sink so they couldn't see. When I came back they were both staring at the mantelpiece.

"Wow," said Jin-Jin.

Behind her, Sharon said, "Where did *that* come from?"

I blushed. I'd forgotten about my redecoration. Don's old trophies and medals were set out in a clever display. A display of his cleverness. I hadn't expected anyone to see.

Jin-Jin walked closer. "Are these yours?" she said.

I glanced at Sharon. "I own them," I said, carefully.

Jin-Jin picked up one of the medals. "State Sudoku Championship 2005 . . . Regional Finals 2004 . . . Germaine. I didn't know you were this good."

"She's not," said Sharon.

I didn't like the tone she used. As though it was impossible—

when in all likelihood I could have been world champion if someone had encouraged me.

"I don't understand." Jin-Jin looked closer at one of the trophies. "National Final 2006 . . . Alan Cos— Oh."

I crossed my arms and held on to my elbows, rocking from side to side. I don't know why they both had to come over. I didn't invite them.

"I am confused," said Jin-Jin.

Sharon put the Tupperware she'd been holding on the coffee table and started picking up parts of the display herself. "Alan Cosgrove . . . Alan Cosgrove . . . Alan Cosgrove." When she put the pieces down she didn't put them in their correct position and she didn't roll the ribbons on the medals right. I had to go and straighten it all.

Sharon and Jin-Jin both gave me pitying looks.

"Who *is* Alan Cosgrove?" said Sharon. "Why do you have all his trophies?"

"He's a friend of mine. He gave them to me." What was it to them? I could decorate however I liked.

"Why did he give them to you?"

"*Because*, Sharon. Stop talking about it."

"You're not a serial killer, are you?" Sharon turned to Jin-Jin. "Because I've often wondered."

I told her she wasn't funny.

Jin-Jin said, slowly, "Are you and Don—"

"*Yes*, what does Don think about"—Sharon gestured at the mantel—"*this*."

Sharon didn't know Don was Alan, and I wasn't going to tell her. She'd only make more comments and ask more questions.

"I mean, it's a bit weird, isn't it?" said Sharon. "It reminds me of a Buddhist offering. All you need is a bowl of rice and—"

"Shut up, Sharon."

Yelling was very effective. The room went quiet. There was no noise in it at all.

Except for when I said, "I'll make the tea now."

Jin-Jin said, "Maybe I should go."

"And you will drink it."

I put the kettle on. While I made the drinks those two talked. Jin-Jin mentioned the homework club. I'd told Sharon about it ten times, but of course she hadn't listened.

"I didn't know you were *volunteering*," she said.

Jin-Jin said, "Germaine's there every week. She's the best tutor there is . . . The best tutor there *was*." Her expression was glum. "Do you think we can stop the council from selling it?"

"No," I said.

Sharon opened her mouth. I gave her an icy stare, and she closed it again.

No one looked at the trophies.

Sharon sipped her tea and said in a careful voice, "Back in eighty-two when we were protesting the Franklin Dam, we tied ourselves to trees and stayed there, even as the bulldozers rolled in."

Jin-Jin was in awe. "We didn't try that. We put chains on the wheels of cars once, but that is all."

"You what?" I said.

Jin-Jin shifted in her chair. "Pardon?"

"I *knew* it."

Jin-Jin looked to Sharon for help. "I think I was not supposed to say that."

My eyes narrowed. "Did you or didn't you?"

"I prefer not to answer this question." Jin-Jin went and put her mug by the sink. "I have to go now. I have homework to do. Nice to meet you, Mrs. Johnson." She gave a small bow and left before I could commence her cross-examination.

Much as I didn't feel like talking to Sharon, I found myself telling her:

1) how Celia had lied to me about chaining up the golf club members' cars,

2) how I knew she'd been lying,

3) how I'd given her the chance to tell the truth, and

4) how if she hadn't lied, none of this would have happened.

Sharon was not the picture of righteous indignation I'd hoped for. "I suppose she had her reasons," she said.

Reasons. That's Sharon for you. Always mitigating circumstances.

She went and got the Tupperware she'd brought and handed it to me. It was blue on the bottom and had a clear top with holes. Inside, two goldfish were swimming around in water.

"Thought you might like some company," she said.

They didn't look like much in the way of company. Better company for each other than for me.

"I'm still mad at you about the Douglas," I said.

She pouted. "You're always mad at me about something."

"Not everything's a joke, Sharon."

"I didn't say it was."

"Sharon."

"Fine, *I'm sorry* . . . But isn't it liberating? You can do anything, Germaine. You don't have to . . . I sometimes wonder if you only clung to the idea of him because he was, in your mind, the opposite of . . ." She looked into the container. "They should be okay in there overnight. You have to keep the lid off. And don't forget to feed them."

"The opposite of what, Sharon?"

"Well . . ." She kept her eyes on the fish. "The opposite of me."

I didn't speak. I watched her watch the fish.

"It's just a thought," she said. "I only thought of it then . . . I haven't been thinking about it for long."

Her purple dress had a thread hanging from the sleeve. I reached and pulled it. For a moment, the thread connected us. Then the thread came off. But I held on to it.

"I'm not trying to be the opposite of you," I said.

"Okay." Sharon's gaze remained fixed on the container.

"I'm not."

There was another pause. I wanted to keep being annoyed at her, but it was harder now than before.

"Thanks for the fish."

If I was going to get a fish, any fish, I wouldn't have chosen gold-fish. I would have picked something with a bit more personality, like a Mexican walking fish or Siamese fighting fish. But now I had them, they seemed okay. They had some redeeming features. They were certainly resilient.

But even survivors can be vulnerable. I'd have to remember that when I transferred them to their new bowl.

"If you don't want them you don't have to have them," said Sharon. "I just thought you might like them . . . You might like being reminded what you're capable of."

"I'm capable of keeping two fish alive?"

"*Germaine*. You saved eighty-four fish from certain death."

"*We* saved eighty-four fish."

Sharon put her hands together. "Yes, it was a team effort. We did it together."

I pulled the container with the fish towards me. I wasn't sure where I was going to put them, the mantelpiece being so full.

"Don *is* Alan," I said. "They're the same person . . . It's compli-cated. But Don gave me his old trophies because he knew how much I liked Alan."

Sharon was listening, a novel and enjoyable experience for both of us. Until she said, "Who do you like better? Don or Alan?"

Her question caught me off guard. "I like them both . . . *They're the same person.*"

"Yes, but if you had to pick."

"But I don't have to pick."

"Hypothetically."

She didn't understand. She was confusing me.

"Okay, okay. Forget I asked." Sensing I was getting annoyed, Sha-ron changed the topic. "Jin-Jin's nice. She seems to really like you."

I shrugged. "Jin-Jin likes everyone."

"And she goes to the homework club, does she?"

"A lot of people do."

Sharon drummed her fingers on the table. "You know you were

there, at the Franklin Dam? We tied your pram to a tree. Some people said that's why they didn't start bulldozing. Because of you. You were at the rally in town, too. Protesting's in your genes, Germaine."

Honestly. That was not how genetics worked. "I could lose my job, Sharon."

"You can get another one. And if all else fails, you can move in with me."

I thought I would have shuddered, but my body didn't have that involuntary reaction.

I didn't go to the senior center in the morning. I went to work, played solitaire on the computer, and came home again.

I was putting my slippers on when there was a knock at the door. I answered it even though I knew who it was going to be.

"Hi, Jin-Jin," I said.

"Where were you today?" Uninvited, she came in and took her shoes off. "You didn't come to the meeting."

She walked past me to the lounge room and made herself comfortable on the couch. The fish were in a new bowl on the coffee table, but she didn't notice them. "Everyone is very upset."

"Are they?"

"*Yes*. It will probably get closed down."

"I think so." I didn't sit down, stayed standing. "Still, they've had a good run, haven't they? That club's been operating more than fifty years."

"Yes, fifty years. But don't worry. Celia has a plan."

"Does it involve chaining up car wheels?"

Jin-Jin cringed. "I wasn't meant to tell you that."

"I knew anyway. I know a lot of things, Jin-Jin. A *lot* of things."

Jin-Jin wasn't paying attention. She said they'd organized a working bee on Saturday during the time normally allocated for the homework club. "Do you want to come? If you want to come, can you drive me? And Celia, she doesn't have a ride."

I said no. I wasn't some kind of taxi service. And anyway, I had a prior engagement.

"Can you change it? When is it? Because the working bee goes all day. Maybe you can come after?"

"It's long. It goes all day."

Jin-Jin was confused. "Don't you want to come and help?"

"I *want* to come, but—" I tried to explain what a complex situation it was. Unfortunately, I chose an advanced metaphor (based on Fermat's last theorem), which Jin-Jin failed to comprehend.

"Doesn't seem that complicated," she said. "Seems simple."

Maybe I was a better explainer than I gave myself credit for.

"What are you afraid of?" said Jin-Jin.

I looked her square in the eye and said I wasn't afraid of anything.

Jin-Jin smoothed the fabric on the arm of the couch. I wished she'd leave.

"This is the first time you invited me over," said Jin-Jin. "I mean, I came yesterday, but that was only because of your mum."

"Technically, I didn't invite you this time. You just came in."

"I invited you lots of times. I always felt sad for you, being alone in here all the time. But now I think, *Oh, well. It's your choice.* You want to be alone, be alone."

The air around me thinned, like a force field was malfunctioning. "I'm not alone."

"Invite me in; don't invite me in. Come; don't come. No impact on me. Only on you."

"I didn't say I didn't *want* to come. I said I *couldn't*. There's a difference."

"Sure." Jin-Jin started getting up. *Now* she was getting up.

She walked towards the front door.

"Wait," I said, but she kept going.

I didn't want her to go. I wanted her to understand.

It was easy for her to say *What are you afraid of?* Asking questions is simple; answering them is much harder. She didn't know what it was like.

Jin-Jin started putting her shoes on, first one and then the other.

She was having a bit of trouble with the laces on the second shoe, but she was going to leave soon if I didn't say something.

I opened my mouth, and some words fell out. "My career is very important to me, Jin-Jin."

"Why?" she said.

My first thought was of Professor Douglas, who had been such an important role model for a child growing up with Sharon. In order to teach at Harvard he'd had to give a few things up. Like a daughter.

Then I remembered he didn't give up a daughter. He and I weren't related.

Then I didn't know what to think. I supposed I would have to think for myself.

Jin-Jin paused midshoe. "Do you like the homework club?"

"I don't hate it."

"Do you like going to the center?"

"It's okay. Nothing special."

There was a row of hooks along the wall near the door. I fiddled with the car keys, hanging in their allocated position, third hook from the end. "You guys don't need me anyway," I said.

Jin-Jin gave an exasperated sigh. "No, we don't need you. But we *want* you."

"Pardon?" I moved the keys innocently. "What did you say?"

"You heard me, Germaine."

"I didn't."

"*Fine*. I said, we don't need you, but we want you."

I was in high demand for once, first the mayor and now this lot. If only they could coordinate themselves and pull in the same direction instead of having a tug of war. It would be much more efficient, less net expended energy.

"Come on, Germaine."

I started to waver—they probably did need me. People hadn't got *so* much better at mathematics as to render my help superfluous.

And it was only a working bee.

"You'd have to put in for petrol," I said.

"Okay."

"And tell Celia if she's not ready at half past eight, I'm leaving."

"I will."

"And Jin-Jin?"

She stopped in the communal hall.

"Thanks for coming over."

We got to Celia's, a double block of old-style brick flats, and I beeped the horn. I gave her ample time to come out, at least seven seconds, but she didn't appear. I started driving off, but Jin-Jin stopped me. "I'll go get her," she said, and undid her seat belt.

"Two minutes, then I'm leaving," I called as Jin-Jin went up the drive.

While I waited I busied myself with the radio. It was a long time since Celia and I had seen each other. I'd thought about her, all those times putting the sudoku in the postbox. I'd wondered what she was doing, but I never allowed myself to dwell. If you dwell on one thing, then you attract other dwellable things. Negative thoughts are like filings to a magnet, and it wasn't my fault she got kicked off the committee.

Jin-Jin appeared with Celia behind her. Jin-Jin came around the back to the passenger's-side door. She opened it but, instead of getting in, held it for Celia.

Celia entered the car bottom first, then feet. Once she was sitting she used the handle above the door to shift and make herself comfortable. She put her handbag, a tan-colored triangular prism, in her lap.

All this I ascertained using only my peripheral vision. I was facing forward, looking out the front window, avoiding eye contact.

"Thank you, Jin-Jin," said Celia, once Jin-Jin had sat down in the back. "You know, you refugees are much more respectful of your elders than the local kids. And more community oriented. Not many of them spend their weekends volunteering."

"I'm not a refugee, I'm studying marketing at the university," said Jin-Jin.

But Celia wasn't listening. She clicked her belt on, and then she opened her handbag. Inside was a bound document I recognized even at a sideways glance. It was Ralph's and my report. I don't know how she got a copy.

She waved it at me. "Did you write this?" she said. It was the first thing she'd said to me the whole time. No *Hello* or *Thanks for picking me up.*

"Yes," I said.

Celia didn't comment on the content of the report, but the way she shook her head, I could tell she didn't like it, even though it was accurate and extremely well written.

"Today's going to be great," said Jin-Jin, in the back seat. She was very optimistic. I felt duty-bound to point out her attitude was unfounded.

"Hate to break it you," I said. "But this isn't going to work." I had a theory about why, but Celia agreed without hearing it.

"For once, Germaine, you're right," she said. "Well, you're half right. The working bee won't be enough. For one, we need a new roof, and if past experience is anything to go by, the council's not going to fork out for that. What we need is an income stream. Then we can maintain our independence."

"What sort of income stream?" said Jin-Jin.

"I don't know. Do I have to think of everything?" She gave an irritated sigh and wound down the window.

As appealing as an income stream might sound, it wasn't going to save them from certain closure. I knew because I'd run the numbers. Ever since I told Jin-Jin I would come along and help, I'd been worried it was the wrong decision. I kept wishing I could flash-forward and see what was going to happen, how it all turned out. And then I realized: I could.

I had a way of predicting the future. Sort of. The relative likelihood of one future over another, anyway.

I could calculate the probability that the senior center *would* be sold and compare it with the probability it would *not* be sold. Whichever probability was higher was the more likely outcome. And if one was *significantly* higher than the other, it was safe—or safe-ish—to assume that one would occur.

The only challenge was to identify the variables in each scenario. The *outcomes* were different, but what were the factors that determined them?

I had to think about that for a while, but once I realized it, it was obvious. Like all the best theories, it was very simple: What differed was the people involved, specifically the beneficiaries.

The people were either:

I = Important (the mayor, Don)
N = *Not* important (senior citizens, participants of the homework club, etc.)

For the scenario in which the senior center was sold:

Beneficiaries = I
Nonbeneficiaries = N

For the scenario in which the senior center was *not*, the converse was true.

Beneficiaries = N
Nonbeneficiaries = I

It wasn't hard to argue the probability that important people being victorious was much higher than the probability of unimportant people being victorious:

$Pr(I) \gg Pr(N)$

Once I realized that, I felt better about attending the working bee. The mayor wouldn't mind, nor would Don. I was helping out in a futile activity. It wouldn't change what was going to happen.

Now, as Celia rested her arm along the open window, tapping her fingers, I explained my theory. "The reason you won't be able to save the center is because you, and to a lesser extent me, are not important. We are nobodies, and nobodies don't get listened to."

Celia seemed to take great offense at the word *nobody*. "That's the stupidest thing I've ever heard."

"I've done the calculations. It's like I told Jin-Jin the first time we met, at the homework club."

"Actually, we'd met before that," said Jin-Jin. "By the communal bins?"

"You can't predict exactly what's going to happen in the future," I said, "but you can get an idea of what *might* happen or what's *most likely* to happen. It's like flipping a coin: You can't say it'll be heads or tails, but you can say half the time it *should* land on heads and the other half on tails. This is the same. Numerically, the probability of stopping the center being closed is low. Very, very low."

Though my calculations and underlying assumptions were correct and neither of them had completed a bachelor's degree majoring in mathematics, they still felt qualified to argue.

"That doesn't make sense," said Celia.

"Which bit? Probability theory or how I worked out the end result? It's easier if I show you on paper, isn't it, Jin-Jin?" I tried to catch Jin-Jin's eye in the rearview mirror, but she didn't look at me.

I was annoyed. I expected more from her.

"This is exactly what I was saying before," said Celia. "These days people have no idea what's important. Their values are all wrong."

Was she that naive? I'd *checked* the values. Double- and triple-checked them. "Look," I said, "importance is made up of four things: status, career, money, and personal connections. If you want to maximize the probability of success, you need to maximize each of those things, and that's what I did. I explored different options and got figures for each. It took a bit of time, let me tell you."

Celia turned to look at Jin-Jin. They exchanged a knowing look. "There's more to life than money," said Celia.

It was as though she wasn't listening at all. Hadn't I just said there was status and career and personal connections? I started to go over it again, but she interrupted to list a range of things she thought were important, ignoring the fact that none of them were measurable.

"*Fairness? Happiness?*" I said. "I can't calculate those things." It was getting hot in the car. I turned the air-conditioning on. "All I'm saying is, the probability of closure is high, very high. High enough to be considered certain."

Celia went to argue, but Jin-Jin piped up from the back. "Based on probabilities, you said I wouldn't break up with Lee."

"It had a lower likelihood, yes. But like I said, you can't actually predict—"

"Ha! See. You can't predict."

I clicked the wrong blinker on; I was getting flustered. The way they were cherry-picking my arguments made it difficult to concentrate. "And anyway, Jin-Jin, you gave me crappy data. Can't calculate anything with crappy data."

"What if *your* data's crappy?" said Jin-Jin.

"It isn't, though, is it? Look, I'm only trying to help. I don't want people to get their hopes up, that's all."

They wouldn't listen; they were impossible. The two of them were being willfully ignorant. I said nothing further on the subject.

There were dozens of people at the senior citizens center and they weren't all old. Everyone from the homework club was there, too, out in the blazing sun, wheeling barrows, sweeping leaves into piles, and picking up rubbish.

Inside, Gladys, Betsy, and others were sorting things for a market stall. It was Gladys's idea: She wanted to sell everything that wasn't being used: chairs, books, other "trash and treasure."

Celia poked through a box of random cutlery. "Trash and trash, more like it."

"No harm in trying, Celia. And besides, it's *retro*. Everything old is new again."

"I'm old," said Celia.

"All right, not everything."

Charlie appeared, holding a pile of books so tall he was resting his chin on the top. Vera was behind him. Charlie kept his chin in place, moving his upper head to ask Celia if he could keep them.

"One book," said Vera. "If it's okay with Celia, you can have *one* book."

Charlie glared at her. *"Mum."*

"What? You have thousands of books. We're *literally* going to drown in old books."

Charlie's glare intensified. "You're using the word *literally* wrong."

"Charlie."

"You are. Isn't she, Germaine?"

I didn't want to be the official adjudicator, but when Vera turned her back, I gave Charlie a tiny nod. *Correct.*

Celia started telling everyone what they had to do. Vera was to help paint outside; Gladys was to continue sorting items for the market stall; Betsy should start cooking morning tea and lunch for all the volunteers. Celia and Charlie were going to supervise the garden cleanup. I offered to help them.

"No, Germaine," said Celia. "We have a special job for you."

I didn't like the sound of that.

Betsy said, "Follow me," and led me to the office, where there was a large pile of paper on the desk. They were James's pension forms: He'd made copies, Betsy explained. "Now, I know you said you *tried* calling already, but guess what? The department's phone line is open until two p.m. on Saturdays. Do you mind?"

- 33 -

I sat in the office at the desk in front of the window. Outside I could hear everyone having fun and enjoying themselves. Inside it was stuffy and cold.

I knew the department's number by heart by now, and most of their recorded selections. I pushed 3, 2, 4 and then had to hold again.

This time the music wasn't soothing. It was an irritating mix of electronica. Why couldn't they play something more interesting, or have someone read out fun facts?

I started feeling lonely. I'd been holding the phone receiver to my ear, but my arm was getting tired so I balanced it on the table and lowered my head onto it.

I kept holding. Listening. Having worked in the industry, I knew it was inevitable a caller would have to wait; you couldn't expect to be answered straightaway. But you could expect to be answered eventually.

After a while there was a ringing sound. I picked up James's form, ready to inform them of their mistake. Only it was a recorded message:

Press 1 for family payments . . . Press 2 for income reporting.

Somehow I was back at the start. I had to press 3 again for pension payments, then 2 for outstanding payments, then 4 for an operator. Or rather, 4 for more hold music. This happened twice more. Seemed I was stuck in a circular loop, a kind of never-ending, electronic maze. I wanted to throttle the phone. Or the person who designed the flow on which the automated system had been based.

Meanwhile, there was a delicious smell in the air. Morning tea. Some kind of biscuit was being distributed. Anzacs? Butter? Melting moments? Eva would have known.

Eva. She didn't know many things, but she would have known that. All at once, I remembered what else she'd claimed to know: how to short-circuit the automated system and go straight to an operator. Ha. How ridiculous. It wasn't possible. That wasn't how the system worked.

And yet.

What was the code? Star . . . star . . .

"Great biscuits, Betsy," I said. Not only were they butter, but she'd remembered me, in the office, on my own. Just as I hung up from the Department of Social Services, having sorted James's pension payments, she came in with a pot, two mugs, and a little tray of golden biscuits.

She put the tea strainer on one of the mugs. "Thanks for calling them. I know it's a pain, but you guys are better at it than us; I never get to speak to anyone. James'll be so pleased."

"It's easy once you know the trick." I picked up another biscuit. "Actually, Eva told me how."

"Eva? I *knew* she'd done it before." This was essentially an *I told you so* but the way Betsy said it, it didn't sound like one.

In fact, I found myself freely admitting that Eva had told me ages ago how to bypass the recordings, but I hadn't believed her. "Eva's so . . ." I wasn't sure of the word. I had a few words that were applicable, but I didn't want to use them in front of Betsy. She was nice to everyone; I wanted to at least *appear* to be the same way. "I made a mistake," I said.

"Everyone makes mistakes." Betsy moved the tea strainer to the other mug.

"Well, that was *my* last one. From now on, I'm not making any more."

"I don't know. They're not the worst things."

"What mistakes have you made?" I asked. Hardly any, I bet.

"I've made mistakes," Betsy assured me. "But some of them were worth making."

That didn't make sense. How could a mistake be worth making? Wasn't that why you called it a mistake, because you got something wrong?

"It's like this chutney I made. With ginger? I thought I'd try something new, but it turned out to be a real flop. That was last year. Needless to say, I didn't get a ribbon." Betsy finished pouring the tea and put the pot down.

"Bet you regretted that," I said.

She surprised me by saying no. "I wanted to try something different. I was willing to take a chance."

"Risking big to win big. You'd make a good gambler, Betsy."

"No, it wasn't that. It's more . . . I guess you have to pick what—or how—you want to win. Like, I could have made my normal chutney and done very well, but I didn't want to."

That was easy to say if you won things all the time. If you didn't, every competition was much more important. Anyway, winning was not just enjoyable, it was an efficiency: a kind of shorthand for showing people how great you were.

I sipped the tea, watching her over the top of the mug.

"You're pretty famous, you know."

This was a fact. She hadn't just won CWA competitions *one* year; she'd won several years in a row. Betsy had articles online and in magazines about her, with her own recipes listed. She'd even been on TV for a while, on a cooking show.

"None of it's real," she said. "I mean, it's great. It's nice and all that, but it doesn't mean anything."

"Have you ever cheated?"

"No."

"Have you ever thought about cheating?"

"No."

"Why not?"

She made a face: *I don't know*.

"Maybe you're afraid of getting caught," I said.

"Maybe." She didn't look like she thought this was the answer.

"What would you do if you *did* get caught?"

"Don't know. Probably apologize. Probably be mortified and spend a lot of time trying to make up for behaving so appallingly."

That was an interesting approach. But Betsy was an anomaly: She was unusually nice.

Betsy swirled her tea and drank the last of it. Then she looked in her cup like she was going to read the leaves, but there were no leaves, as she'd strained them out. "Like I said, Germaine, everyone makes mistakes. It's what you do after that counts."

"What did you do after the ginger chutney? Did you go back to making normal chutney?"

"No. I kept working on it, and now I'm pretty close to the final recipe."

Late in the afternoon, when most people had gone home, Celia called the committee (and Jin-Jin) together to talk. The topic for discussion was the "income stream" Celia had mentioned in the car.

"The working bee's all well and good, but we need money, ladies. And Tom. Any ideas?"

The ideas were few and few between. The good ones were particularly sparsely distributed.

Gladys mentioned her market stall, and Jin-Jin talked about something called "crowd funding." Then Betsy suggested a cake stall. This wasn't the worst idea that had been put forward, but by then Celia had had enough. She was scathing. "A cake stall? Come on, Betsy."

Betsy got upset. She seemed to take Celia's opposition as a reflection on her cooking skills. Gladys stuck up for her. "I think Betsy's cakes would do very well. Have you had her banana bread? It's excellent."

"It *is* good." Celia was in angry-sounding agreement. "But we need *fifty thousand dollars*, Gladys. We're not going to make it baking cookies."

I didn't offer my opinion, but I knew Celia was right. The money for cakes and biscuits was in bulk sales and distribution. A couple of one-off stalls wouldn't have (a) the economies of scale or (b) sufficient total turnover.

Jin-Jin, who obviously didn't understand basic economics, thought it was a great idea. "I've got a very good Japanese cheesecake recipe," she said.

Celia pressed her fingers to her temples. *"We're not doing a cake stall."* It was a large room, but her voice managed to fill it. Everyone went silent.

While they were quiet I offered some helpful advice. "If you're going to think of something, you better do it quick. Time's running out. The mayor's going to announce the closure at the mayoral ball."

"That's next month," said Gladys.

Exactly, I thought. It was the perfect moment to ensure they understood the futility of the situation. But I felt my previous efforts had been underappreciated. No, I wasn't going to put myself out.

"The other thing we can do," said Celia, "is go to the papers. Try and get something in there about how important this place is. Maybe we can take some photos, try and drum up some sympathy."

The papers? Interesting. I tuned out for a moment to think about it.

In my calculations I had assumed the status of unimportant (and, indeed, important) people were constants. But what if these were, in fact, variables? In harnessing the power of "the media," unimportant people might be elevated in their importance. And vice versa.

"I've drafted something," said Celia. "It's short but contains all the pertinent information. What I've said is that the council is 'secretly moving' to get rid of the senior citizens center. Can I say 'unscrupulous'? Too much? I was going to use 'debauched,' but I don't want to come off as a loon. And so many people have a limited vocabulary these days."

If status changed over time, then it couldn't be represented as a single figure, rather a function . . . This was very subversive, part of an alternative paradigm. I couldn't quite . . .

"We've tried that before," said Betsy. "They've never been receptive."

"No, they wouldn't be." I was thinking out aloud. "Not unless you had proof something sinister was going on. And I am *not* doing anything to hurt Don."

"Don?" Celia's face scrunched, the way it did whenever his name was mentioned. "Who said anything about Don?"

"If he buys this place, he shouldn't be punished for it."

"If he what?"

Oh, dear.

They were all wide-eyed. It was very disconcerting, their level of interest in this piece of information. Had I made another mistake? Or was I just about to? I tried to backpedal. "Look, I don't know anything . . . I didn't say . . . I think we should go ahead with the cake stall."

"Germaine." Celia's voice was calm. "Is this place being sold to Don Thomas?"

I blew out my cheeks. "The mayor said that *could* happen. It was *possible*."

They all exchanged looks, multiple looks in multiple directions, like tram tracks at a confusing intersection.

"I *knew* it," said Celia. "Haven't I said all along that was happening?"

"Is that nepotism?" said Gladys.

"I'd say corruption," said Betsy. "I'm no expert, though."

I was willing to admit it sounded curious, but that was all I was willing to admit. "How much do you know about coincidences?" I said.

Celia ignored this, pressing for more information about the sale. "Did the mayor tell you that verbally or via email?"

"Verbally. I might have misheard."

"I'm sure there'll be something in a file somewhere." Celia was getting excited. They were all getting excited; there was a palpable spike in energy. "You guys have lots of files. Don't you."

"Not that many. And the archiving system is not documented. You can never find what you're looking for." I shouldn't have said anything. Even if . . . which it wasn't . . . Besides, all the files were confidential, I couldn't leak the information. That wouldn't be fair to the mayor. She was the only person who'd ever believed in me.

Well, her and one or two people here.

I would like it on record that I said no. And I meant it, too, in that specific moment.

Then, unfortunately, something happened.

- 34 -

I didn't offer Celia a lift home, same as I didn't offer Jin-Jin a lift home. But at the end of the meeting, as the sun was setting and everyone began to leave, the two of them followed me to the car. When the doors unlocked, they let themselves in, put on their seat belts, and sat with an air of expectation. I could have prodded them out and pointed them to the bus stop, but it seemed easier and quicker to drive.

None of us spoke as I went through the car park and down the long drive that led to the main road. We were too busy thinking. I was also wishing I hadn't disclosed certain pieces of information, as they'd been misinterpreted. You never knew what people would find interesting. I said interesting things all the time and was very rarely asked to elaborate.

That said, I *was* concentrating on the road. When we got to the end of the drive, I stopped at the stop sign. I looked left and right and ensured it was clear in both directions before proceeding. But when we were only partway out, a black car came careening around the corner, hugging the wrong side of the road like it was in its own private grand prix. Even at a glance I could determine it was going faster than the speed limit and—more pertinent—too fast to correct its arc in the distance available.

Its path, in short, was going to collide with ours.

My foot stamped down on the brake. We were all thrown forward; I felt the seat belt cut across my neck. Celia grunted, Jin-Jin cried out. Rubber screeched against asphalt. We braced, bodies tight, eyes shut. Waiting for the impact.

Waiting, waiting . . . And . . .

I opened my eyes.

Celia was beside me. Her glasses had fallen off her nose and hung around her neck. In the back, Jin-Jin was bent forward in the brace position, her head buried under her hair. When she lifted it up, her face was pale.

The three of us sat very still.

Outside, the black car was still moving, only slowly.

It stopped. The driver's-side door opened, and a man got out. He had gray hair, dark sunglasses, a lean build.

"Don Thomas," said Celia. "Now there's a surprise."

I could see that it was Don, and Celia said that it was Don, but I couldn't quite comprehend it. The world was electrons and neutrons and light and sound, but none of them had come together yet. Slowly, they stopped trembling randomly in space and began to coalesce.

Don was in the car.

It was Don's car.

Don was coming towards us. Should I be angry or excited? My neck hurt and so did my shoulder.

"Sorry," he called. "Are you okay? I didn't mean to—" He flicked his glasses back and squinted at me. "Germaine?"

The sound of my name, the sound of his voice saying my name. I rolled my head on my neck. The muscles in my back seemed to loosen.

"Are you all right?" Don was at the window. "Germaine, I think your nose is bleeding. Do you need a tissue?" He went to open the door. Don wasn't afraid of blood. He wasn't afraid of anything.

He opened the door.

He was right there in front of me. I could smell him with my bleeding nose.

"Celia?" he said.

And I had another wish: that she wasn't there.

Celia raised her hand in a sort of wave.

"She's okay," I said. "She and Jin-Jin are fine. It's me . . . I've got a bloody nose."

"Right," said Don, a beat too late. "Good. Are you sure?"

"We're fine," said Celia. If only she hadn't spoken. If only she'd been very quiet, maybe he would have forgotten she was there.

But he didn't forget. He asked again—were we all okay—and apologized, again. And then, when he was satisfied we weren't injured, when I had a tissue, he said goodbye, and when he said goodbye, he used our names, one by one, in turn:

Goodbye, Jin-Jin.

Goodbye, Celia.

Goodbye, Germaine.

I dropped Celia off. That left Jin-Jin and me alone in the car.

She leaned forward in her seat. "Germaine, do you think Don would tell the mayor . . ."

"*No*," I said.

"I didn't finish."

But I knew what she was going to ask. "Don and I are friends," I said, and with each word felt more certain. "Very good friends. I'm better friends with him than I am with you."

"Okay." She sat back. "I was only asking."

– 35 –

Privately, however, I had some concerns, the primary one being: What did Don think I'd been doing?

He must have been shocked to see me with Celia. I hoped he didn't think I was working against him. Because I wasn't. I was only kind of mucking in because I know it wouldn't achieve anything. Nothing was going to change. Don must know that. But if he didn't . . .

I picked a trophy up off the mantel. A gold statue of a man, holding a notepad and pencil. I stroked its gold-plated hair, pretending it was Alan himself, hoping this might provide comfort. Then I tried pretending it was Don. Neither seemed to work.

The next day, the mayor asked to see me.

Her potential knowledge of the situation was another concern I had identified but placed a lower emphasis on relative to Don. Now, it seemed more pressing.

I put on a brave face, the face of a friend/employee awaiting further instruction. Not the face of someone who'd been caught doing the wrong thing.

I didn't even want to help those stupid old people.

Everything in the mayor's office was the same as always. She was as polite and courteous as ever. If anything she was *more* polite and *more* courteous, which should have made the interaction *more* enjoyable but somehow didn't.

It reminded me of Peter. How in front of other people he'd say things like: *What an interesting insight, Germaine*; or, *Not at all, the level of detail is fascinating*. The way he said it . . . Like he didn't really like me, even though he said he did.

When the mayor asked how I was, the emphasis was different. It was not, "How are you, Germaine?" It was "How *are* you, Germaine?" And she used the voice she used with Francine, not the voice she used with me. She was formal and not candid or funny or cutting. I had to force myself to maintain eye contact and then started having difficulty gauging what was an appropriate amount.

Normally, our conversations took a circuitous route before arriving at the point, but on this occasion she got straight to it.

"Did you hear the news?"

She was deliberately ambiguous, another sign of her change in attitude. She wanted me to ask so she could explain. But when I did, she took her time to answer.

Holding my gaze, she took a long, slow sip of water. "I'm bringing back the biscuits, Germaine."

It wasn't what I thought she'd say. I knew Eva and Frank had presented their petition, but that was weeks ago. Nothing had happened since and nor should it. The biscuits were a waste of time and money; they didn't really matter.

"Yes. *The people have spoken.*" She explained the petition had made her reassess. She'd realized the biscuits were more than just biscuits. They weren't an expenditure so much as an *investment*. "In what, you might ask? Why, in staff morale—and *that* is something you can't put a price on. Can you, Germaine?"

I could have put a price on it. Staff morale linked to employee turnover, which had all sorts of implications for efficiency and wages and training budgets, but the tone of the conversation didn't lend itself to disputing facts.

"Staff morale is very important, Germaine," said the mayor. "Everyone likes to feel appreciated, don't they? I mean, take yourself. You work hard, you're dedicated, and I've tried to show my appreciation.

I've given you an office and a raise, and I've considered you a friend." She stopped talking, and her dark eyes fell on mine.

I confess I felt rather small. I liked the mayor. I really did. I felt sadness, an emptiness akin to losing, but like no loss I'd ever known.

"One thing I've learned is you should never underestimate the power of happy staff, Germaine. Unhappy staff might stab you in the back, but happy ones? Why, they're like nuggets of gold." Her eyes narrowed. "Are you happy, Germaine?"

I didn't know. I said, "Are any of us really happy?" and understood at once this was the wrong answer.

"I spoke to Don on the weekend. He sends you his regards." She was watching me carefully, and I breathed in through my nose, not letting the nostrils move. Was she being disingenuous or had he really sent regards? It was unsettling.

"Speaking of Don—speaking of the golf club," said the mayor, though we weren't speaking of either, not really. "All set for the mayoral ball? Not long now, is it? I had thought you'd be at my table, but now I'm not sure if that will work. We'll see. But I did want to ask you a favor, Germaine. Can you do me a favor?"

I would never normally agree to something without knowing what it was, and yet now I felt I should.

Excellent; she knew she could count on me. She made much of my reliability. That was nice. But she still hadn't said what I was supposed to do so reliably, and now it seemed petty to ask. I was becoming more and more certain that the favor was not work-related, though. It was a personal favor she was asking. How was I going to get out of it?

"You remember I said we were going to make the announcement at the ball? About the senior center? Well, I can tell you it's official now. We voted to sell at a confidential meeting last night, five ayes and four noes. Only one vote in it. Still, one vote's all you need, isn't it? I wanted to tell you the good news myself."

The silence that followed lasted only a second or two, probably. It seemed a lot longer.

"I'd like your help to write my speech, Germaine. I could get the media team to do it, but you know what they're like. All fancy words and no technical accuracy. I want you to be the one."

"Is it definite?" I said. My voice sounded thin.

"Absolutely, positively definite. The decision's been made; there's no going back. Set in stone, you might say. Why"—she seemed inordinately happy when she said this—"God herself couldn't save that place now."

I was tired when I got back to my office. I hadn't slept well the night before. I turned the light off and lay on the floor under my desk.

I had a lot of thoughts swirling around inside, and they weren't nice. No. I wished I could delete them from my brain, or sweep them in a pile and put them in the bin.

The mayor was mad at me. She didn't say so, but I am extremely observant. I didn't like people being mad at me, and I didn't like the *mayor* being mad at me more. It made me question if she still liked me. Or if she'd ever liked me.

It made me question—and this was the worst part—if Don did. It was good I was lying down flat. You can't get lower than the floor.

Don must have told the mayor he'd seen me with Celia. If he told her that, what else had he told her? And what did this say about our relationship? What did it say about theirs?

It wasn't a competition. But if it *was* a competition, I wasn't winning.

Later, Eva transferred a call to my office. "It's for you," she said, and pushed the button before disclosing who it was.

I knew as soon as I heard the voice.

"I'm calling for advice," she said. "About a friend of mine?"

"Celia. This isn't a counseling service."

"She's a bit thick. Thinks she knows everything, but she doesn't know much at all."

"I'm sorry"—*doesn't know much at all*—"but I don't have time to talk."

"Bad luck, running into Don. Still, I guess it helps you work out who your friends are."

"How's that?"

"Well . . . Did he tell her?"

I kept my mouth shut. I didn't know for sure Don told the mayor anything, and if he did it was probably an accident. It was easy to say something you didn't mean to say. Didn't mean you didn't value the relationship, or weren't secretly in love with the person whom you got in trouble.

"I'll take that as a yes. It's a sign of his character, Germaine. He's weak."

"You don't know him like I do," I said.

"You're better than he is. You're better than both of them."

Better? How?

But Celia wasn't divulging. She wanted to know if I was coming to see them. "Betsy and Gladys are planning their ridiculous cake stall, but I thought you and I could talk some more about this newspaper article."

"No, thank you."

"Germaine, come on. Don't you think it's important?"

"Yes, but so's having a job and a place to live."

"Your career. Of course. I forgot." Celia's tone was no longer jovial. "Can't risk that to help a bunch of *nobodies*."

She'd misunderstood what I said in the car. She and Jin-Jin hadn't paid enough attention. "I didn't mean you didn't matter or you weren't important," I said. "I meant you're not well connected; you don't have any influence." If it was true when I first said it, it was even truer now.

Celia sighed. "Germaine. What is wrong with you?"

That again. "Nothing. This is just how I am."

"No, it's not." She stopped talking for a moment, then she changed the subject. "You sent me those letters."

"What letters?"

"Don't be stupid; no one likes sudoku. Thank you for the letters, Germaine."

If it was a trap she was setting, I wasn't sure what would spring it. I slipped my hands under my legs to protect them.

"It just goes to show you're more than career oriented. You are *also* a person who sends letters."

Even though they weren't letters—they were sudoku—this was still a frightening idea. Because Celia wasn't the only one who sent a lot of items in the post: So did Sharon. Was I more like her than I thought?

Celia hadn't spoken for a bit. "Are you still there?" I said.

"I'm here."

"Thought you might have gone already."

"No, I'm not going anywhere."

Then we just breathed together. It was very weird, but I didn't hate it, actually. Knowing she was there.

At lunchtime I went for a walk and somehow ended up at the café over the road, the one where Jack and I used to go, and where I hadn't been for quite a while. And where he was, right now, the one time I wanted to be alone. And with him were Eva and, of all people, Marie Curie. How annoying.

I tried not to let them see me, but they did. Jack called out and came up to the register.

"Germaine," he said. "Where have you been? Haven't seen you for ages."

"Nowhere. Working."

It was my turn to order. I asked the woman at the counter for a hot chocolate and a donut. She said, "Eat in or takeaway?"

Jack said, "Eat in. There's room on our table."

I told the woman takeaway. "I have to get back to work, Jack."

I'd decided that I wasn't going to socialize with colleagues anymore. I was going to maintain a professional distance. It was too hard otherwise.

"What's so important it can't wait ten minutes?" said Jack.

"Everything. You wouldn't know what that's like because your job is just computers. Mine is much more complex."

"Has something happened?" he said. "You look upset."

"I'm fine."

"Were you okay the other day, about the article? Marie was just helping."

"Okay." The lady behind the counter was waiting for me to pay. I looked in my wallet and found I didn't have any money. "Is card all right?" I said.

"Minimum purchase is ten dollars."

Jack got his wallet out and paid with a note. "She'll eat in," he said to the lady. He was trying to be nice when I didn't want him to be, and now I was trapped.

I went and sat down with Eva and Marie. "Why are you here?" I said to Marie. "Don't you have a job?"

"She's your replacement," said Eva.

"You're the temp?" I said.

"Actually, they're considering making the position permanent," she said.

I couldn't even. I didn't want to know. I emptied my wallet on the table and started counting the coins, moving them one by one to make a pile.

Marie put her hand on the table. "Did you get the article I sent?" she said in a sweet voice. Sickly sweet, like fake sugar.

"Yeah. Thanks."

"So interesting, I thought," she said.

I glanced at her, face like stone, then waved her hand off and pushed the pile of coins to Jack. "Don't worry about it," he said. "My treat."

My order took ages to come. Eva and Marie Curie were talking about the biscuits.

"It's a big investment the mayor's making," said Eva. "Biscuits are not cheap, especially when you factor in how many we need."

"I know," said Marie Curie. "I found out a lot about catering when I researched it for Lucy's wedding, remember, Jack? You'd be amazed how much they charge. Some of them even make you pay for delivery."

As the seconds ticked over I found myself getting even more annoyed with all of them. They cared about such stupid stuff. Nothing that really mattered. I had an urge to point this out.

I interrupted Eva and Marie to say the senior citizens center was going to be sold soon. "Not that you guys would be interested."

"I'm interested," said Jack.

"Why wouldn't I be interested?" said Eva. "Marie Curie probably isn't, but I am."

"I'm interested," said Marie Curie, looking at Jack.

They were just saying that. They didn't know anything about the place or the people, not like I did.

My hot chocolate and donut arrived. I asked if I could have them takeaway after all. The waitress picked them up in a swift but resentful movement and carried them back to the counter.

Jack asked what happened. I said it was a long story and a lot of it was confidential so I couldn't say. But Jack kept probing and the lady transferring the hot chocolate into the paper cup was astonishingly slow, so I told him.

He and Eva were shocked. That is probably not too strong a word.

"What are they going to do about it?" said Jack.

"They're talking about holding a cake stall," I said sarcastically.

"Betsy is?" Eva got excited. "Really? Because her banana cake'd be in my top five cakes of all time." She thought about it. "Maybe even top two."

"I don't know if you'd make much money at a cake stall," said Marie Curie. "Do you, Jack?"

"I've got no idea." Jack turned to me. "But Germaine—"

And no one will ever know what he was going to say because the lady came back with my hot chocolate/donut, and I took them and left. I carried them back to the town hall and consumed them in an office so quiet I could hear the saliva form in my mouth as I chewed.

I'd hardly got inside my front door that evening when Jin-Jin knocked. I was still deciding if I was going to answer when she said, "I can hear you." I felt obliged to undo the latch. She walked in.

"Remember how I said Lee and I broke up? Well, he called. I

didn't answer and he didn't leave a message. What do you think I should do?" She went and sat on the couch, putting her feet on the pouffe.

I stayed by the door, holding it open. "I'm busy, Jin-Jin. And anyway, didn't you say probability functions have their romantic limitations?"

"Oh, I'm not asking for any mathematical insight. I just wanted your opinion. You know, as a woman."

I said, without any kind of false modesty, that I didn't think I was the best person to ask. But she persisted.

"When I saw it was him, I didn't answer. I thought I'd make him suffer. But he hasn't called back, and now I'm not sure what to do. Do you think it was an accident? Maybe he was scrolling. But even if he was just scrolling, it still means he was looking at my name, right? What would you do if Don did that?"

I didn't want to talk about Don. I didn't want to talk full stop. I wanted to be on my own. It was my natural state.

"Listen, Jin-Jin," I said. "I don't know how it works in China, but here in Australia being a good neighbor means you say hi and bye and that's it. You don't invite yourself in. You don't talk at people and make them listen. It's considered very rude."

"Oh." Jin-Jin's face broke in half.

It didn't feel as good as I'd hoped, being mean to her. But she was the only one there: I had no one else to pick from.

Jin-Jin got up from the couch. "I'm Japanese, Germaine. I already told you that ten times."

I thought to myself, not for the first time, that I couldn't get anything right, could I?

– 36 –

Over the next few days I refocused my energies. I asked Ron Steven, who was head of Records, if he and I could switch offices for a week so I wouldn't be interrupted. Ron's office was downstairs in the basement. Not prime real estate. "If you want to swap for good, let me know," he said.

I tapped away on my keyboard in grim surrounds. I had only two things to do—write the mayor's speech and advise the seniors club on the date of closure—but they were taking a long time.

I felt bad. Very bad. So bad I was able to feel bad about contradictory things. Like guilt about the senior center and simultaneous remorse about letting the mayor down. I felt bad about hurting Don's feelings *and* I was mad at him for hurting mine.

Jack emailed multiple times:

Have to talk to you about something.

Germaine, it's important.

WHERE ARE YOU?

He called, but I let it go to voicemail.

I had a new way of being: competent, aloof, distant. Pretty much my old way, really.

Thursday afternoon I went upstairs to get a cup of tea from the kitchenette, and guess who was sitting in a chair waiting for me? Eva. She called Jack on her mobile.

"Found her."

I walked away, no tea, but she followed me, narrating an ongoing commentary to Jack on our whereabouts.

He was in the basement two minutes after we were.

"Where have you been?" he said. "I've been trying to reach you all week. We both have. Didn't you get my emails? Didn't you see I called?"

I didn't look at him. I noticed there was a mark on the floor and scuffed it to see if it would shift.

"You could have been dead for all we knew," he said.

"Marie Curie thought you *were* dead," said Eva. "She owes me a dollar now."

"I was busy." I would never admit this to anyone, but I found their irritation oddly endearing.

Jack said, "We've got something to tell you."

I didn't know that I wanted to hear what it was, but they were both so pleased with themselves. "I'm listening."

Jack lowered his voice and cocked his head in Eva's direction. "She had an idea."

"Oh."

Eva had ideas all the time. Mostly conspiracy theories, but sometimes pointless inventions she thought she might patent.

"No, this one's good," said Jack.

I tried to stop him from speaking. "Don't bother. I'm not interested. It's nothing personal."

Eva said, "I had the idea recently, when the mayor said she'd bring the biscuits back. I was pleased, for obvious reasons. I missed those rice crackers. And my pants were getting loose; I thought I was going to have to buy a belt. So when the mayor said she was placing an order, I started thinking about which biscuits I was going to eat first and how I'd structure my breaks. Marie Curie's a bit uptight when it comes to breaks, Germaine. She's not like you, not like you at all."

I was pleased to hear disparaging words about Marie. Just because someone sounds like one of the most intelligent women who ever existed doesn't mean they are.

"It was on one such break," said Eva, "that I had a brainwave. It came to me right out of the blue, like a lightning bolt. *Why get the same biscuits as before?* I thought. *Why not get something different, something better?*"

I wasn't really listening. I was just watching her mouth move.

"And then in the café you mentioned Betsy. Do you know who Betsy is?"

"Yes, I know who Betsy is."

"She's the best baker, no, the best *cook*, in the whole of the Southern Hemisphere. Have you tried her biscuits? Her banana cake? That cake is something special. It's unbelievable. It's moist and sweet but not sickly. The crust on top is crunchy but never dry. It's—"

Jack hadn't said much up until this point, but now he cut her off. "A *catering company*, Germaine," he said.

"*Hey.*" Eva hit him on the arm: not hard. But not soft either. "I was about to say that."

The two of them looked at me expectantly, and when I didn't respond straightaway, Jack began to explain.

It wasn't necessary. I understood at once. *A catering company*. Celia's income stream.

The idea *did* have potential, but they should have had it earlier. It was too late now.

"The council's already voted."

Jack said, "They can unvote. I'm sure we can change their minds."

Given how long he'd worked there, you would have thought he'd have a better understanding of the political system.

"It's not that easy. Nice idea, but I wouldn't bother."

Jack didn't make a sound, but his negativity felt CAPITALIZED. He glanced across at Eva, who was wearing the same confused expression she had when she was on the helpline. "Are you joking?" said Jack.

"Nope. Quit while you're ahead. That's my new mantra."

Jack began to get nasty. "Quit while you're ahead? How exactly are you *ahead*, Germaine? No, go on, tell me. I want to know. What aspects of your life are going so incredibly well you don't want to risk compromising them?"

"This is the new me, Jack. I've decided I need to lower my expectations."

A pause.

"The new you sucks, Germaine."

"Well, the new me doesn't think you're so great either."

Jack went quiet. Maybe he was thinking about how he shouldn't judge other people's life choices when he wasn't making great life choices himself. Or maybe he was wishing he'd been more supportive of me in my successful period, berating himself for being a jerk. Or maybe he was thinking about Marie. Whatever it was, he thought about it for a moment and then seemed to make a decision. He turned towards the door.

But before he could open it, Eva put her hand on the doorknob. "That's what people said about the biscuits," she said.

"Forget it, Eva," said Jack. "She's not listening."

"They did; they said there was no point trying to get them back. People were angry, but they just thought that was the end of it. Tony Lam in Finance told me I was wasting my time. And now look what's happened. I mean, if everyone had rolled over and accepted there were no more biscuits, then there'd be no more biscuits, would there? But there *are* biscuits. Well, not yet, but as of next week there will be—and not just biscuits but *better* biscuits. And that's because of me. I'm living proof there's a point to kicking up a fuss. You know six hundred and four people signed my petition?"

I got annoyed. "There's a big difference between a biscuit contract worth a couple of thousand dollars and a senior citizens center worth millions. You can't compare those things; they have nothing in common."

"They do have some commonalities," said Jack. "Well, one: the mayor. And she's what you'd call a 'known variable,' isn't she, Germaine?"

I didn't give him the satisfaction of eye contact, but I will admit I felt a surge of goodwill. *Known variable.* Jack knew me.

"The thing about the mayor," Jack went on, "is she's predictable. She'll always behave the same way: i.e., in pursuit of her own self-interest."

"I like the mayor," I said, and I meant it.

Eva didn't hear me. "I thought you were going to say me, Jack," she said. "That *I'm* common to both because *I* did the biscuit petition and *I* had the catering idea. And I can do more than just have the idea, Germaine. Jack and I came to help."

More annoying goodwill surging.

"You and Jack?" I cast a sidelong glance at him. He was fiddling with the pocket of his shorts.

"Betsy will have lots of recipes," said Eva. "Her banana cake is her magnum opus, but there are others. I've had her chocolate pudding, her sticky date, her sausage rolls. She does a mini-quiche that is very good."

"It doesn't matter," I said. "Even if we could change the mayor's mind, which we can't, the council has *made* the *decision*. It's too *late*."

"But the *biscuits*," said Eva.

I rubbed my temples for twenty-seven seconds. When I stopped, the two of them were still there. Waiting.

"All we can do is try," said Jack, which was a most un-Jack-like thing to say.

"I'm telling you," said Eva. "It's a great idea."

I looked at their hopeful, expectant faces. I wasn't thinking clearly. I'd been feeling so bad, and now here was a sliver of good.

"It's not the worst idea," I conceded.

People say two brains are better than one. I always thought it depended on the brains involved, but maybe that's not true. Maybe you get better ideas when there's a spread of personalities and intelligence levels. Like a random number generator in which fractions as well as whole numbers can come up: Suddenly. there are infinitely more possibilities. Though there were lower IQs involved, discussions at the senior citizens center were (initially) fruitful. Of the seven of us huddled in the office, Gladys was the most enthusiastic. "Oh, wow," she said, clapping. "Wow, wow, wow. I knew Betsy's cake stall was a good idea, but this is brilliant."

"Yeah, I thought of it," said Eva.

Betsy was less sure. "I don't know. It would be a lot of work. Would people really hire us? Food is so fancy these days. You don't see my kind of cooking in the restaurants."

For someone whose diet consisted of Slurpees and complimentary crackers, Eva was very authoritative. "That's why it *will* work. It's all in the wording. You just need to make it *sound* fancy. It's not *beef*, it's *Wagyu*. It's not an egg and bacon sandwich, it's *free-range*, *organic* egg and *hickory-smoked* bacon."

Gladys jumped in her chair, surprisingly agile. "Exactly. It's an *award-winning* banana cake. It's a *secret family recipe* handed down from generation to generation. Maybe even *artisanal*. Ooh, and we can leave one ingredient off the list so no one can ever try and make it themselves."

"Well, no. You'll have to include all the ingredients. It's a requirement," said Ralph. Yes, Ralph. Jack had insisted we invite him along. "There's no point doing something if you're not going to do it properly," Jack said, at which I'd done an actual double take. I'd never heard Jack talk with such drive, such perfectionism. Or any drive or perfectionism. It made him oddly attractive. I found myself thinking about what other appealing attributes might be concealed beneath his polar fleece vest.

In the senior citizens center office, I outlined the plan I'd formulated in the car on the way over. "Jack can do the website and I can coordinate the financials, cost per item based on ingredients, labor, markup, et cetera, et cetera. We also need someone to do the marketing, to make it look professional."

"Jin-Jin does marketing," said Gladys. "At uni. And she's such a lovely girl. Maybe we can ask her?"

Jin-Jin. I squirmed.

Jin-Jin and I hadn't spoken since she came over that last time. I'd seen her twice outside the lifts, and both times she walked straight past. She had a blank expression on her face, as though she couldn't see me. It would be a lot easier if she wasn't involved.

"Is there anyone else? I said.

"Why not Jin-Jin? Jin-Jin's great," said Betsy. There was a murmur of agreement as to how wonderful she was.

"Maybe you call her, Gladys," I said.

"I don't have her number. Do you have her number, Betsy? No, no one has her number. I thought she lived near you, Germaine. I remember her saying how nice it was to have a friend so close by."

Fine, I said. I'd ask Jin-Jin. "But you and Betsy will need to work with Ralph on the registration. We also have to—" I had plenty more to say. Thinking of everything and telling people what to do were two things I was very good at. But then Celia, who'd been uncharacteristically quiet, spoke up.

"You realize nothing's actually changed? Just because it's a catering company instead of a biscuit stand, we still have the same problem. We need fifty grand for a new roof, and we're not going to make that selling baked goods. I mean, if we sold each biscuit for a dollar we'd need to sell fifty thousand biscuits."

That was incorrect. I said that if we sold each biscuit for $1, our profit would be *less* than $1 because of production and delivery costs. We'd need to sell *more* than fifty thousand biscuits to make $50,000.

"Okay," said Celia, "we need to sell *more* than fifty thousand biscuits," which, though accurate, was not exactly the point I'd intended to make.

Eva spoke up. "As president of the biscuit committee at council, I can make a recommendation about which biscuits they purchase. There's also a catering committee, and they select the sandwiches. Frank's on that. He'd be very supportive."

Celia was dismissive. "Even if you did sell enough biscuits—"

"*And* sandwiches," said Eva.

"*And* sandwiches, they're not about to pay up front, are they? And the mayoral ball is just around the corner." Her negativity was infectious. A feeling of dejection and uncertainty began to creep into the room.

Celia looked around with apparent satisfaction, then turned and rustled through some files lying on the desk behind her. When she turned back, she was holding a copy of the *Deepdene Courier*. I had a terrible sinking feeling.

"I don't want to go to the paper," I said.

"I don't want to go to the paper either," said Celia.

The ensuing silence was heavy.

Celia put the paper on the table. "You know what's better than going to the paper?" she said. "*Not* going to the paper, that's what. See, I've been thinking. The thing about politicians is, they're all the same: motivated powerfully and exclusively by the well-being of number one. We don't need to *defeat* Mayor Bainbridge—we need to *recruit* her. Get her on our side. Give her a reason to keep this place open."

"Haven't we tried that?" said Gladys.

"Yes, but what I'm proposing is a little less about lobbying and a lot more about leverage."

"Celia." I swallowed. "You're not suggesting some kind of blackmail?"

Celia was offended. "No, no. It's like this one said"—she gestured at Eva—"it's all in the wording. It's not *blackmail*, it's a *reciprocal relationship*. A friendship, if you like: *mutually beneficial*. We just need to find something that demonstrates the benefits of that friendship in the most convincing manner."

I wasn't sure about this; I wasn't sure at all. What about my résumé? I could massage dismissal, but there were few lights in which a criminal conviction for blackmail would appear favorably. I looked around the room, trying to gauge what everyone was thinking. Gladys and Betsy looked concerned, but Ralph didn't. Was he considering the idea? It looked like it. Eva was nodding. And Jack was also nodding.

Where was the collective indignation? The evidence of moral quandary? Had I fallen in with a criminal element?

Celia pointed at Jack. "You. You work in computers. Can't you check her email? Bound to be something incriminating there. I mean, Verity's not exactly the sharpest tool in the shed. I'm sure Germaine can help you out."

"I'm sure she can't," I said. There was no way. It was unthinkable. I couldn't do that to the mayor. She'd helped me, *nurtured* me. I owed her something.

Before I could respond there was a loud *thump*, and a bird bounced off the window. It was fine; it flew away unhurt. But the seven of us were left looking at the view.

We could see the car park and, beyond it, the golf club. There was a large billboard out the front. It said, LORD MAYOR'S CHARI-TABLE FOUNDATION BALL—SOLD OUT and had a photo of Mayor Bainbridge. She beamed across at us.

"There's not enough time to raise fifty thousand dollars," said Celia. "But there's plenty of time to have a conversation." She looked at Jack. "I mean, how long would it take to check some email? See? Not long."

Checking the mayor's email was not a good idea; really, it wasn't. It wasn't like there was going to be anything incriminating anyway, she and Don being innocent of the crime they were suspected of.

"There's no harm trying, then," said Celia.

Even as I sat there, spouting excuses, I knew Jack would do it, and I knew if he asked me, I'd help him.

What was happening to me? It wasn't so much that I'd changed, more that they seemed to think I was already that sort of person. The sort who wrote letters and took risks, even when they made no sense whatsoever, just to help other people.

What a terrible way to live. I was playing right into their deluded expectations.

I told myself I'd go and see Jin-Jin as soon as I got home. Then I said, *After a shower*, and then I said, *After dinner*, and then, *After one more sudoku*. It was eleven o'clock when I tiptoed into the corridor holding a typed note to slip under her door in the event she didn't answer.

I knocked softly, but the door swung open anyway. For a moment, Jin-Jin was a dark figure silhouetted against the light from her kitchen.

"Hello, *Germaine*." Her voice was not friendly. She held on to the door like I was an Oxfam collector.

"Hi. Can I come in?"

Jin-Jin waited a beat before responding. She was not a tall person, but I could feel her looking down at me. "*Can you come in?* I thought good neighbors didn't invite themselves in."

"I—"

"That's what I was told recently. By a 'good neighbor.'"

People forget things all the time, but the one occasion you're slightly out of order they'll remember forever. "I may have been . . . a bit rude to you, Jin-Jin."

"*May* have been?" She was wearing one of her cartoon jumpers. It made her look friendly and approachable, an appearance in contradiction to the sharpness of her voice. This was a side of Jin-Jin I hadn't seen before. If it had been directed at someone other than me, I would have enjoyed it more.

"I *was* rude to you."

Jin-Jin said nothing. Down the hall the lift doors opened and the man from number 24 appeared. We waited in silence as he walked past. When he was gone, Jin-Jin looked at me expectantly. *Well?* she seemed to be saying. I looked closely at the doorjamb, which, as expected, wasn't very interesting.

"I've got an assignment to do, Germaine." Jin-Jin started to shut the door. I put my foot out to stop it from closing.

"Wait."

It wasn't that I didn't think she deserved an apology. She did deserve it. But I could feel my apology lodged there, inside my clamped lips. I was concerned that if I opened my mouth, *all* of my inner thoughts and worries would tumble out, not just those that pertained to Jin-Jin.

"Germaine?"

"Okay." I swallowed. "Look, I'm not very good with people."

Jin-Jin didn't respond, but her grip on the door softened.

"I'm like a mathematics textbook. *I got problems.* Ha. That's a joke . . . Okay, look . . ." Another swallow. "Jin-Jin, I'm sorry."

"For."

"Being rude. And not just that one time, for some other times, too. Which is not to say I want you to hang around all the time but maybe occasionally, sometimes, every now and then. It wouldn't be completely unenjoyable."

"Not completely unenjoyable?" The kitten on Jin-Jin's jumper was not to be underestimated. It might have been pink, but it had claws.

"Maybe sometimes I'd like it," I said.

Jin-Jin weighed this up and seemed to find it acceptable. "You're a funny lady, Germaine."

"Am I?" I felt less encumbered, like I'd taken off a heavy backpack. It wasn't that hard, apologizing. Maybe my thing was people after all.

"Not funny ha-ha, the other funny. Funny strange. But thank you."

The next day Jack and I went to the café. We ordered sandwiches and sat in a corner booth so we could see everyone in there: the guy making coffee, the lady on the till, people at their tables talking. It seemed like a safe place. No excuse for Jack to be so blasé, however.

"I logged on to her email," he announced to me, to everyone. "Ran a search on Don but— What? I'm not being obvious. *You're* being obvious, I'm being normal." Grudgingly, he lowered his voice. "*Fine.* Is this better? I ran a search on Don, but there was nothing."

"Did you try *Donald* Thomas?"

"Yes, I tried Donald Thomas. And senior citizens center and just senior citizens and . . ."

He listed all the words he'd searched. It was a serious business and I should have been concentrating, but I found myself losing the thread. The problem was we were sitting so close. It was a two-person table. One person was meant to sit on the bench and the other on the chair opposite, but when I sat on the bench Jack shifted the seat so instead of sitting at 180 degrees, we were at 90. There should have been ample leg room, but we had not quite enough. Our knees were almost touching.

"I even tried *old people* . . . I don't know what else to do, Germaine. *Germaine.* Are you listening?"

"I'm listening." I was listening. I was. He'd searched the mayor's email and there was nothing. I had the vague sense this wasn't right, but I couldn't pinpoint why. I was distracted. Why was Jack wearing a long-sleeved shirt? He never wore long sleeves. And was that after-shave I could smell? It was subtle but pleasant.

"So?" He was waiting.

"I'm thinking."

Right, focus.

The mayor and Don . . . No emails. Now I thought about it, some-thing was odd. There was an anomaly somewhere, a misstep in the pattern. I went back to the beginning and plotted all the points:

$(x1, y1)$: my first day

$(x2, y2)$: meeting the mayor and Don. i.e., the first complaint

$(x3, y3)$: meeting with the mayor after she received the second complaint—

Then I had it, my "aha" moment. Don *had* sent the mayor an email, complaining about the banners. Photos attached—the mayor had shown them to Francine and me. If Jack couldn't find it in his search, she must have another email account with a different address.

When I said this to Jack, he said, "Interesting."

Then we were interrupted by the waitress. She put the plates on the table side by side. I picked up my sandwich.

Jack waited until she was gone and said, "What are you doing tonight?"

Bread lodged in my throat. "Nothing. Why?"

"We should get together."

"Us? You and me?" What would Marie say?

"To get into her email," he said. "We could go to the mayor's office after everyone's gone home and check her search history. Hey—are you okay? You've gone all red."

What a tense afternoon. I was wound up like a spring. When Jack came to get me, I said, "Maybe you want to do this by yourself?"

"Relax," he said. "Everything will turn out fine."

Of all the sentences in all the world, that has to be my least favorite. But I went with him: Up the stairs and down the corridor, the town hall was quiet and still. Everyone had gone home, and the only sound was the soft pat of our feet on the carpet.

As we entered the mayoral suite, the air seemed to get cooler, the silence more eerie. It was dark outside and the long glass window reflected our faces back at us. Mine did not look relaxed.

We stopped in front of the mayor's door. Jack held a security pass above the lock. "This is unexpected, eh?"

"Can you hurry up? I want to get this over with."

"Calm down. Stacey said Bainbridge is in Canberra all week. And anyway"—he said this louder: *acting*—"we're just updating some software."

Jack pushed the card in the slot. A green light appeared, there was a faint clicking sound, and the door opened.

The room was dark. As our eyes adjusted, we could see the outline of the mayor's desk, her computer, the filing cabinet. It wasn't until I saw there was no one there that I let go of the breath I hadn't known I was holding.

Jack flicked the light on and went and sat himself in the mayor's chair. "This is comfortable. Ooh, this is very, very comfortable. Germaine, you have to try— *Okay*."

He turned the computer on, and the sound of it whirring to life filled the room. It was so noisy I was sure the whole world could hear it. Or if they couldn't hear that, they could hear me, my heart beating so hard and so loud in my chest. It was like a drum sounding across an amphitheater, echoing, echoing, echoing.

"I just have to log in as her and then we can . . ." Jack whispered to himself and tapped at the keyboard. I stayed where I was, by the open door.

The air was cool, but a clammy sweat formed and began to run down my back. We were going to get caught. I was one hundred percent sure of it. Would they call the police? Life would not be worth living if I went to jail. Even if I survived the experience, when I got out, I'd have trouble finding a job and forming relationships. It would be . . . Well, strangely familiar. But that was less comforting than it should have been.

"Are you going to shut the door, Germaine?"

"No, I'm the lookout. I have to *look out*."

Everyone knows the lookout is an *accessory*. My role was to stand where I was and say: "They're coming," if perchance they *did* come. And if that happened, then I would enact my second role, which was to *deny all involvement*. If I shut the door, I'd go from being an *accessory* to being an *accomplice*. An accomplice gets a much longer sentence.

"You won't believe what her password is," said Jack. "VerityforPrimeMinister. Yep, one word, capital V, capital P, capital M."

"Hurry up, Jack."

"I'm going as fast as I can."

Imagine if I had to shower in front of other people. And in a communal bathroom.

"Can you shut the door, Germaine? It's a one-way corridor. If someone comes, you're not going to be able to escape that way."

Jack was not being helpful. In fact, he seemed to be rather enjoying himself.

I went and stood behind him, hoping to hurry him along.

On the screen, the council logo appeared and the mayor's official mailbox opened. Jack closed it and clicked the Internet browser instead. When it loaded, he went to the history tab and scrolled across until he found a line that said *In-box–Verity Anne Bainbridge*. He pressed Enter.

The mayor's personal email opened and rows of emails filled the screen.

"I would have thought you could do that remotely," I said.

"You probably can . . . I don't know how, though. I did a six month course, but that was in the nineties. Technology's changed since then." Jack moved the mouse to the search bar. "You want to do it?" he said.

For the record: I liked the mayor. Even if she was using and/or lying to me, I still felt gratitude towards her. A kind of gratitude—it was complicated.

I typed D-O-N-space-T-H-O-M-A-S into the search box.

A tiny hourglass appeared. It was only there a couple of seconds, but each second seemed to take much longer than usual.

There were no results for that search.

I tried D-O-N-A-L-D T-H-O-M-A-S.

There were no results for that search, either.

And then: A-L-A-N C-O-S-G-R-O-V-E

Bingo. A match. Multiple matches.

The screen filled with emails from Verity Anne Bainbridge to Alan Donald Cosgrove and from Alan Donald Cosgrove to Verity Anne Bainbridge.

Jack clicked one open.

From: Verity Anne Bainbridge

To: Alan Donald Cosgrove

Don,

> Special project to proceed.
> How are you going to make this up to me?
> Verity xx

"Huh," I said.

"Yes. That's very—"

From: Alan Donald Cosgrove

To: Verity Anne Bainbridge

I can think of a few ways. The first involves—

"Oh." I patted my hair flat, suddenly self-conscious.

"That's fucked," said Jack, and then he did something very unexpected. Instead of patting my hand in a consoling fashion or giving me a pitying shoulder rub, he began to laugh. And his laugh made me laugh. I don't suppose I even knew what we were laughing at. The situation was absurd.

"I thought you and Don were an item," said Jack.

"I thought we were, too."

It was confusing. I was laughing, but it wasn't funny.

Jack's voice softened. "I never liked him."

"I did."

I didn't want to read any more emails. I stood up and told Jack to print whatever he thought would be useful. I didn't want to touch the keyboard myself. It seemed dirty.

Jack said, "I told you he was an idiot."

"Just print the emails. I want to go home."

"There's one small problem. A technical glitch. Tiny, really, but I should have thought of it before. Anyway, the mayor's not connected to the printer network. Because she's got an assistant and the connection was at capacity, and we had to remove all nonessential staff. Yeah, I know. But it's okay, I'll just set up a new email address, and we can forward them there. It won't take a minute. What should I call it? *The email*. It can be anything. Nope, that's taken. That's taken, too. Let me think . . ."

He set about creating a new email address and forwarding the mayor's and Don's emails to it. I did nothing except try not to think about Don. Or about anything.

Then all at once, there was a noise outside. Voices in the hall.

Jack and I froze. He turned around. *Who's that?* he asked using only his eyebrows.

I don't know, I replied with mine.

The voices grew louder and came closer and grew even louder. Jack and I had the same thought in the same moment. He pointed and I dropped to the floor, crawling between his legs so I was wedged between the chair and the front panel of the desk. In the same instant, the door opened.

"Come through— Jack?" It was Stacey, the mayor's assistant. I recognized her voice. "What are you doing here?"

"Just updating some software." Jack slapped at the keyboard.

"I thought Roland did the updates."

"Roland's sick."

"Okay . . . I just came to get a file—"

The cabinet was behind us.

"—for Francine."

Francine? I curled forward, pressing my cheek to the floor so I could see through the gap between the bottom of the desk and the carpet.

In addition to a pair of black heels (Stacey) there were two brown orthopedic sandals. Unmistakably Francine.

Stacey said, "You'll have to move, Jack." Her black heels started walking across the room while Francine's brown flats stayed by the door.

In five seconds Stacey would see me.

In four seconds she'd see me.

Jack said, "I'll get it," in a desperate voice and rolled forward, knocking into me. My elbow thumped against the front of the desk. His knee was in my back.

"What was that?" said Stacey.

Jack rolled back, giving me some room. "What was what?"

She was coming closer.

I *knew* this was a bad idea. I should never have come.

"Wait, Stacey," said Francine.

"Can you move, Jack?" said Stacey, still walking.

My career flashed before my eyes, short and unremarkable but very precious now that it was about to end.

"*Stacey, STOP*," said Francine again. This time quite loud.

Stacey stopped.

"I, ah, just remembered," said Francine. "I do have the file. I don't need you to get it. It's in . . . in my bag. Look, that's my bag, on the floor over there." Francine was talking about *my* bag. I must have dropped it on the floor when we came in.

There was movement as Francine went and picked it up. A zip opened. "Yes, here it is. Sorry, Stacey. I shouldn't have—"

If irritation was represented on an analogue meter, Stacey's needle was flickering somewhere between annoyed and seriously fucked off.

"Are you *kidding* me?" she said. "Shouldn't have, what? Got me to come in from home? Shouldn't have made me turn around and drive back in to print something out? You said it was urgent, Francine."

"Sorry, Stacey."

"Sorry? Jesus. What a waste of time. You people think I have nothing better to do."

The light went off, their voices faded.

I drove Jack home.

"That was close," he said.

I didn't comment; I had to concentrate on driving. The chance of having an accident increases when it's dark.

It's also elevated when people drive in an emotional state. Like if they're upset or feeling heartbroken. I held the wheel tight and watched where the dotted white line was going.

We didn't talk until we got to Jack's house. Then Jack said, "Don's an idiot, Germaine."

Maybe he was, maybe he wasn't.

Maybe I was.

Jack undid his seat belt, and it slipped back to its holder. He turned towards me. The silence was heavy and low hanging, like fruit rotting on a tree.

"Want to come in?" said Jack.

"Not really."

"Please? I want to show you something. It'll only take five seconds."

It wouldn't take five seconds, it would take many more. But even though Jack's voice was soft on the surface, underneath it was pushy and imploring. He seemed determined that I see whatever it was. I realized it would be easier and quicker to go in than to argue. I pulled the keys from the ignition.

I knew Jack lived in a bungalow out the back of his mother's house but had assumed it was accessible via some sort of side gate—I'm sure that's what he'd told me—but this was not the situation. We had to go through the house to get there, which I did not feel like doing. I planned to walk very quickly behind him with my head down, so if anyone was there, I wouldn't have to talk to them. But unfortunately the front door opened straight into a lounge room, i.e., there was no hallway.

As if the atypical layout wasn't off-putting enough, there was something even more perturbing inside—was this what Jack wanted to show me?

Two women were sitting on the couch watching TV. One I took to be Jack's mother, by her age. The other—and this seemed very insensitive of Jack—was Marie Curie.

Jack lived with Marie Curie.

"Germaine," said Marie, getting up. She waved at Jack's mother to pause the television or turn the volume down but Jack's mother clutched the remote to her chest and kept watching.

"*Mum*," said Marie, trying to get her attention. "*Mum*, it's Germaine."

Jack's mother did not respond; she didn't even seem to hear, which was weird.

It was also weird that Marie was calling her *Mum*.

When I was small, Sharon made me call her friend Marion "Auntie Marion," even though we weren't related, so I supposed there was some precedent for this, but it was still odd. Typical Marie. I was annoyed with Jack. I should have known he was going to show me something stupid.

Jack said to Marie, "How is she?"

Marie, who'd come over to us by now, looked behind her and said, "She didn't have a good day. She kept saying someone came in and stole a bag of onions. I had to put the TV on to calm her down."

Jack glanced at his mother and said, "She was like that on the weekend."

"It's getting worse," said Marie. "Maybe we should think about—"

I interrupted. "I should go." Now I'd seen "the thing"—Marie living there—I should have been free to leave, and that's what I wanted to do, quick as possible.

But Jack said, "You haven't seen it yet."

There was more? I wasn't sure if I wanted more. I felt very worn.

Jack told Marie we were going out the back. She was happy about this, nodding at me meaningfully. "It's good to see you, Germaine. I'm glad you're here," she said.

Sharon used to say, *If you have nothing nice to say, don't say anything at all*. She didn't offer much in the way of useful life advice, but this I tried to follow on occasion. I kept my mouth shut.

We had to go through the lounge to the kitchen and then there was a hallway that led to the back door. At the other end of the yard was a small building with an outside light on.

Inside, it was one big room divided into sections like a motel, without the folded towels on the bed. The *single* bed. Jack and I sat at the table between the microwave and the bathroom.

"Want a cup of tea?" he said.

"No."

"Beer?"

"No."

I looked around the room. There was a ukulele in the corner on a stand and a poster of a comic book character I didn't recognize. On top of the TV was a laptop and papers, but not many other personal effects. I was glad there weren't photographs of Marie. Having just escaped her, it would have seemed particularly grueling to have to sit in a room where she was staring at me from all angles.

Jack said, "Mum's . . . unwell. That's why Marie and I are here."

"Okay." I didn't care where he and Marie lived. I wanted to go home to my apartment. "Did you have something to show me?" I said.

"*Yes*." He went and got his laptop then sat beside me so we could both see. The screen was much smaller than the one in the mayor's office. I wondered what Marie would think, the two of us sitting so close. Probably nothing. She seemed to have very liberal attitudes.

Jack said he wasn't surprised about Don and the mayor.

"I don't really feel like talking about it."

"This isn't about that," said Jack. "It's something else." He clicked through to find a file on the computer.

It was an old newspaper article entitled "Sudoku Champion Pays Large Sum in Confidential Settlement Agreement."

Jack said, "I did some research on that sudoku incident." He pushed the laptop to me, wanting me to read. When I said I didn't feel like reading, he paraphrased.

According to Jack, Alan had paid the World Puzzle Forum a lot of money in early 2008. "So?"

"So then everyone shut up about his cheating. It stopped being an issue."

"Maybe they realized it was all a big misunderstanding."

"Maybe he paid them *to* shut up about it."

"So?" I said.

"So he lied to you."

It was very late. I wished I was home in bed, curled up in a ball with the air-conditioning on.

"Well?" said Jack after a bit.

"Well, I guess you think I'm pretty dumb."

"I don't think you're dumb."

But I *was* dumb. I was stupid. Maybe even insane, by Albert Einstein's definition, doing the same thing over and over again and expecting different results. First Peter, now Don. I was the common denominator in both equations.

"You're not dumb, Germaine. I think you're . . . optimistic. You gave Don the benefit of the doubt. I think you thought he'd changed."

"People don't change," I said. Wasn't that what I'd told Sharon?

"People can change," said Jack, but I shook my head.

He gave me a condescending look. "You don't know anyone who's ever changed? No one?" The way he was saying it was like there was an obvious answer, but there wasn't. Or there was, and this was just another example of what a halfwit I was.

"Would you have ever thought *you* would be working on a telephone helpline?"

"That's not changing. That's getting a different job."

"But you *chose* to do it."

"No." I swallowed hard. "I didn't *choose*."

The cover on Jack's bed was brown and had shaggy edges that touched the ground. It had probably never been washed, but I had the urge to rip it off and hide beneath it. Bury myself in darkness, ignoring the old skin cells and whatever bacteria.

"There were some extenuating circumstances," I said.

Jack didn't move. The computer screen turned black as it went to power-saving mode.

"I had some challenges with my references." A familiar, queasy feeling returned. There were aspects of my relationship with Peter that I was loath to talk about. I couldn't think of them without feeling nauseous.

I'd never told Jack about Peter. With the exception of Sharon, I hadn't told anyone. Peter asked me not to, and in those quiet moments when it was just the two of us, that didn't seem to matter.

I remembered how it was having Peter's hands on my shoulders, his hot breath in my ear. He'd say, "Is the pressure okay?" when he was massaging, which it never was. It was always too soft, but that wasn't only his technique, it was also because he didn't want to hurt me.

Peter was quite sensitive. He worried, for instance, that other people teased him for dyeing his hair. He used to ask me all the time if anyone had. I'd say, "Who cares?" and he'd say, "I'm not as strong as you, Germaine."

I told him no one ever said anything, even though they had, they said it all the time. But he didn't have to know—what purpose did it serve? I didn't care if it was dyed. I would have dyed it for him if he'd asked.

"That's nice," said Jack, sounding strained.

But that was Peter's problem. He worried too much what other people thought. Certain other people, I should say. Not me.

Figure 2 (Persons at Fault for the Incident) is incorrect; the Incident was not caused by other people. Peter was just a straw on the back of the camel. If you have a logarithmic function that tends towards a number, all you need is a small amount to tip it over. It was a lot of things over a long time is what I'm saying.

"Peter sounds like . . ." Jack shook his head as if to say, *An unpleasant person*, or stronger words to that effect. "He sounds like *Don*" was how he eventually put it.

"See?" I said. "It's the same situation. I *am* stupid."

"Not stupid. Maybe a slow learner?" Jack folded the computer screen down, got up, and moved the laptop to the sink. Then he shifted his chair so he was sitting opposite me.

"You might not have *chosen* the helpline, but you're good at it."

"Yeah, yeah."

"It's true." Jack held his hands out, as if to ask for mine. I didn't give them to him, but slipped them under my buttocks. He let his fall to the table, turning the palms down.

"You're probably the best person on the helpline, you know."

There were only two helpline workers, three if you counted Marie, but still I blushed. Jack seemed to enjoy my blushing because he tried to exacerbate it.

"Maybe I'll nominate you for Employee of the Year," he said, even though he was the one who told me there was no nomination system, it was all up to the mayor.

"Hey, are you hungry?" said Jack. "There's three-fifths of a tomato inside, and I could probably cook some pasta."

"I'm okay." I was still tense, stomach clenching.

I looked around the room. The key feature was the single bed. "Do you guys top and tail?" I said.

"What?"

"You and Marie." I flapped my hand in the direction of the bed, very quickly, like I was flicking something disgusting off. "Do you top and tail?"

Jack looked horrified. I knew how he felt; I wasn't even sure why I was asking. "Marie's my half sister," said Jack.

Oh, God. "Is that legal?"

"We're not in a relationship, Germaine."

"Oh. *Oh*."

Jack's face was still contorted, like he was having trouble removing the image from his brain. I felt a bit better myself. Maybe it was helpful, this talking.

"She seems quite nice," I said.

Jack shook himself.

I could have stayed longer but then I wouldn't have got eight hours' sleep. I had to go for this reason. Jack walked me back to the main house. Before we went in I said, "Jack, you might be able to get some help for your mother, you know. You could call the helpline."

"Germaine. You know there's no nomination system, don't you? You are aware of that?"

"Are you sure, though? I'm just saying maybe check."

– 38 –

On the way home I was wide awake, buzzing like I'd had multiple cups of coffee. I turned the radio to a popular music station. I didn't know any of the words so I repeated them after the singer, a few beats behind, and wiggled on the driver's seat in the way of chair aerobics but with fewer leg lifts.

Marie was Jack's sister. I had a bit of a laugh to myself thinking about it. She *was* a nice person, actually. Fairly interesting, and had lots of helpful comments. I was glad they didn't top and tail in a single bed.

It was a very quick trip home. I got all the green lights, and the elevator at the apartment block was at car park level, just as I needed it. Everything seemed okay, what happened in the mayor's office moving from short- to long-term memory, until I walked in the door of my apartment and saw the trophies on the mantelpiece. A heavy coat the exact size and weight of Don Thomas fell across my shoulders. It buttoned itself up and couldn't be removed.

How embarrassing. Despite what Jack said, I wasn't a slow learner; I was a fool.

I didn't get my eight hours' sleep. I tossed and turned in bed, dredging up unpleasant memories—and what a lot there were, half buried in the sludge of my subconscious. The times Don and I talked and how what I *thought* he was thinking was not what he was really thinking. How he'd probably been thinking about her—the mayor. How the mayor used to like me but didn't anymore. How that was the course of most of my interactions with other people (except for the ones where people hadn't liked me to begin with). How it had been the course with Peter.

How I was not likable; how flawed I was and in what specific ways. E.g., bad at sports, terrible at board games. Even my hair: underwhelming in both color and style. I was unattractive. I had never not been unattractive.

There was nothing new in any of this, but cataloguing it all at once created an ugly picture.

When I was with Peter and he'd said, "Let's keep this a secret," at least he'd acknowledged there was a "this." Even if only in private.

Don hadn't. Because there was no "this." Sharon's words came back to me: *You have a way of latching on, Germaine.*

I began to doubt myself. What if I was *latching on* to Jack as well? Maybe my enjoyment had been one-sided. He and Marie could be discussing me right now.

"I couldn't get rid of her," Jack was saying.

"She is very strange," Marie was answering.

I put the pillow over my face and told myself, *Germaine, you will not make the same mistake again. You will not make the same mistake again.* I kept repeating it like counting sheep until I fell asleep.

In the morning, on the way to the office, I realized the one benefit to my relationship with Don ceasing to exist/never having existed was I didn't have to worry about hurting him anymore. I could try to stop the senior citizens center from being sold without any of the internal angst that previously characterized the situation. *Isn't that great?* I told myself.

Betsy had sent me the recipes they planned to use for the catering company and I had to work out how much they cost. It was simple. I just had to convert the wholesale price for each ingredient into a per-recipe figure and then divide by the number of serves. The only fiddly bit was converting the units. I had to write some basic algorithms based on weight-to-volume ratios. They were easy but for some reason I kept typing the formulas wrong.

Francine interrupted me. "Germaine." She was standing at the door, holding my handbag aloft. "Is this yours?"

I squinted at it, as though it might not be. "Yes." Then I dropped the pretense. "I can explain."

Francine shook her head, her fuzzy hair moving in a single Lego-like block. "No explanation necessary," she said.

But I did want to explain, at least partly. I shuddered to think what Francine might have thought we were doing in the mayor's office. An incorrect assumption could have been more embarrassing than the truth.

"Germaine." Francine held her hands up to stop me from speaking. "I don't need to know. All I want to say is: Be careful. The mayor's got enemies, but she's also got friends."

"Yes, *friends*. That's what I'm saying about Jack and me. We're friends. Less than friends, even. He's like a brother I don't even like. We weren't doing anything—"

Francine came in closer and put the handbag on my desk. Her enormous front teeth bit into her lip. "There's something else you should know."

"Okay." It didn't sound good.

"I told the mayor about your spreadsheet, the one with all the data. It was ages ago now, but she just sent an email. She's thinking about automating the helpline, making it all recorded messages." Francine adjusted one of the handles on the bag.

"Oh." When I'd imagined this moment, I thought it would be very different.

"She wants you to send it to me."

"I can send it," I said, slowly. "I just have to . . . fix a few things first."

When Francine was gone, I opened up my lovely spreadsheet. All that beautiful data, all those graphs and charts. It was so satisfying, the way I'd constructed it, how I'd linked the formulas, how I'd used different tabs for different types of analysis. I'd built a very clear picture, a convincing argument based on the evidence. Professor John

Douglas would have admired it greatly—not as a father, but as a fellow mathematician.

I clicked on the raw data page. There were rows and rows of information; almost every call I'd ever taken was listed there.

I scrolled down to look at them. A call from James, one from Betsy, one from Celia . . . They weren't all annoying. In fact, I noticed the "annoying" flag, the one I hoped would help identify people and numbers to block, had reduced in usage over time. It was as though fewer annoying people were calling. But this wasn't actually the case. The population hadn't changed; what had changed was how irritating I found them. They weren't strangers anymore, which made them harder to dislike.

It still broke my heart to do it.

I highlighted every single cell on every single sheet. When the screen was a dark color I pressed:

DELETE.

Then I saved the empty file.

− 39 −

In the afternoon there was a meeting at the senior center. Everyone was going, even Ralph, even Eva, even *Jack*. I didn't want to drive with the three of them, but we'd agreed to go together the previous day. There was no easy way of getting out of it.

Jack was driving and I was in the seat behind him. I didn't say one word the entire journey, just looked at the back of his head and avoided his eyes in the rearview mirror. He must have had limited visibility, because he kept turning around and looking out the back window.

Celia was thrilled with what Jack and I had discovered. She called the emails between the mayor and Don "leverage." She said now we had "leverage" there was no way the place would ever be sold. "Of course, we still need to discuss the matter with the mayor, and this catering business will be important if we're going to be self-sufficient, but that's all just details." She pointed at me. "You're going to have to talk to her."

"Me?" I didn't think it had to be me. It could be any of us. I was no more articulate than the next person, as I'd often been told.

"Oh, please. Don't be stupid. Germaine has to, doesn't she?" There was no formal vote but everyone present seemed to agree.

"There's just one small logistical problem," said Jack. "Bainbridge is away. I checked with Stacey and she's not back until the day of the ball. In fact, Stacey said the mayor's going straight to the golf club from the airport."

"Oh, dear," said Gladys.

But I was relieved. "That's okay. I'll email her."

No one was convinced by that suggestion. Jack pointed out that we might not want evidence of our own involvement, an argument others seemed to find compelling.

Celia said, "You'll have to talk to her at the ball. It's the only way."

There was another spontaneous nonvote: everyone (else) in favor.

"I wish I could be there," said Betsy, most out of character. "I'd love to see her face when you show her those emails."

"Me, too," said Gladys. "I wish we could *all* be there."

I didn't wish that. I was glad the event was sold out. I didn't want an audience for what was bound to be a sensitive conversation. What if I broke down and started crying?

"Wait." Eva's face lit up in a way I found troubling. "I have an idea."

"Maybe keep it to yourself?" I said.

"What if we *catered* the event? Wouldn't that be great?"

I shouldn't have let Eva come. It was only because she was so enthusiastic that I'd thought to include her. Now she was getting ahead of herself—quite a long way ahead—and wasn't everyone delighted? Weren't they all jumping about, saying, *Good idea, Eva* and *Aren't you clever?*

"It would be great exposure," said Jin-Jin. "We could get a few testimonials for the website."

I alone was the voice of reason. "Bit late now," I said. "I'm pretty sure they'd have their catering organized already. Can't do much about that, can we?"

Ralph coughed. "I have known instances in which licenses for food provision were suspended for short periods due to noncompliance. The list of terms is long and, *ahem*, open to interpretation."

I was shocked. One would have thought a health and safety inspector would be scrupulously impartial and beyond reproach, but it appeared this was a view only I held.

"Perfect," said Celia, and there was an energetic hum of approval for this blatant manipulation of power.

One would have also thought the main actor—the one person who was doing more than anyone and had a number of concerns (i.e., me)—should have had a greater say.

Apparently not.

After the meeting, en route to the car, Jack said, "Germaine, do you feel like walking back?" Ralph and Eva were ahead of us and gave each other looks. The looks were not discreet; I had to disabuse them of what they thought they knew.

"Jack and I were discussing the importance of moderate exercise as it relates to life expectancy," I said. "I have a pedometer on my phone."

For once, Eva didn't comment. All she said was, "Ralph, can we get Slurpees on the way back?"

But I told Jack I couldn't walk as I'd pulled a muscle in my knee—I wasn't going to make the same mistake twice. Then I ran to catch up with Eva and Ralph. "Yeah, can we, Ralph? I've never had a Slurpee."

- 40 -

I was not involved in the health and safety inspection but I knew it occurred because later that week Ralph advised me that the golf club's food and beverage license had been suspended until further notice. They'd been given a reprieve for the night of the mayoral ball, which was rapidly approaching, so long as an "external provider" was responsible for the catering.

I was nominated as the one to suggest that Don use the Olde World Catering Company, which, since Ralph had streamlined our accreditation, was up and ready to go.

I could have emailed Don or called him, but I went to see him instead. There were things I wanted to talk about in person.

I dressed carefully. I put on the shirt Don once said was "impressive." The mayor didn't have a shirt like that. No one did. It was a limited edition from ten years ago. I polished my shoes and wore tan-colored stockings.

I wasn't sure how I felt about seeing Don. My emotions had been a roller coaster. One minute I was embarrassed at how I'd thrown myself at him; the next I was furious he'd led me on. I didn't know what the truth was. You could argue either way.

I found Don in the bistro area of the golf club. He was in a booth up the back, doing paperwork. I tapped him on the shoulder and he jumped. "Germaine, you scared me."

"Did I?" I didn't apologize.

"It's okay. It's good you're here; I've been meaning to call you. I feel terrible about nearly running you over."

"You mean nearly killing me."

"Well . . . Killing's a bit much, isn't it?"

"Is it, Don? Is it?" I was in a picky mood. I don't know what I wanted him to say, but he wasn't saying it. Everything he said was wrong. Even when he said, "I'm glad you're okay."

"I'm glad you're glad," I said.

Don put his pen down, carefully, like the table was a miniature battlefield full of tiny land mines. "Germaine, *are* you okay? You seem . . . I don't know. Not yourself?"

"Not myself? How can a person *not* be themselves, Don? Isn't that exactly what they are? Don't they have to be . . . *themselves*?"

A cautious laugh. "That's a bit deep for me," he said.

I *was* myself. It was only because Don hadn't met the real me that he wasn't able to recognize it.

He tried to move us on to a new topic. It was his favorite: "Remember in 2006 when I was about to go to regionals? Did you know I got interviewed for *Lateline*? Have you seen that interview? It's still on YouTube." He swallowed. I watched his Adam's apple go up and down. "It comes up if you google *Alan Cosgrove Eastern Region Sudoku Melbourne 2006*. Anyway, it doesn't matter. Hey, how are my trophies going?"

"Want to see?" I said with assertive—possibly aggressive—enthusiasm.

He moved back about thirty-five millimeters. "Yes?"

I got out my phone and showed him a photo: Gauss and Archimedes in their bowl on the mantelpiece. Just those two, nothing else. No trophies, no medals, no certificates.

"Ah . . . I don't understand," said Don.

"*I've been meaning to call you* . . . I feel terrible . . . I had to get rid of them."

I enjoyed watching his face. How it went from shock and disbelief to horror and then sadness.

"Yeah, I binned them. *All of them.* I tried selling them, but no one was interested. You know if you mention the name Alan Cosgrove, people's first thought is 'cheat.' Or sometimes 'liar.'" I put a hand to my chin, thoughtful. "But you probably *do* know that, don't you?"

Don fussed with his collar. "Have I done something to upset you, Germaine?"

"I don't know, Don . . . have you?" I stared at him.

He coughed. "I told Verity I saw you and Celia in the car. It just came up in conversation, I wasn't . . . I didn't *suggest* anything."

"You and Verity seem close."

He flinched. "We are close."

"Very close."

Don examined the hands in his lap. They were his hands, the ones he'd always had: i.e., they did not warrant such consideration.

"I heard you had a problem with your kitchen," I said.

"Yes. Health inspectors. I don't know why . . . But don't worry. Verity's going to fix it. She'll turn it around. Eventually." He gave a half laugh. "Don't know anyone who will cater a ball on short notice, do you?"

I felt like people didn't really acknowledge what a feat it was, getting him to say yes. When I told the committee (et al.), they acted like it was a foregone conclusion.

"Our menus *are* world class," said Eva.

"We just have to practice cooking them," said Betsy.

"And find some people to wait the tables," said Gladys.

"And order uniforms," said Jin-Jin.

"And get a refrigerated van," said Ralph.

"*Also*: Don's an idiot," said Celia.

Only Jack seemed impressed. He came to see me in my office and said, "That was quite complicated maneuvering, what you did with Don."

I agreed. "It *was* complicated."

"But you did it. I knew you could." Then he asked if I wanted to go for a drink to celebrate. By drink he meant alcoholic beverage.

I wasn't opposed to the idea. I said I'd be happy to, and we organized to meet at a pub on Friday, after work concluded.

Before Jack left, I asked him if he intended for other people to attend the drink. He said it would be just the two of us. It was only when he confirmed this that I understood it was what I'd been hoping for.

There is a lot of research on relationships but not enough of it is empirical; far too much is qualitative. That's why I don't think psychology is a science. It's a humanity, maybe even a form of fiction. I read every article in the *Australian Journal of Psychology* and its American equivalent from 2016 to the present day and *still* I was uncertain as to the categorization of my relationship with Jack. I was determined not to make a fool of myself.

What I needed was some way of understanding what was currently going on and the likely future trajectory. Trajectories are tricky though, as evidenced by Figure 1 (Career Trajectory), which pertained to my career. Just because you *think* something might happen or you want it to doesn't mean it will.

Not that I wanted anything to happen. I was simply interested, as one party *in* the relationship, in what its nature was.

One way of understanding this was to consider my scoring system.

The research said that people are attracted to other people who are as attractive as they are. In crude terms: If I was an 8 and my significant other was a 7, regardless of the specific scale or system of ranking, then I would always think I could do better. Conversely, if I ranked my partner a 9 and me an 8, then I would always think I was overachieving. If we were both 9s or 8s or even 2s, then we'd both be happy.

But I knew that a person's appeal could fluctuate.

People can be more or less attractive the better you know them. Take Don/Alan Cosgrove. In the days when he was sudoku champion, a man I greatly admired, he was a 9.999 recurring. Now he was a 1.6. *Most* of the time I was an 8.8 but I'd been as high as a 9.2. During that black period after I left Wallace's I went down to a

4.3. My lowest ebb was the day I looked into the eyes of a butcher, elbow deep in pigs' tails, and winked.

The question was: What was Jack's number?

When I first met him, I decided he was a 3.7. But he'd improved since then. At the picnic he was a 6, and at his house he was a 7.5 (refer to Figure 6).

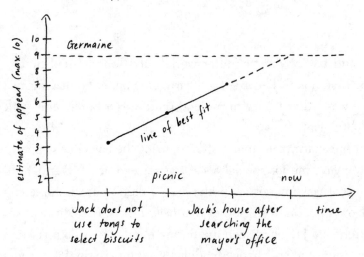

6. Jack's Appeal (Subjective Attractiveness) Over Time

There was a line of best fit, but could I extrapolate it out? Or was this an incorrect application of the theory?

I ruled it inconclusive, but it was my current favorite graph. I thought there was something very pleasing about it.

Jack and I were meeting after work, but I found I had time to go home first, mainly because I left early. One benefit of having my own office was I didn't have to pretend there was a family emergency: I could just leave.

At the apartment I took a shower, using the lavender-scented soap Sharon gave me for special occasions instead of the Dettol antibacterial that was my normal preference. I didn't put the same clothes back on. I put on fresh clothes that *looked* the same. This was so that if perchance Jack had seen me during the day he wouldn't know I'd come home and got changed. I didn't want him to think I was making an effort; he might get the wrong impression. Or at least an impression he didn't reciprocate.

Was I really an 8.8, or did I have an inflated sense of self?

The tram into the city was slow and nervous, but even so I was in Swan Street ten minutes early. I checked the location of the pub again on my phone. It hadn't moved, it was still down a side street near the supermarket.

I didn't mind if I was the first one there. It meant I could sit down and plant The List in a discreet location, maybe tape it to the leg of the table. I'd never needed The List with Jack before, but this time I decided to bring it with me—a modified version—just in case. I felt it in my pocket, a comforting wad of folded paper.

I don't know what I was concerned about. Sometimes when we had lunch Jack and I would sit in silence *most* of the time; we might hardly speak at all, and it didn't matter. Those silences felt effortless and not just because we were chewing. We weren't thinking about what to say next or worrying what other people thought. We weren't thinking about anything, really. We were just . . . being, which was probably complacent of us and certainly typical of Jack.

The pub had two levels, and Jack had said to meet on the top. I took the stairs, three at a time.

When I came out there was a small undercover area, a holding bay where people could gather if it was raining or if there were a lot of people going up and down. Neither of these things was occurring, but Jack was sitting there anyway, waiting for me, on the one and only bench.

When he saw me, he stood up.

I couldn't believe what Jack was wearing. I was glad I'd been home to freshen up. In fact, I regretted not having put something different on because not only did Jack have a T-shirt with a printed tie on the front (bow variety, black) but:

Pants.

I pointed at them and Jack grinned in a way that could only be described as "goofy."

"Aren't you hot?" I said, regretting the sentiment the instant it slipped out; but Jack's only response was that he'd been misinformed about the rate of heat loss via exposed limbs.

We left the undercover area and approached the bar. The sign said it was HAPPY HOUR, inaccurately, as it went from five p.m. to seven p.m. During this time pots of beer (285 mL) were $2.50 and jugs (1 L) were $8.

Jack asked for two pots but I stopped the bartender from getting them. I said to Jack that based on cost per liter the jug was the better option. He said that jugs were problematic. According to him, a set proportion of the beer in any receptacle went flat by the time you got to the bottom. This proportion was manageable in a single serve (it was just a mouthful or two) but in a jug the issue was magnified.

"It's not worth it," he said. "No one wants a flat beer, do they?"

This was disappointing. It not only showed Jack as a spendthrift, but also suggested that when he'd said "a drink" he really did mean "a."

Jack paid for the drinks and we carried them to a table. When we were sitting down, he raised his glass and said, "To the Olde World Catering Company's first gig."

"And my ability to convince Don to take us on."

We chinked our glasses and sipped the beer.

"So, tell me. How did old Greg Norman take the news? What did he say when you told him you knew what he and the mayor were trying to do?"

As stated previously, whereas everyone else had been blasé about my meeting with Don, Jack was very interested. We hadn't discussed the specifics of it yet because, strangely, once he suggested we have *a* drink, we'd stopped talking. Normally we sent emails multiple times a day, or he'd call down either on the phone or in person, but for the past three days there'd been none of that. It was very unusual.

At the pub, Jack said, "I hope he was worried. I hope he thinks he's going to jail for corruption. He could get fifteen years, you know."

I wiped my upper lip. "We didn't really talk about it," I said.

"Oh." Jack seemed disappointed. "Did you tell him you knew about the sudoku competition?"

"No."

"Oh." Jack looked in his beer, as if for answers. "I guess he did it as a personal favor, did he?"

"I'm not sure." There was a reason "Don" was not a topic of conversation on The List. I tried to think of what *was* on The List, but it was stuck in my pocket. I should have got there earlier. You can never be too early. "I don't think he had a lot of options. And Betsy is surprisingly well known."

Jack nodded. He didn't look very happy about Betsy's level of fame. I tried to think of things that he might be happy about. Maybe it would have been better if we'd invited other people along to the pub. A group.

"Nice tie," I said, pointing at his top.

Normally, Jack would have recounted the story of the top's origin. Like *My mum got it for me* or *It was free with a six-pack*, but he was awfully quiet. All he said was, "This one?" Followed by: "Did you *want* to tell Don you knew he cheated at sudoku? Because I can give you all the information."

"No, I don't really . . ." I lifted my shoulders up and let them fall again. "I don't care. I already knew Don wasn't who I thought he was."

It was as if I'd proven Betsy *wasn't* famous: Jack was very pleased.

That's when I remembered something from The List, the modified version. It was a topic I'd thought about for a while but hadn't mentioned yet. Whenever I went to, it seemed stupid and unimportant, but now I wanted to tell him.

I ran my hand along the tabletop. "Remember that picnic you did?"

"Yes."

"I didn't say it at the time but . . . it was a very nice picnic."

I didn't look at him, just at the table, but I knew he had the stupid grin again, the goofy one.

"Was it?" he said.

"Probably the best one I've been to," I said.

"Really?"

"Yeah. But I haven't been to many."

– 42 –

Though Jack had said "a drink" and chose a size of beverage that rein-forced this idea, we had more than one. We had several and he paid for all of them, even those consumed after happy hour, when there was a thirty percent increase in the price.

By the time we came out of the pub it was dark outside and all the streetlights had turned on. In the sky the moon was visible, a cres-cent shape. It was not a comma but a tick: approving.

Jack said, "Maybe we should go for dinner?"

I said, "The Red Emperor's open until nine."

We started walking to the tram stop, two abreast on the footpath. When we reached the main road, Jack cut around the back of me to be on the outer side, closer to the cars. As he did, he caught my hand and squeezed.

I squeezed back, but harder.

Then he squeezed harder, then I did, then he did, then I did, then we had to stop because otherwise someone* was going to break a finger.

There was a lot of work to be done in a short space of time. So much so, I relocated from Ron Steven's office in the downstairs basement of the town hall to the one at the senior center. It was easier, less commut-ing. I didn't mention my transfer to Francine. I just put a sign on the door that said BACK IN FIVE MINUTES. No one seemed to notice.

At the center, Betsy was working hard on her recipes. She had a

---

*It wasn't going to be me.

lot of sweet ones but had to expand her savory repertoire. Eva came periodically to help, which was not as bad as you would have thought. Her palate was surprisingly refined. She knew if a dish had a pinch too much salt or insufficient butter. She even came up with the idea of separating a sausage roll into parts and calling it "deconstructed." And she *loved* Betsy's ginger chutney. They were working on a jam line.

Eva's presence didn't negatively impact the helpline, either, and not just because of how useless she'd been. Back at the town hall, Marie Curie was staffing the phones on her own. I was glad Marie was helping, and glad I didn't have to be around her. My opinion of her hadn't improved *that* much.

I was trying to source some branded serviettes when Betsy came to get me. She'd changed out of her apron and had runners on. "You coming?"

"Sure am."

Chair aerobics. I'd been going every day, and the muscles in my legs were building; you could see them when I walked. I'd verified this in the mirror, when trying on my dress for the mayoral ball, which was "black tie."

The dress was not new; I'd worn it previously, at my high school formal. It still fitted—pretty much, though Jin-Jin said purple velvet was kind of dated, and Sharon said, "You don't have to wear a tie as well, Germaine," but what did those two know about dress codes?

Betsy and I got stuck in the hall, behind a woman walking with the aid of a stepper. She was very slow. When I hissed, "Can't we go around?" Betsy shushed me. "They won't start without us, Germaine."

The class was nearly full: There were only three seats left in the room and that included Betsy's up near the front. Of the two other seats, one was the second best in the whole room. It was next to James, who was in the first best. He'd been getting to classes earlier and earlier.

The woman with the stepper approached the good seat, but James put his hand on it. "This one's taken," he said, and looked around her to me. He was a much nicer person since his pension payment got sorted. Stress does funny things to people.

The woman with the stepper hobbled off to the other chair, which was right down at the other end. It took her ages to get there.

When I got back to the office, Celia was there, on the computer. If it had been a Tuesday or a Thursday, Charlie would have been with her. Those days she brought him in after school, but this was a Wednesday so it was just the two of us.

"I'm nearly done," she said, jabbing the keyboard with her index fingers. "Just getting this newsletter finished. Gladys has been too busy with all this fund-raising for her presidential duties."

I started stretching, an unusual stretch to begin with, involving covering both ears. It made me feel awkward when Celia mentioned positions on the committee, particularly the presidential one.

"Not long now." Celia was staring at the computer screen. "Until the ball, I mean. Excited?"

I was not excited. Talking to the mayor used to be the highlight of my day but it was no longer something I was looking forward to.

"I'd love to be the one confronting her," said Celia. "But no one seems to think I'm the right person."

I did a different stretch, this time arm-related.

"If I was the one talking to her, I'd say, I know that policy was a lie. I know you just wanted to get rid of me."

And back to the ear-covering "stretch." It wasn't very good at blocking out the noise. I could still hear Celia's voice.

"I'd say, Don't you have anything better to do than kick little old ladies off committees?"

I mumbled something into my arm.

"What's that?" Celia stopped typing.

"I said . . ." I coughed. "It wasn't the *mayor's* idea to remove you from the committee."

Celia frowned. "Whose was it then?"

I put my head down and winced at the floor. "Mine?"

Celia said nothing. I wondered if she'd heard. I lifted my head up. "It was mine."

- 43 -

The morning of the ball, Celia called a committee meeting. We came together in the kitchen and lined up along one side of the long silver bench. Celia paced back and forth on the other: a general briefing the troops before battle. "Betsy, what's the status on food? Estimated time of departure is four o'clock."

"We'll be ready." Betsy wiped her hands on a tea towel. "The mini-quiches are almost done, and the rest is just prep. We have to cook or assemble it over there. Right, Eva?"

Eva was wearing an apron that said KISS THE COOK; she made it herself using a tea towel and a Sharpie. "Right," she said. "Except for the bacon brioches, but they're going in the oven shortly."

Eva really did seem to have found her calling. Not only did she display a level of enthusiasm over and above anything she'd shown previously (including as related to the biscuit petition), she also had a knack. I didn't use the word *genius* often, and I certainly wouldn't have used it to describe her. But she was very good with flavors. Her weird and (often) delicious combinations—grapefruit on goats cheese with almond sprinkle or chicken liver parfait cones and mar-malade topping—gave the Olde World Catering Company what Jin-Jin described on the website as a "modern edge."

There had been some debate about the phrasing.

"How can you be 'olde world' if you have a 'modern edge'?" I said. "You're old or you're new; you can't be both."

"It's called 'fusion,'" said Jin-Jin. "And it's very important to the target market."

"It's called a 'contradiction in terms.'"

"Germaine," Jin-Jin said, in an almost Jack-like way.

In the kitchen, Celia did an about-turn and marched in the opposite direction. "Jin-Jin, Jack. The waitstaff?"

Jin-Jin and Jack were responsible for "front of house." Jin-Jin because she'd waited tables in the past and Jack because he insisted on helping and it was that or get him to play the ukulele. He didn't have the most versatile skill set, though he had been quite helpful with the web design. He and I had to interact a lot over that. Quite a lot, actually.

Jin-Jin and Jack had recruited an enthusiastic but not overly polished team from the homework club. "They'll be here at three," said Jack.

"And they know what they're doing?" said Celia, peering over the top of her glasses.

Jack thought for a moment. "More or less."

Celia ticked "waitstaff" off her list.

"Now, Gladys. The meet and greet. Are you ready?"

Gladys was responsible for liaising with Don when they arrived, working out where to park the refrigerated van, where to come in, all that boring stuff. This meant Betsy and Eva could get on with the cooking, and it would free me up, when the time came, to speak to Mayor Bainbridge.

Speak to Mayor Bainbridge. As though it was just a conversation. Like the future of this place and everyone in it didn't depend on that one exchange of words and ideas.

No pressure.

Celia stopped pacing and looked at us one by one.

"This is it," she said. "You know what to do. Betsy and Eva, keep cooking. Jack, Jin-Jin, make sure the service is top-notch. Gladys, ignore Don if he gets annoyed. And Germaine—"

All eyes were on me.

"Good luck?" said Betsy.

"Germaine, just remember who your friends are," said Celia.

She might have still been a bit annoyed with me. I don't know. Just a thought.

I had to go home to get ready. I told Jack I was leaving, and he walked me to the car. When we got there, I stood against the driver's-side door with my hands behind me. "What do you think's the probability we'll pull this off?" I said.

Jack said, "Two hundred percent."

"There's no such thing as a probability of two hundred percent."

"*Germaine.*" Jack came closer; he wanted to lean against one of the car doors, too. Thing was, he chose the same door, so my body was in between. He pressed into me. "You know what I mean," he said.

I try to discourage the use of incorrect hyperbole, but on this occasion I lowered my standards.

"Yeah," I said. "I know what you mean."

When I got back to my apartment, I had two hours to get ready. I would have had a bath, but Sharon was coming over, for reasons unexplained. She'd called earlier in the week to inquire about the well-being of Archimedes and Gauss, who were not only alive but thriving. "Maybe I'll come and see them on Saturday night," she said.

"You can, but I won't be there. That's the night of the ball."

"Oh," said Sharon. "How exciting." She was being sarcastic. I hadn't told her about the reordering of my priorities vis-à-vis the senior citizens center.

When I explained how the situation had evolved, she went quiet. I had to check the call hadn't dropped out. "Are you there?" I said.

"I'm here. It's just . . ." Sharon was never lost for words, but this was one occasion on which she was.

She found them eventually. "I can't believe you're single-handedly stopping the sale of an old people's home."

"I'm not," I said. "It's not an old people's home; it's a community center. It's not single-handed; there are others involved. And we probably won't succeed."

"But you're trying," said Sharon. Then she got a frog in her throat and had to hang up.

Now, she buzzed, and when I let her in, she was carrying a black suit bag on a wire hanger. "This is for you," she said, handing it to me.

The bag was old and crumpled. From a secondhand shop, I could tell, which made me want to put on gloves and a disposable mask.

However, I held the hanger while Sharon unzipped the bag. I was braced for the worst, which was also the most likely because Sharon had terrible taste, as characterized by her love of cheesecloth.

"I have a dress already," I warned her as the bag came off.

But it was pretty nice at first glance.

It wasn't cheesecloth, and it wasn't paisley. It was long and red, and when I held it up, the fabric seemed to shimmer.

"Turn it over. There was a tiny problem at the back, but Marion helped me fix it."

What a shame. I knew then it would be terrible, with some major issue made worse by Sharon and Marion trying to reduce the magnitude of the original problem. Those two had a very lax approach: not just zero attention to detail, but also a willingness to look foolish in public. They were very embracing of that.

I turned the dress over. On the upper-upper back, the fabric was red. Around the middle-back was where they'd performed their alterations. A large square of fabric had been sewn on. Most people would have done this in red. Typically, Sharon and Marion would have chosen a shade of red close to but not exactly the same as the rest of the dress. On this occasion, however, they'd picked a white satin. Then, using black sequins, they'd sewn nine small boxes on it, three across and three down. Two-thirds of the boxes had numbers in them, the rest were blank.

"It's a level six," said Sharon. "I got it off the World Puzzle Federation website."

"A level *six*? But I've never—"

"I think you can do it," she said.

It would be hard to do while wearing it; I might have to look in double mirrors. But I didn't mind that. Seeing myself from a different angle.

"Do you like it?" said Sharon. "You don't have to wear it if you don't like it."

"No." I looked at it again, then at Sharon. "I like it."

Sharon dropped me at the golf club on her way home. "You're very quiet," she said on the way there. "Something up?"

"No. I'm just thinking." It was an important night. There were a lot of logistical elements involved, and I had to keep track of them.

Jack had messaged when he and the senior citizens and the homework clubbers got in the buses to go to the golf club. I was glad I wasn't there when they arrived. I didn't want to see Don's face when he realized whom he'd hired. I hadn't lied, as such, but I had excluded fifty-one percent of the relevant information.

Predictably, the car park at the golf club was full, and there was a long line of cars waiting to drop guests at the entrance. In the distance, we could see the red carpet running down the steps and the large banner that hung from the portico. It had a picture of the mayor.

Sharon wound her window down. "That her, is it?" she said.

"That's what it says, Sharon. In quite big letters."

From here, the mayor looked perfect: Her hair was straight, her face was symmetrical, and her teeth were as good as ever. But sometimes looks could be deceiving. Like you wouldn't know my dress had a level six sudoku on the back if you were looking from the front. Like you wouldn't know some crappy old building had some pretty nice things inside (not including furniture but including people).

Sharon patted me on the knee. "I'm proud of you."

"Why? I haven't done anything yet."

"Doesn't matter what happens. Even if this is a spectacular failure, which it probably will be, I'll still be proud."

It was the stupid dress. There must have been dust on it, or some other allergen, to get my eyes watering like that.

I should have worn the mask.

- 44 -

The nice moment didn't last. When we got to the front of the queue, Sharon wouldn't let me out of the car until I promised to call her at the end of the night and tell her what had happened. She locked the doors and everything, even after I agreed—she was being "funny." I didn't wave at her as I went up the steps and into the building.

Inside, the foyer was full of people—men in black tuxedos and women in long shiny dresses. Mine was the only one that served a dual purpose, which was not unexpected. It didn't seem like any of them noticed, though. Me or my attire.

The catering staff stood at intervals along the wall, holding trays of food and drink. I recognized their faces from the homework club. It was heartening how professional they looked, especially given how challenged most of them were in other ways, e.g., numerically.

"Champagne?" One held his tray out. It took me a second to realize it was Jack. He was wearing pants again. I pointed at them.

"Yeah." He moved his tray to the side to look down. "They're part of the uniform. You'd be happy about that."

I did like pants; they were what most people wore in most situations, certainly in the workplace. However, I wasn't sure if I liked them on Jack. His knees were one of his best features: Why cover them? When I said this to Jack, he seemed very pleased. His chest puffed up like a peacock.

I took a glass off Jack's tray and drank some wine, hoping the alcohol might have a relaxing effect. It didn't seem to. My stomach was still folded along a series of invisible dotted lines.

"Good luck," said Jack.

I gave him back the glass and continued down the hall.

Don had shown me the dining room on our tour of the clubhouse, but that was when it wasn't decorated. Now it had been transformed. All the tables had white tablecloths and white napkins and little vases with white flowers and glasses that seemed to twinkle in the light. The chairs were covered in fabric and had bows around their middles.

The mayor's table was up the front. I had to sidestep around people to get there. It was empty, save for one person. His face did not light up when he saw me.

"Germaine," said Don. "I wish you'd told me."

"Told you what?"

Don gave a disbelieving look, but it was lost on me. I was immune. I felt nothing for him.

"If I'd known who it was, I wouldn't have hired them," he said, which was obvious. Don was not as clever as I'd thought. I was glad I didn't love him; his stupidity would have been wearing, in time.

"I thought we were friends," he said. Once, I would have cherished these words, dissected his every inflection. Now I found I didn't care to.

Don went to say something further, but then his eyes shifted and his expression changed.

The mayor had arrived.

The sea of people seemed to part as she moved through it, from the foyer, past tables and more tables to our table.

"Hello, Don." She did not acknowledge me, but kissed him on both cheeks. He held her arm lightly, and they stood close together. The spatial orientation of their bodies with respect to mine seemed to confirm how distant we'd become.

I cleared my throat and called across the abyss: "Hi, Verity." It felt weird saying that. Like calling a teacher by her first name.

She didn't answer, so I said it again. "*Hi*, Verity."

"Germaine. What a lovely outfit."

"Thank you."

She made a shrill sound, a bit like a laugh, but not a laugh. "I'm surprised you came."

"You invited me," I pointed out.

"That was *before*. The situation has changed, don't you think, Germaine?" Her mouth twisted in a cruel way. "But maybe you're not capable of independent thought?"

She was trying to wound me with her little barbs. But I had my force field up. "I have something to tell you," I said.

"Not now, Germaine. Not a good time." She leaned into Don, murmuring in his ear: "Is the premier here?"

"Not yet," he said.

I was not enjoying this. They were being . . . the only word I could think of was *mean*. But it didn't affect me. My heart felt full. I wasn't hungry for something to top it up.

"It involves both of you," I said.

"Are you still here?" Her voice was mocking.

All of us had jobs, and mine was to impart the message. I had to make her listen, and soon. The dinner was scheduled to start any minute. I could raise the amplitude and/or frequency of my voice, but the issue was sensitive. My proposal might be misconstrued; whereas if I kept it private, I could maintain plausible deniability. I remembered Celia saying, "It's not blackmail; it's a reciprocal relationship," but sometimes these fine distinctions can be obscure to the untrained eye.

I had to think. But in emergency situations the amygdala floods the cortex with adrenaline, triggering a fight-or-flight reaction—not a thinking one. I started getting flummoxed. Also, the champagne had affected my mental agility.

Then Celia appeared.

And beside her was Betsy. And beside Betsy was Gladys, and behind them were Jack and Eva and Jin-Jin and Vera and a long line of catering staff. All of them, on my side of the equation.

"Oh, God," said the mayor. "Can we get security?"

"I'd hold that thought if I were you," said Celia. She gestured to me, and I bent down to unpin a piece of paper from inside the hem of my dress. I began to read aloud.

"Email dated May seventh, last year. Sender: Alan Donald Cosgrove. Dear Verity, Can you get those old people to stop parking in that car park? I thought you said you'd have them out by Christmas."

I didn't need to look to know I had captivated my audience. The mayor might have thought she was an unstoppable force, but I was an immovable object. What would happen if we collided?

The mayor seemed equally unsure. The look she gave Don didn't require a cryptographer to decipher. "Perhaps we should take this conversation elsewhere," she said.

I said I didn't mind where we had the conversation.

Celia said she didn't mind either. Actually, none of the seniors center affiliates were all that particular.

The mayor asked Don for the keys to his office.

We followed the mayor to Don's office. All of us, including most of the catering staff. (I hoped the water carafes in the dining room had already been filled; we didn't want to jeopardize our Responsible Service of Alcohol certificate.) On the way, the mayor seemed to undergo a metamorphosis. By the time we got there she was calmer and there was less hissing. Her voice was like silk: "Welcome, everyone. Thanks for coming. It's always a treat to meet with my constituents." She extended her arms in an inclusive fashion. "How can I be of service?"

I was succinct in our list of demands. They were very modest, I told her. Only a commitment *not* to sell ONE (1) senior citizens center and a guarantee that ONE (1) senior citizens center would not be sold in the future.

"I'm listening to what you're saying, Germaine. I am listening, *however . . .*" She winced to simulate sympathy. "It's not that easy. You might think I'm all-powerful, but I'm not. The council's voted."

A voice up the back, near the door, called down: "That's what you said about the biscuits."

"Is that Eva?" The mayor tried to find her, looking over people's heads. "I must say I'm disappointed to see you here."

Eva was not affected by the mayor's disappointment. "Could you please stick to the specific line of questioning at hand?" she said.

"Fine. The council didn't have to vote on the biscuits. That was *within my discretion.*"

Celia said, "What a coincidence. We have some emails that are *within our discretion.*"

Normally the mayor was unflappable, but this seemed to flap her. Her mask began to slip. "What emails? I don't know how you . . . If those are . . . I don't believe those were obtained in a legal manner."

Don, who'd been silent until now, chimed in. "Yes. I'd like to understand how you came to be in possession of them."

Celia said we couldn't comment on the method of obtaining the emails, but the *Deepdene Courier* was *very* interested in their content.

The mayor's lovely hair had frizzed around her forehead, forming an ironic crown. "It's not how it looks. It's all very aboveboard. There are a lot of complex processes, internal checks, and things you wouldn't know about going on behind the scenes." She was sweating now; there was a sheen on her forehead. "Isn't that right, Don?"

Don agreed. "Oh yes. Very complex."

"That's okay. The *Courier* is well versed in these kinds of issues," said Celia. "Remember the exposé they did on petrol stations and money laundering? Those guys went to jail, you know."

The mayor pressed her lips together. Her face was impassive, but her eyes looked like an angry tiger was trapped inside.

"In fact"—Celia was enjoying herself—"their reporter will be here any minute, if you want to explain more fully."

"That's not necessary," said the mayor. "We're all reasonable; I'm sure we can sort something out. Why don't we talk about it next week? Germaine, call Stacey. Ask her to set something up for Monday or Tuesday. Whatever's convenient."

She was delaying: That was her tactic. Jack said she'd try this so she could clean up her emails, delete the ones that were incriminating. "It would be easier if we talked about it now," I said. "No time like the present."

The angry tiger inside the mayor was ready to come out. It was being held back by the barest of threads. "Look, this is all one big misunderstanding. But I can see you're upset. You don't want the center sold, and that's understandable. Unfortunately, at this point in time, even if I *wanted* to stop the sale, I couldn't. Once the council votes, it's almost impossible to *un*vote. Isn't it, Don?"

Don had no particular expertise in local government standing orders, but the way he agreed, you would have thought he did. I couldn't bear to look at him.

I said, "*Almost* impossible is not the same as *im*possible."

The mayor had been trying to hang on to her calmness, but now it seemed to get away from her. "Germaine," she said, "you're an intelligent person, aren't you? Surely you understand there are limits to what I can do."

"Actually," I said, "I don't know *that* much about democracy. You probably know more than me, in fact." This was quite generous, given the circumstances. And I encouraged her further: "If anyone can do it, you can."

My faith was apparently not a solace to her. She said, "You're not the only ones in the municipality, you know. There are other people . . . They don't all want to hang around a senior citizens center."

"I don't know why," said Celia. "We have a very varied program. And an employment scheme, too, now."

The mayor didn't listen to her. "Germaine." She lowered her voice. "What's all this about? You don't want to go back on the helpline? Fine. You want to stay in that office? No problem. You want an official promotion? *I can organize that.*"

I wasn't even tempted.

Don said, "Would you like a complimentary golf membership? On the house, no fees for ten years. What about my 2008 medal? I was meant to hand it back, but I never did."

"*Don.* No one wants your stupid medal," said the mayor, and he recoiled as if scorched. I felt a small amount of sympathy for him. He only wanted to be noticed. That's all he'd ever wanted. It was a shame he had to go about it in such an annoying way.

The mayor said, "Germaine, think about this . . . You don't want to burn bridges. It's not what it looks like. Do you really want to . . . For these people?"

I looked around the room. They were all there: Celia, Betsy, Gladys . . . Eva, Jack, Jin-Jin . . . Vera . . . Others whose names I hadn't bothered to learn.

"Yes," I said. "I quite like these losers."

"Germaine," said Jack.

"What?"

I turned back to the mayor. "It would be good if you could make the announcement today. The reporter is coming to attend the speeches."

Celia added, "And it would be nice if you remained in your current position as long as is practicable. We're quite attached to you, Verity."

The mayor lowered herself into Don's chair. She put her head on the desk a moment.

Don whispered, "Do it, Verity. I don't want to go to jail."

The mayor's voice might have been muffled, but her sentiment was crystal clear: "Shut up, Don."

- 45 -

We had to save our celebrations until after the event. The Olde World Catering Company saw every single guest in attendance as a potential future customer, so we left the mayor and Don in Don's office and everyone returned to their allocated duties.

My duties had officially concluded, and Celia didn't have any—aside from acting as escort to the *Deepdene Courier* reporter, and he hadn't arrived yet—so the two of us went and stood at the entrance to the dining room.

We watched the waitstaff mill around and top up people's glasses. It was okay for a while, but once the entrées came out we were in the way. Though hungry, I was not inclined to go and sit at the mayor's table. She and Don had entered the room the back way, via the stage. They were now seated, and, periodically, the mayor would turn and glare at Celia and me.

Celia and I went out to the foyer. There were a couple of chairs near where reception was. We sat on them, side by side, with a plate of Betsy's manchego and gorgonzola straws.

"That didn't go too badly," said Celia. "Considering."

I thought so, too, but I was glad it was over. The conversation with the mayor had been difficult. A level six in sudoku terms, maybe even a level seven, if such a thing existed, because it involved feelings. These were not only unpredictable; they could be very unpleasant, which was why I generally tried to avoid them.

On some occasions, though, when you pressed them down, they popped straight back up.

Like now, for example. I started folding my serviette into rectangles. I was glad Celia and I weren't looking at each other.

"Celia," I said.

"What?"

I coughed. There seemed to be a crumb stuck in my throat.

"Well . . . I think maybe I was wrong."

She didn't respond straightaway. There was a low murmur coming from the dining room, but it was not so loud I couldn't hear the chair creak as she uncrossed her legs and put both feet on the floor.

I clarified. "I probably shouldn't have made a fake policy and used it to get rid of you."

"Don't worry. I've already forgotten about it."

"If you've forgotten about it, how do you know what I'm talking about?"

Celia looked up at the ceiling. "Maybe we were both wrong," she said. "Maybe there were some occasions, a few, perhaps, when I got . . . overwrought. Those letters I wrote . . . Maybe some of them, one or two, were unnecessary."

I couldn't see Celia's face, but I felt very close to her. We *were* close—our elbows were nearly touching.

We sat in silence for a minute. Then I said, "How many of the letters do you think you got wrong?"

"I don't know, Germaine."

"Twenty percent? Thirty percent?"

"Fine, twenty percent."

What an understatement. She was way off. But I was okay with it. If I could be half wrong, she could be sixty to seventy percent incorrect also. I'd give her that.

Darren Hinkley from the *Deepdene Courier* came at exactly eight o'clock. The speeches weren't expected to start until around half past, so we had a bit of time.

Celia, Darren, and I went down to the kitchens to see Betsy and Eva. I asked Darren if he wanted to take some photos of the newest catering company in the municipality, but he said he was the politics reporter and it wasn't relevant to his beat.

"When are you going to give me this big tip-off?" he said.

"Soon," said Celia.

Don was the host of the evening's official proceedings. He got out of his chair and stood on the stage in front of a lectern. He was handsome in his suit; I could still see the glimmer of Alan in him, but it was an older, sadder, more pathetic version. He'd lost his sparkle. He seemed preoccupied, too. Maybe he was thinking this might be one of the last times he'd be able to make a speech in his precious golf club. Who knew what would happen to it now?

Oh, well. He'd reinvented himself once; he'd have to do it again.

After Don introduced her, Mayor Bainbridge got up. I hadn't written a speech for her; it seemed like a waste of time. She must have written it herself, and of course she now had to ad-lib in some new bits. I felt I could make allowances, but it was clear she should get professional help in future. The speech was quite long-winded and very boring, even for someone listening as intently as all of us.

"On behalf of the Deepdene Council, I'd like to welcome you here today. As you know, proceeds from tonight's ball go to the National Dementia Foundation. Dementia is an issue that I'm sure has touched us all." She cited some facts about it, but since none of the source material was disclosed, no one knew if any of it was true.

Then she told a very convenient anecdote.

In a voice dripping with sincerity, she began to talk about her great-aunt Ethel—allegedly, her favorite person in the whole world.

"Can't imagine anyone but Verity Bainbridge would be Verity Bainbridge's favorite person," said Celia under her breath.

"Great-aunt Ethel began to forget things." The mayor dabbed the side of her eye with an open palm, and elaborated that this was "tragic" and "heartbreaking."

"Some government bodies see older people as a drain on resources. Well, not here. In the City of Deepdene we like to look after our older citizens; we think they're an important part of the community. Who here has heard of the senior citizens center?"

A smattering of hands went up. Celia nudged Darren and mimed taking a photograph, and he gave her an irritated look.

The center was a "wonderful place," said the mayor, despite her failure ever to have visited it. "They do very important work. It's not just a place that people go to, though. It's a second *home*." She was laying it on thick, but, even so, when she announced the council planned to retain the senior citizens center in perpetuity, it didn't get much of a response. It got zero response, in fact. But that didn't matter. It was On Record now, though Darren didn't seem overly interested. "Why am I here?" he whispered to Celia.

By the time the guests were gone and the cleaning was done, it was after midnight. Celia asked everyone to gather in the empty dining room. She told Jack and Jin-Jin to pour the leftover champagne into glasses for a toast, then she made a speech about what a good job everyone had done, the importance of teamwork, blah, blah, blah. It was getting late.

Eventually, she said, "There's one person I wanted to thank in particular . . ." I guessed it was going to be Betsy for creating the menu, or Eva for helping her, or maybe even Gladys, who'd worked hard to create a newsletter to communicate with volunteers. But Celia said, "Germaine."

Germaine. That's what she said.

I was the center of attention. I tried to hide behind my glass, but there was a disparity between the size of it and the size of me.

"Where's the certificate, Gladys?" said Celia, and Gladys came forward holding a sheet of paper. It was laminated and had a gold ribbon drawn in the corner.

It said:

GERMAINE JOHNSON
EMPLOYEE OF THE YEAR

It wasn't the official one, but it was pretty close. It looked genuine if I wanted to include it in my portfolio. "I think it normally comes with a voucher," I said, but there didn't seem to be one.

Celia said, "One thing I was wrong about was *you*, Germaine. You're . . . different."

"Everyone always says that."

"Yes, but I mean in a good way."

My face went the color of Eva's tomato sorbets. "You're not going to hug me, are you?"

She said she was happy to leave it as a verbal—but sincere—thank-you, and all present raised their glasses. To me.

Jack and I stayed back and put the bottles of unopened wine in the back of his car. When the boot was full, we sat on the hood, drinking the last of the leftover champagne and looking at the stars. Flashy things, they were, sparkling for us.

Jack pointed at a constellation. "Look, the Saucepan," he said.

I pointed out a better one. "Southern Cross."

Jack kept looking, but he didn't know any others. I might have, but I was sick of stars. Something else was on my mind.

"Hey, Jack."

"Hey, Germaine."

"You know that night in the mayor's office? You know how Francine came in? I didn't tell you, but she said something funny after."

"What'd she say?"

"She said, 'I didn't know you and Jack were *friends*.'"

"That's not *that* strange," he said. "We are friends."

"It was *how* she said it. Like . . ." My voice stopped talking.

"Like . . . ? Oh, my God, do you think she thought . . . you and I . . . ?"

"I don't know. God, I hope not. How embarrassing. I mean, I'd never."

"No, of course not," said Jack, quickly.

And then: "Never?"

"Nothing to do with you. You're a moderately attractive man." I thought about stressing this point by touching his trousers. His leg in the trousers. But I didn't.

"You're moderately attractive, too," said Jack. He thought about it. "Perhaps a bit more than *moderately*."

"But we're friends," I said. "Right? And the parameters of friendship are well defined."

"Absolutely." Jack topped up our glasses. "We're friends."

We sipped in companionable silence.

"Never, though . . . it's a little over the top, don't you think, Germaine? I mean, it's not like it would be impossible."

"Nothing's impossible. Well, some things are, but not that. I suppose, hypothetically, if I were drunk. And probably you'd have to be drunk, too—"

"Yes—?"

"Well, if we were both hypothetically drunk enough . . . Maybe. Possibly. Not saying yes, but potentially."

He said nothing.

I said nothing back. We looked at the Saucepan for a while.

Then Jack said, "I'll open another bottle, will I?"

"All right," I said. "Might as well."

Two weeks later, Sharon was in my apartment. "Isn't this fun?" she said as she wrapped a plate in newspaper and put it in a box.

"Not really." I eased an old sudoku workbook carefully into an individual plastic slip, then added a piece of cardboard backing to make sure it stayed flat. I didn't want the edges to curl on the way to my destination.

When I told Sharon I was going on a pilgrimage to Japan, the spiritual home of sudoku, she said, "Did you lose your job again?"

"I didn't *lose* it; they ran out of work. I don't think they expected me to achieve so much in such a short space of time."

The morning after the ball, when I checked my email, there was a message from the mayor. The subject line was: YOU'RE FIRED.

The email elaborated:

As per the conditions of your employment, specifically Clause 4 re-garding a probation period of six months, your contract is terminated—effective immediately.

Goodbye, Germaine.

Sharon folded the top of the box and pushed it to the side. "Have you heard from Kimberly?" she said.

"Not since last time."

Cousin Kimberly had called a day later. "Fuck you, Germaine," she said, "and double fuck you if you think I'm ever helping you get a job again."

Once again, I utilized my Wallace Insurance training. "I understand where you're coming from, Kimberly," I said. "I'm hearing you."

"Verity's not talking to me, Germaine. She said, 'I rue the day I ever gave that cousin of yours a job.'"

"She didn't *give* me a job, Kimberly, I earned it. Hey, are you planning any parties or ceremonies in the next little while? I know a good catering company."

I didn't get a reply before she hung up.

I was sticking down the top of the plastic slip when there was a knock on the door. It was Jack. He'd offered to come and help Sharon and me. "I can drive your stuff to a storage facility if you like," he said. "I've got a friend with a van."

Jack had seemed enthusiastic when he proposed this idea, but now, when he came in, his expression was glum. I asked him what the matter was.

"Nothing." He hovered by the door, his head hanging like a burst football. "How long are you going for, again?"

"Not sure. Depends how much I like it."

"Don't outstay your welcome, Germaine," called Sharon from the kitchen. "Jin-Jin's parents aren't going to want you to live with them forever."

I'd asked Jin-Jin if I could stay with her and her family in Japan. Accommodation there is horrifyingly expensive, and Jin-Jin was going home for the university holidays anyway. I told her I'd be a great guest; they wouldn't even notice I was there except for when they had to come along and translate things for me.

Sharon came out of the kitchen and said hi to Jack. "It's nice of you help," she said. "Isn't it, Germaine?"

I was busy putting another workbook inside a plastic slip, which required concentration and a steady hand. When Sharon nudged me, it knocked the corner out. "Aren't you going to thank Jack for coming?" she said.

"He hasn't done anything yet," I pointed out.

"Germaine."

"What?"

Jack was still by the door, standing with his hands by his sides. All of a sudden he reached behind his back, and out of nowhere appeared a single rose, wrapped in brown paper. He must have had it tucked into the back of his shorts.

He held it out. "This is for you."

"What's it for?"

"I don't know, I just saw it."

I went and took it from him, holding the stem with two fingers, like pincers—I didn't know precisely how it had been positioned in relation to his underwear.

"Don't know where I'll put it," I said, looking around for a receptacle.

"Go and get a glass from the kitchen," bossed Sharon.

"*You* go and get a glass."

Sharon turned to Jack. "You're too good for her, Jack. Honestly. She's not worth it."

That's what she said. My own mother.

When Sharon returned with the glass of water, she put the rose in it and set it on the mantelpiece, next to Gauss and Archimedes. Then she went and got her handbag. "I'm going for a coffee." Sharon didn't normally drink coffee; she must have just started.

After Sharon slammed the door, Jack sat on the couch and took his cap off. It held its shape, a curved outer, like half his head was still inside.

"I wish you weren't going so soon. We've only just . . ." His voice trailed off, and he looked at the floor. Trying to hide the welling tears, probably—I watched closely, hoping I'd see one drop—because he'd been very emotional about my leaving.

He said for the eleventh time, "Why don't you wait until after Christmas? I could get leave for all of January."

"Because I want to be there for Sudo-Con."

"But there's another Sudo-Con then. If you waited, we could go together."

"You and me?" No tears yet, but I could sense a lot of pent-up emotion. Maybe I could tip him over the edge . . .

"What about your mum?" I said.

"She'd be okay. Marie will be there."

"Yeah, that's what I meant." Imagine living with Marie Curie all the time.

For a bit we didn't speak; Jack was presumably too distraught.

Maybe now was the time to tell him I wasn't going anywhere. Not anywhere international, I mean. Japan is horrifyingly expensive *full stop*. I wasn't going to waste that kind of money on stuff I could see in a book.

But I was moving, and I wanted to surprise Jack with the location: It was a romantic gesture. Those aren't easily quantifiable, of course. There's no international standard unit of measurement, for a start. But turning up on someone's doorstep, the family home they can't leave because their mother is so unwell, with everything you own would have to be one of the biggest. The floor plan would be a challenge, but if we pushed Jack's single bed up against the wall near the bathroom, my double could go in the middle of the room, in front of the TV.

Jack said, "I'll miss you, Germaine."

"Do you wish I was staying?"

"It'd be nice to spend some time together, that's all. You know, hang out a little."

"Or a lot," I said.

"Well, you know. A reasonable amount. You don't want to get sick of each other."

"No, you don't want to live in each other's pocket," I said with a very serious expression.

Then I had to grab a cushion off the couch and stuff my face into it, so he couldn't see me laughing.

He was going to be so excited when he found out.

Acknowledgments

My deepest thanks to:

My agent, Jacinta di Mase, who was an advocate of this book very early on, and has been instrumental in making great things happen. I feel very lucky to have you in my corner.

My Australian editor, Mandy Brett, who not only got the jokes but made them better. You said I would learn a lot, and I have. Thank you for making *The Helpline* the best version of itself, but also me a better writer.

To Mandy, publisher Michael Heyward, and the team at Text Publishing—this has been a dream and I am very grateful.

To Tara Parsons, Kaitlin Olson, Jo Dickinson, and the teams at both Simon & Schusters, for their enthusiasm and support.

My writers group, Kate Mildenhall, Kim Hood, Emily Brewin, and Meg Dunley. Also, to very early readers Alice Drew and Kate Harding.

The ACT Writers Centre, via their Hardcopy program.

Varuna, the Writers' House, where parts of this novel were written.

Students and teachers in the Associate Degree in Professional Writing and Editing program at RMIT, where parts of *The Helpline* were workshopped.

Stan and Marianna Kucharski, who have provided much in the way of practical help and support, and whose family I feel very lucky to be a part of.

My parents, for all the books, even the ones that were too old for me. Thanks for your encouragement, positivity, and the many (many) things you've done to help along the way.

Matilda and Oscar, for making life more fun, more interesting, and me a better person.

But most of all, to Carney, who, more than anyone, has listened, supported, provided perspective, and only occasionally asked, "Are you finished yet?" Carney, if not for you, I would never have started writing this book in the first place. Thank you.

About the Author

Katherine Collette is a Melbourne-based writer and sewage engineer. She once worked at a council, and her experience there informed *The Helpline*, her debut novel.